The McJeffers Act

By D.A

GW00994190

To Jack, George & Ted with love

To Chris and Marsha for your help and guidance

For Mum and Dad

Table Of Contents

Chapter Twenty-One – The pigeon, the boot and the mess that followed

Chapter One – Robin McJeffers

Robin McJeffers was fifty-eight years old. A man of slender, but respectable build, his appearance was that of a fit and healthy forty-odd year old, but with the greying hair of an elder statesman. Life was good for Robin. Currently the highest profile Lord in the land, the focus of media attention the world over and pretty much oblivious to it all. His unassuming character meaning that he was able to simply shrug off all of this attention and enjoy his home life with Elizabeth, completely unaffected by the chaos he had caused around the planet.

As a child he had attended the Marian Vian School in Beckenham, Kent and had moved to his senior school, Langley Park School for Boys, which was situated about a mile up the road, when his age dictated that he do so. In both schools his reports spoke of "dreaming" and "minimal concentration," but rarely noted "outstanding achievements," which every parent hoped to see. By the time he'd arrived at his first career decision, that of staying on for sixth form and further education or leaving for the outside world, Robin McJeffers knew what he wanted. Out, no question about it.

School life had bored him and he had wished for no

more. He'd not applied himself to his work because the subjects that he'd faced had held no interest for him. Lectures on crop rotation merely sent him to sleep. Lectures on First and Second World War battles, including the events surrounding them, made McJeffers sit up but, as it seemed to him, no sooner had he sat up than the subject had changed and the class were in the middle of a discussion on farming techniques in the sixteenth century. McJeffers would slide down in his seat, asleep again.

And so, wishing to escape the tedium that education had bought to his young mind, Robin McJeffers left school at the age of sixteen and took a train to London in search of employment. He found his first position in the illustrious and fame-soaked New Scotland Yard. His first desk, in this glorified office block, gave him his first taste of job contentment. He was to stay there for a few years, idly whiling away every moment in a grey looking office, rarely doing anything of much consequence. He'd gained several promotions and internal moves before finally deciding to draw the curtains on his police career, due to boredom setting in, as it had during his school life.

Many, many positions followed, along with many, many changes in direction. Every change brought with it a temporary respite from monotony, but temporary was all it was. Administrative, sales support, sales itself, cleaning, sales again, driving, in fact all sorts of things burned their mark on his c.v, until a tasty little number in a printing company made him feel as though he was set for life.

He had been drawn to the company by its slogan. Being somewhat of a dreamer, McJeffers had assured himself that he was the man for the job and presented his best image to the company. Once taken on, he felt that a slogan of his own, maybe on his business cards, would pull in the punters. After taking delivery of his first few boxes of business cards, McJeffers rushed home.

All the while he was sitting in traffic he was re-assessing his slogan; creating it, thinking for a while, stripping it down, and then re-building it, better than before. Every time he amended it in his head, there would follow a mental list of plus and minus factors, which would lead him back to the drawing board. By the time he'd reached home, he'd cracked it and so, rushing through the door and somehow managing to combine a hug and a kiss with Elizabeth, taking his coat off and reaching for a pen, McJeffers sat down that evening, much to the amusement of Elizabeth, and carefully wrote in ink his slogan, "Give me your dream...I'll give you reality!" in the small space between the company name and his own.

Elizabeth had sat there, dumb founded at first, when her husband started on number one of a box of two-fifty but, by the time he'd started number ten, she was hysterical with laughter. Now, Elizabeth McJeffers had always supported her husband in everything he'd undertaken, but this latest futile attempt at breaking into the house of genius by the toilet window was just too much for her and she had collapsed, banging her fists on the kitchen table, laughing loudly.

In fact, her laughter was such that it began to cause pain, practically from the beginning, and soon she began crying because of it. Her husband, on the other hand, had not been amused by this and, being the man of the house, had decided to end this display of contempt from his wife by merely pushing fifty or so cards across the table, offering her a pen, and saying in a firm voice "Now write carefully, Darling!" With that show of manly control, the sort of display usually seen by the elder baboon on a wildlife program, who would bring the young baboons down a peg or two when their behaviour became mischievous, Elizabeth had regained control and begun to write.

At first, the cards, complete with slogan, had worked well. Sales were good, but these had dried up once McJeffers had serviced the needs of the few oddballs who had held purchasing positions within his customer database. Anyone of reasonable mind found McJeffers just too far "out there" when it came to putting their dreams to print. They would start by explaining, in what they thought were basic terms, pure and simple, exactly what their requirements were. McJeffers, at this point of the meeting, would be still and silent, absorbing the brief, writing a few notes and generally behaving in a professional manner.

The problem came when the customer muttered the words "What do you think?" Those four words rapidly began to act as a kind of trigger mechanism for McJeffers to spill the contents of his brain into his customer's lap. He would describe images that were to him, so vivid, but to his customer, very concerning. He would become animated, waving his arms about in a similar fashion to that of Hitler or Mussolini in their prime. He would elaborate on his customers' ideas for sure, but to a greater extent than his customer ever wished for.

At first, he'd be quietly asked to leave. This was followed by the 'escorted from the building' period, which was swiftly followed up by a series of complaints to his manager, who was also the Managing Director. McJeffers' head was on the block and within days the axe fell. He wasn't violent or abusive. He was just a dreamer, dreaming his way through each meeting. His customer would feed him the initial thought, the backdrop so to speak, and then he'd fill in the foreground with his dreams, which were dangerously vivid and far beyond anything any normal dream contained.

They were neither of his wife, Elizabeth, nor of their future plans together. Robin McJeffers' dreams were full of wondrous creations. Cars, planes, ships, buildings, in fact you name it, it was in there. Questions too, such as "What if?" and "Supposing?" His imagination took the role the writer. He'd pose the question, set the scene, build the props and create the characters. He'd failed in a position that he'd had no experience or training in, but for which he knew, deep down; he was the right man. He'd been asked to leave the company, which he'd been attracted to by it's slogan, and it had been those words alone that had brought this man alive. Up until then he'd been a drifter. One job to another, no real plans, as long as Elizabeth and he were ok then that was all that had mattered.

But now, he found himself unemployed and although this concerned Robin, it hadn't bothered Elizabeth too much, as she had seen her husband grow strong and self assured through this latest position and smiled to herself knowing that his future would bring him success. Thumbing through the recruitment pages of the Guardian that first time, McJeffers knew what sort of position he was looking for. His mental list of criteria read, "need a job, with reasonable salary, to support Elizabeth and myself, not too high up the ladder, 'cos I'm fifty-five now and, oh yes, not too much stress!" Of course, he was unable to explain these things to Elizabeth. She just carried on with the cooking and cleaning, while he sat at the kitchen table scanning each line on each page.

He'd reached the final two pages and knew that time was running out for this paper. Pretty soon it would be condemned to the wastebasket in the corner of the room. But, just then, at that precise moment, he saw it. He smiled to himself and marked it with the exactness of an enemy position being circled on a map, for he knew that that was the one. Sitting there at the foot of the page was the advertisement, "Postal Clerk/Messenger required." He liked that already, but the place of work was just what he wanted, The Houses Of Parliament. If he got this job then he could still bring home a salary, just about high enough to support him and his wife, as well as feel like an important cog in the gearbox of England. He'd also be able to wander the corridors, steeped in history, dreaming to his hearts content. Yep, that was the one for him.

So he rang the number on the advertisement, listened to the recorded message and followed the instructions.

Within a few days the letterbox nearly shattered, as the application pack arrived on his hallway carpet, by being rammed through it with great enthusiasm by the local postman, seventeen and obviously still drunk from the night before. This had become apparent to McJeffers, as he had just watched the young lad walk back down the path and attempt to mount his trusty bicycle and ride off to his next point of delivery. He'd managed to mount his bike, but had assumed that the basket on the front was mounted on the mudguard and not on the frame and so, with his front wheel pointing in an easterly direction and unbeknown to him, the young lad kicked off and instantly tumbled over the handlebars into the hedge.

McJeffers, watching from his lounge window, had stood staring in amazement at this exhibition of drunken gymnastics, before rapidly bringing himself back to reality and hurrying off into the hall to collect the package that had nearly destroyed his front door. A quick bit of arranging and a five-minute read of the covering letter brought a smile to his face. In seemingly no time at all, before him on the kitchen table, spread out and organised in a ridiculously thorough fashion, was the in's and out's, up's and down's and, above all else, an application form for what Robin McJeffers knew, was his ideal job. The job that would make him a household name around the world.

He completed the forms and returned them promptly. He was pleased to read, although deep down he knew, that he'd been selected for an interview. He attended and was given the tour and, whilst walking round with his interviewer, smiled to himself knowing that he'd got the job. Sure enough, a few days later, the postman, now clearly sober and sporting some intricate facial cuts, brought the letter bearing the news he always knew would come. He'd got the job and been given a start date. It was now only a matter of time.

His first day as "a cog in the gearbox of England" gave him a smile and a sense of satisfaction that would serve him well and keep his blood pressure down for years to come. The only thing asked of him was to ensure that the Lords, MP's or other esteemed V.I.P's received whatever documents he had for them, as quickly as possible. He soon became acquainted with a few and began to converse quite freely with his "esteemed colleagues," as he'd refer of them to his wife, finding his way around and becoming more confident in the corridors of power day by day.

So by the time his first year was up, McJeffers was one happy chappy. He'd been right about having the opportunity to dream to his hearts content and it would be on one of these occasions where, in the past it had brought him redundancy and before that a nice security guard to escort him from the building, but this time, in this job and on this occasion, it would bring him promotion and fame, whether he wanted it or not.

Chapter Two – A day to remember

It was about half past two on a Friday afternoon and Robin McJeffers had not long been back from a lazy lunchtime in the park. His lunch had comprised of cheese sandwiches and a couple of bottles of beer, which had been lovingly packed in a cold bag that morning by his wife. He had just returned his briefcase to its usual place under his desk when his manager, "Tone," asked him to rush an important package through to one of the Lords "Loitering in the same place as they're always loitering in!"

Being the ever-willing employee that he'd become over the past year, Robin took the package and, without question, set off down the corridors that always seemed to trigger a dream in his mind. The cold and never ending grey floors just couldn't dampen his spirits, as he set off in search of Lord Hooey of Edenbridge.

Swiftly he walked, turning left this way, right that way, occasionally stopping to ask someone if they knew where Lord Hooey could be found. It was one of these "someone's" that suggested the main chamber but, on arriving there and finding the place deserted, the realisation of where Lord Hooey and, indeed, all the other Lords would be sank in; The Lords Bar.

The Lords Bar was a medium sized room, set aside for the various Lords of the day, who wished to drink themselves into snoring wrecks. None of them ever left there sober, due to the plain and simple fact that none of them ever had to drive home; a chauffeur being a valuable perk of the job.

In appearance, The Lords Bar was a cross between a Gentleman's Club and a normal family living room. It had the homely appearance of a room a regular family might spend their time in, but was furnished with large, deep red, leather armchairs. It was these armchairs that the Lords liked to retire to after a hard morning in the main chamber, which usually involved falling asleep during Prime Ministers question time, which they listened to through a speaker system, checking the form guide whilst the "the old fart on the other bench" said his bit, that sort of thing.

There were only two laws, both unwritten, which hung like a chandelier above the Lords Bar. Number one centred on membership or entry to the Bar. The rule was that anyone with the word "Lord" in their name could step foot in the room. A Lords name was never questioned or challenged, which meant that a security guard by the name of Simon Read had, in fact, taken the alias of "Lord Of All Dancing Chickens" for the past seven years every time he had stepped into the room. Until his face became familiar, a newcomer to the Bar would be asked his name by the Barman and thus, the check on the word "Lord" appearing in his title.

Rule number two, centred on freedom of speech. When the Lords had installed their own meeting place, ten years earlier, they had all insisted that they be allowed to talk openly and freely, on any subject that they desired, without fear of retribution or betrayal. What they said outside that room, either to the press or in debate in the Main Chamber, was not, they felt, necessarily their true feelings on the subject. And so they felt that they needed somewhere where they could discuss these feelings and, with that desire, came the formation of The Lords Bar.

On arrival at the Bar, McJeffers peered in and found the place heaving with Lords, or at least, gentlemen with the word "Lord" in their name. Over on one side of the room sat Lord Charrington, a noble man in his mid seventies, who was renowned for being a prankster but, on this occasion, was to be found asleep by the fireplace, head tilted back, snoring to the gods. As McJeffers scanned around the room he noted a rowdy bunch gathered at the far end of the bar. There seemed to be all manner of gesticulating going on and, from where he stood, he could just make out the dashing figure of Lord Hooey Of Edenbridge.

Although he couldn't make out what all the shouting was about, he knew that it was passionate and probably highly political. On recent visits to the bar to deliver packages or documents, McJeffers had been present at such proclamations as "Yes, Yes, Yes, that's all very well, but I see no reason why they can't fit a horse inside a Formula One car" and "Supermarkets have been fitting spy cameras into bunches of bananas for years, you know!"

Now, to gain entry to the Lords Bar if your name or title didn't contain the word "Lord," meant that you had to collect a small badge that sat in a bowl on the table outside the bar, attach it to oneself and then enter. The badge bore the legend "Guest Lord" and that was good enough to allow McJeffers to enter the Bar and approach Lord Hooey. As he got closer, he could make out the additional figures of Lords Rothschild, Huntingdon, Briars, Nelson and a certain Anthony Lord who worked for a small Travel Insurance company across the road.

On arrival at the far end of the bar Lord Hooey greeted him.

"Ah, Robin, my friend!"

"Lord Hooey!"

"What have ya got for me today then?"

"I'm not sure Sir, but Tone asked me to get it to you, ASAP!"

Lord Hooey took the package, examined it and, without opening it, placed it on the bar. Satisfied that he knew what it was, he continued with the discussion raging all around him. With his mission seemingly over, McJeffers turned to make his exit when a hand grasped his shoulder and the voice of Lord Hooey beamed out once again.

"Don't go Robin, stay and give us your thoughts." Before McJeffers could answer, Lord Hooey continued.

"Come on, join in, lad. It's quite amusing really. Old Nelson here's telling us what he thinks should be done with the Navy, you know."

Lord Nelson's only link with the Navy was his famous name. If asked, he'd willingly declare no interest in the Navy or indeed, in anything that floated. He was fast approaching ninety and felt that, because of his famous name, he was entitled to have a say in how the Navy was run. He'd lived the life of an eccentric, constantly producing strange and quite useless inventions and now, in his latter years, he felt the Navy could benefit from his maturity. Being a well-respected member of the Lords Bar, he had once called for, and secured, a two minutes silence for one of his inventions, that had met an untimely demise.

This curious old-timers' life could quite easily be broken down into periods, whereby he'd "wandered along various avenues," as he had once been quoted as saying. Amongst the many avenues, previously wandered along, there lie periods such as the "sports fanatic period" and the "novelist period." It was the novelist period that had brought him much wealth and fame, although it was to be another period, the "dress as a yellow-feathered bird and stand outside the local retirement home" period that would bring him more fame and attention than he'd wished for and the 'matter,' as the Police described it, although it was actually a six month period, was drawn to a close and hushed up, quickly.

It was a lazy Sunday, during the "radio control" period of his inventive life and Lord Nelson had just emerged from his garden shed with his latest, and to him, most beautiful creation. A radio controlled, flying duck. It had taken him two years to build and a further eight months to perfect, but after two weeks of flight trials and a further three days of waddling trials, Lord Nelson felt that his "bird" was ready for take off. He had named it "The Albatross" and had let her loose that sunny June day from a field near his home in Kent.

He'd stood there, proud as punch, working the controls and watching his "bird" fly around and around in large circles. These had begun to widen, taking "The

Albatross" out over surrounding fields. To him, seeing this yellow mechanical monster gamely limp by recalled visions of Spitfires and Hurricanes and "The Few." Ok, he'd not been able to perfect its wing movement, but it flew nonetheless.

Or, at least, it had flown until a local farmer in one of those surrounding fields had become so irritated by the yellow, fake feathered, mechanical monster, which kept circling overhead, that he'd gone to his barn, retrieved his shotgun, and with careful aim had chalked up a score for "Blighty." Lord Nelson had been overcome with grief at the sight of the first, then the second, shotgun blast ripping through "The Albatross." The first shot had removed the fake beak, but she still flew more or less unhindered. It was the second shot that removed the mechanical duck from aloft and sent it spinning in flames into the local river.

His first day back at The Lords Bar after this incident had moved Lord Nelson to ask for two minutes silence from his fellow Lords, in memory of his "Albatross." His request was duly granted and what a sight it had been to see twenty-five grown, and supposedly noble Lords, or gentleman with the word "Lord" in their title, stand heads bowed, in honour of a duck they never knew.

"I'd love to stay, Sir, but I think Tone would have something to say about it."

22

"Oh nonsense, Robin!"

With that, Lord Hooey motioned to the barman.

"Harry….I say, Harry, old fruit...pass the phone will you, my man!"

Harry duly obliged, passing him the telephone from under the counter. Lord Hooey instantly dialled Tone's number or rather the number of the Post Room. It rang and was answered by the man himself, almost instantly.

"Post room."

"Aahh, Tone, my good man!"

"Lord Hooey, has Robin found you yet?"

"Yes, yes he has Tone….and I've got some important business to attend to and I'd like Robin to accompany me. Is that okay with you?"

"Yes, Sir, that's not a problem."

"Thank you, Tone, you're an absolute god send!"

"Thank you, Sir!"

With that both men hung up. Lord Hooey turned to McJeffers.

"Right then, Robin. Now Tone's off ya back, will ya stay and join in?"

McJeffers reluctantly agreed and both men re-joined the rowdy rabble at the end of the bar. As they approached the group they just caught the end of Lord Nelson's picture of his "new Navy."

".... and that's why I think it should be restructured....totally changed!"

Lord Hooey turned to Robin and, whilst putting an arm around Lord Nelson, addressed him and the group at the same time.

"Looks as though we've missed the big picture, my friend. Now then, Charles, tell us all again, but really for the benefit of Robin and myself, just what should be done with the Navy?"

All the Lords, that were gathered there in front of Lord Hooey and McJeffers, stared in horror as if to say, in fact as if crying out with desperation, "Oh my God, Hooey! What the bloody hell are you doing?" Lord Nelson didn't need a second request and was instantly starting his address all over again.

"You see, it's like this. The whole damn thing's too confusing. I mean, all the bloody ranks and phrases and their own bloody way of saying left and right. Even the names of their boats, for God's sake! I mean, "Aircraft Carrier" says it all. Anyone on the outside knows what this type of boat's all about, as they do with a "Submarine," but "Frigates?" Can anyone of you tell me what a "Frigate" looks like? The answer's "no." I know, you see. Unless you're in the Navy, you haven't got a clue. Gentleman, who can tell me the ranks in the Navy and what all those squiggly lines on their shoulders and sleeves mean, or the size, biggest first, of their ships?"

Lord Hooey interjected.

"But Charles! They're professionals, it's their business. As long as they know what's going on, who cares?"

Lord Nelson's facial features now changed to that of a primary school teacher addressing a group of five-year-olds.

"Yes, yes, I agree with you that they need to know. But, don't you see? We're the one's that send them off to war and we don't have a bloody clue what's going on!"

"But we have advisers, Charles!"

"Yes, I know that, but we still don't know anything. They advise us with what they want. It's like another bloody language and we need to change it!"

Some of the Lords, gathered around Lord Nelson, had found this speech amusing first time around, but on it's second airing, they found it positively frightening when they realised that Lord Hooey and Robin McJeffers were found to be in agreement with him.

"Gentleman, Charles has a very valid point. If we're to send people to war, a war or conflict from which they may not return, then surely it is our duty to those service men and

25

women to understand completely their professions and that includes their squiggly signs and ranking structure. Are we not just being ignorant if we fail to understand this? Is it not the least that these brave men and women should expect from their peers?"

Silence greeted Lord Hooey as he finished his speech. On opening his eyes he found all present staring at him and, not wishing to have these sets of eyes dwelling on him for a second longer, diverted their gaze to the man standing at his side.

"Robin my lad. Tell us what you think?"

A chorus of approval greeted this suggestion from just about every Lord in the bar now, as it had become the main debate of the day. Lord Hooey had previously gestured to Harry behind the bar for refreshment and a frighteningly large quantity of brandy appeared on the bar next to them. Robin McJeffers, having been triggered by those key words "What do you think?" felt a bout of nerves coming on and decided to quell them with four straight doubles on the trot. Now, as he fought to stand upright, he began with all in attendance eagerly awaiting his poetic views.

"Gentleman! I would have to say that I am in complete agreement with Lord Hooey and Lord Nelson. I genuinely believe that if the Navy appeared to the outside world, in a more simplified version, then the interest and confidence in it would increase in monumental proportions." He felt very pleased with himself at this point as, not only had he stayed on his feet and curbed his swaying, but had also kept the attention of all before him, as well as keeping his train of thought. He continued.

"Nobody bothers with the Navy because, to understand it, you need a degree in "hullabaloo," for want of a better word! I know for a fact that if you spot a Naval person, you haven't really got a clue who or what he is! All you know is that he's got lots of squiggles all over his coat. I have to ask you, what bloody good's that to anyone? What? Eh?"

Lord Hooey intervened. "Gentleman, I feel as though we've stumbled upon something that requires our utmost attention and debate and I therefore suggest that we adjourn to the Lords Chamber. Harry, shut the bar down and load up the drinks trolley. Five bottles of brandy should do it. You can always come back for more, can't you?"

And with that, the Lords Bar was left bereft of Lords and a barman as the half-cut occupants made their way down the corridors to the Lords Chamber whereby they all took their seats on the benches. Once settled, Robin McJeffers was asked to continue by Lord Hooey, as Harry the barman poured more doubles.

"As I was about to say, Gentlemen, how do you address someone with a mass of squiggles on his arm if you don't have a "Danny La Rue," what those squiggles mean? How can you impress on the youngsters of this great nation the importance of frigates, if you don't have a bloody clue what they look like and what role they play in the modern Navy? Unless you've got time on your hands to go to university and study the ranking system of the British Navy, can anyone tell me the ranks, descending in order, from a Captain? I know we all know that "Number One" is next, because we've all seen "The Cruel Sea" but, seriously, Gentleman, it's not a very good painting is it?"

The assembled Lords sat motionless and still. Mentally reeling from having the absolute truth rammed home by this "genius" of a man that stood before them. Lord Tarter, whom up unto this point in proceedings had been quiet and reserved, stood up and addressed his colleagues. "Gentleman! I have to ask you, just where has this extraordinary young man been? With sounding as he has just demonstrated to us, I feel that we should make him a member of the Lords Chamber, without hesitation!"

A resounding wave of agreement swept through the chamber and it was left to Lord Hooey to bestow upon the surprised and very drunk Robin McJeffers, the title of "Lord Robin McJeffers of Beckenham." As soon as Lord Hooey had draped the red ceremonial cloak (fetched from the stores by Harry) around his shoulders a huge, if not drunken, cheer went up from those in attendance, as Lord Hooey addressed the chamber once more.

"Gentleman, I think that, with this act that we have just undertaken, in securing the services of this special man into our ranks, we have quite possibly saved the country from disaster and, I put forward the proposition to you all, that whatever Lord McJeffers of Beckenham, of the back bench, House Of Lords, now says relating to the Royal Navy, we pass it as an emergency Act, as we have all been empowered to do!"

Another resounding wave of agreement swept through the chamber as McJeffers, who had started the day as a post messenger and was now in line to finish the day as the most important Lord in the House, acknowledged his new colleagues. The small matter of ascertaining just whether they were actually empowered to do this kind of thing had fallen by the way side, or maybe even just plain fallen over.

He realised that, after all his years of dreaming, and the problems that they'd created for him, he was now in a position of real power and it would be his and his dreams alone that would shape the Navy for years to come. Nothing had made him feel as satisfied as this moment and he thought to himself that he couldn't wait to get home and tell Elizabeth what he'd become and what he'd done for that matter! "Please continue, Lord McJeffers, with your thoughts surrounding changes to the Royal Navy."

"Gentleman! Harry! Make mine a double! Gentleman, what I feel we need to do, is abolish this ranking thing that's obviously, for want of a better expression, "getting our goat up!" and bring in a simplified version that the world, and indeed it's whippet, can understand. I therefore suggest a simple numbering system, split across two levels. Level A, being the old farts behind desks with a rum in their hands. Level B being the people that actually matter! Numbering downwards from the top. The top, Gentleman, being number one, descending as number two, three etc. Thus we'd all know where everyone stood. Both levels would be numbered the same, but the difference in rank would be the letter after their number. Thus Number One, Level A being far superior to Number One, Level B. Does everyone understand? And more to the point, does everyone agree?"

Again, a resounding cheer of approval swept around the chamber. Harry, the barman, knew he was in for a long night and popped outside to call his wife and tell her to give his dinner to the dog. On his return to the chamber, not more than ten minutes later, everything had been agreed and effectively, signed, sealed and delivered. Everything, that the now Lord McJeffers had suggested or proposed, had been agreed and passed by his now in-coherent colleagues and, as Harry opened the chamber door to re-enter, he was met by raucous cheering and singing. In that brandy-fuelled couple of hours, the fate and future of the Royal Navy had been systematically installed as the number one priority for the powers that be, when they awoke the following morning.

As for Lord Robin McJeffers of Beckenham, he took his first ride home in his chauffeur driven car to the surprise of his wife, Elizabeth, whom he took inside and sat down at the dining room table, before rushing outside to despatch his driver home for the rest of the night, with a request to return to the McJeffers' household for nine o'clock the following morning. Once inside, he shut the door and rushed into the dining room where his startled wife sat, bleary eyed.

"Darling Elizzibuff."

"Oh Robin! Really! What time do you call this? And, and look at the state of you!"

"Darling Elizzibuff, hic, will you please from now on, hic, Harry! Harry! Make mine a oh, erm, Elizzibuff, my darling."

"Robin McJeffers! In all my years, I've never ever seen you

31

in this state. What happened today?"

"Well, I am now officially "Lord Robin McJeffers Of Beckenham," but still "darling" to you, my dear!"

"Robin? I don't understand."

"Come, sit down, luv!"

Elizabeth had rapidly realised that whatever liquid her husband had consumed, and in the vast quantity that he obviously had, had turned him from mild mannered Robin McJeffers into a kind of Mike Read meets the Sweeney type of character, as he'd just demonstrated by falling onto the sofa, beating the hell out of the cushion to his right and muttering the immortal line "Come, sit down, luv!" His constant beating of the cushion, in a very over enthusiastic manner, suggested to her that maybe sitting next to him was a good idea, if anything, for the sake of the cushion.

So down sat a rather sober and shocked Elizabeth McJeffers, next to her completely smashed and very excited husband, who proceeded to deliver an account of that days events, which took three pints of water, seven visits to the bathroom and had the pace and content of a budget day speech, as Robin had forced himself to speak at less than half speed in order to aid his memory and speech ability.

Over the coming hour or so, Robin relayed the events of his monumental day, just passed, to his wife. Every so

32

often, well every other word, or so it seemed, he'd confuse important characters. Lord Hooey would become "Hooey, the Barman," whilst "Harry, the Barman" would become, if only for a few seconds, "Lord Harry of Barman." After about an hour, her husband had relayed, in some sort of order at least, the happenings that had brought on this now unconscious condition on the sofa next to her. From what she could make out, her husband was now a Lord and had had an Act named in his honour, as he had thought of it. Oh, and that he'd had the equivalent of seventeen brandy's and had walked through the front door at three in the morning completely "twatted," as she'd heard their young postman describe the condition, with a strange man following him and taking orders from her husband.

This man had turned out to be the new chauffeur and she'd overheard, well the street had overheard, her enthusiastic husband despatch this man's services for the night with a request to be picked up at nine the following morning. It was now fast approaching five in the morning. Rising from the sofa to survey the wreckage that lay before her, she quickly made up her mind that her husband would be sleeping downstairs for the remainder of the night.

She hurried upstairs to get a couple of blankets and a pillow and, on her return to the crash site, removed his shoes and his tie and swung his legs around onto the sofa, so that he was now laying full stretch. She lifted his head and wedged the pillow between it and the arm of the furniture and covered him with the blankets before retreating to the doorway. Stopping herself at the light switch, she turned for one last look at her husband. Surveying the scene for the last time, any shock and anger that she may have felt two hours, earlier had left her heart, as a feeling of love once again filled it. This caused her to smile warmly at the crumpled body poking out from under the blankets and, with this smile on her face, Elizabeth McJeffers switched off the lights and hurried upstairs to bed.

Having been dressed for bed for the last seven hours or so, all she needed to do was set the alarm. "The chauffeur will be here at nine," she thought to herself. "He needs some sleep, it's five-ish now, seven should do it, with a lay-in recovery period to half past." With that, organised so quickly and efficiently, the way only a woman can, Elizabeth McJeffers lay down, turned out her bedside lamp and closed her eyes, knowing that she'd only two hours sleep ahead of her. If she felt like it, she could return to bed after the chauffeur had scooped up the remains of her husband from the front room and set out for Parliament in four hours time.

Like most who've had too much to drink and retire to

bed far too late in the night, or morning in most cases, the alarm always sounds just when you think you've closed your eyes. Just get to sleep and off she goes. For Elizabeth McJeffers, the result was no different. Out went the lamp and on went the alarm. No sooner had she closed her eyes and the recent events had started to fill her thoughts, then Radio Two was dulling her brain with some dreary old Simply Red tune. She tried, oh how she tried, to lay there and fight the radio alarm clock, but mighty Mick Hucknall's dulcet tones finally won the day and out of bed she leapt.

As soon has she felt her two feet hit the carpet, the firm palm of her hand crashed down on the 'off' button, situated on top of the alarm clock, and the morbid tone emanating from Mr Hucknall ceased to cause depression and a relaxing air filled her head. "How did that man ever make any money?" she thought to herself. Now, with one dirty job done, her mind focused on the next task on the agenda.

A deep breath, a quick stretch and she was off downstairs. As she negotiated each step, she wondered what vision would be waiting for her in the dining room. Some vomit? A pale looking, half dead husband possibly? Maybe it'd be the sight of her husband, who'd fallen off of the sofa and into the vomit, or onto the cat, who'd probably nestled itself into his face and gone to sleep. Or what if he'd died?

She quickly dismissed that theory and mentally scolded herself for thinking such thoughts. She shivered at the thought of the sight that awaited her and brought herself back to the task ahead. As Elizabeth McJeffers descended the stairs, she noticed a beam of light spreading itself down the hall from the direction of the front door. "What an earth?" Surely, she'd not left the front door open all night?

When her feet touched the hallway carpet, she turned to her left, to see her rather shaky husband, still dressed from the night before, on a stepladder, on the doorstep.

"Robin?"

"Aagh, erm! Morning, dear!"

"What are you doing?"

"It's a respect thing dear. Our neighbours must realise who they're living next to."

"What exactly do you mean, Robin?"

"Look!"

And with that, Robin McJeffers pointed to the pane of glass situated above the front door. Originally, in fact up to half an hour ago, it had said, "Here lives Robin and Elizabeth McJeffers." Tacky for some, but for Robin and Elizabeth, it showed the world that they were proud of their home and of each other. Now, however, it declared, with the aid of some black paint fetched and mixed hastily from the garden shed by Robin, "Here lives Lord Robin and Lordess Elizabeth McJeffers."

Elizabeth focused on the object of her husband's desire, the sign above the front door, which had meant so much for so many years. A wave of emotions swamped her heart. Dejection, frustration, disappointment, they were all in attendance and so many more were knocking on the door, wanting to come in.

"Oh Robin! What have you done?"

"Darling, it's important that everyone knows."

Elizabeth interrupted her husband mid sentence.

"Robin, everything you said earlier was true? EVERYTHING??? Robin?"

Robin looked down the hallway, from the lofty height of three steps, to see his wife in the throes of being overcome with the ridiculous realisation that her husband had become a Lord. She felt faint. The man on the ladder with a paint pot and brush in his hand, on her doorstep, saw this and immediately made for the bottom step, wanting to get to his wife as quickly as possible. However, he was still effectively under the influence of around seventeen brandy's, so the lofty height of the third step on the ladder roughly equated to being on a tight rope at thirty thousand feet for Robin, as he became unsteady and fought to regain some control and balance.

Having, once again, regained the balance thing, he descended the three steps and, having placed the paint pot and brush on the newspaper, which was currently spread out all over the floor, walked down the hall the few paces to where Elizabeth stood dazed.

"Now darling, it's O.K! I'm a Lord, that makes you a Lordess, I think. That sounds great. "Lord and Lordess McJeffers." How cool is that?"

"But, Robin!"

Elizabeth protested feebly at the events and, indeed, the situation, which now swamped her existence. All of which she had no control over. She thought to herself that never again would she pack her husbands' lunchbox with any drink other than water, as two bottles of lager had transformed her and her husbands life forever, for better or for worse, only time would tell, but it felt pretty bad right now.

Pointing at the amended sign above the front door, complete with paint runs, Elizabeth now sat on the bottom of the stairs, confused and concerned, and felt she needed some answers to settle her condition.

"Why, oh why, on earth did you do that? And, and what possessed you to get up in the state your in and do that to the sign? And have you cleaned your teeth yet?"

Chapter Three – A girl called Elizabeth

Elizabeth had been brought up to clean her teeth in the mornings and also in the evenings, as well as any occasions where food and drink had been involved. This last situation, of course, only became an addition when she became old enough to drink alcohol and, apart from having it drummed into her by her parents, had felt that after a drink it was a good thing to clean ones teeth as it gave one a "fresh" taste.

She also grew up with the belief that it saved everyone else around the fate of having "beer breath" cast all over them. These morals had been rigorously upheld throughout her life and, had she and her husband been inclined to have children, then they too would've been raised with these same standards. However, Elizabeth and her husband weren't interested in the children thing and so that situation had never presented itself. All through her teens and early twenties, Elizabeth McJeffers had lead a clean, nigh almost religious existence, with a couple of steady boyfriends, but nothing to really write home about or cause her parents to start planning a wedding. Then she met Robin.

She'd had a passion for the films and the stars that had brought them to life in her younger days and frequently visited the library in Beckenham to see if there were any books that she could gorge on. She particularly liked John Mills and Kenneth Moore as she felt they displayed "a very English charm," as she would describe it to her friends. On one particular day in question, all those years ago, Elizabeth Pellow, as she was then, had entered the library and headed straight for the film section, as normal.

Now, possibly through her upbringing or because of a mild shyness in her character, Elizabeth rarely looked at anybody else in the library, let alone any other section, as she felt that a library was a private thing for each person in there. But, on this day, she couldn't help but notice a man, slightly older looking than herself and standing across the aisle. She thought that he was quite good looking, probably more charming and elegant than good looking, in fact, but then she realised that, in the few seconds in which she'd decided all of this, she'd actually broken all of her own rules for visiting a library and was actually staring at this man.

She couldn't help but feel attracted to him, but it was the book that he was perusing that really made her smile inside. Whereas she was standing there with "Come inside M.G.M," which, she felt, was an honest and informative, behind-the-scenes look at one of the great movie studios, this man, whom she couldn't keep her eyes off of, was actually standing there reading a book which appeared to be entitled, "Am I mad? What the hell do my dreams mean?" by some doctor or professor of some sort.

As soon as she managed to read the whole title she giggled a giggle, which, was meant to be silent and to herself but unfortunately for her, echoed across the sleepy aisle to where this man stood. Once the sound wave of the giggle hit his head he moved his eyes, from deep in the pages of the book that lay open in his hands, to from where and whom the giggle had originated. The vision of loveliness that greeted him far outweighed, in fact completely crushed, the feeling of rudeness that he was about to object to across the aisle. Elizabeth, on the other hand just froze, smiling and staring, unable to move.

A very, very tiny part of her old self was saying "Oh my God! What have you done? Just put the book back and get out quick!" Whereas, the new-found confidence that had just suddenly appeared, was saying to her "keep smiling, walk over there and say in your softest voice "I'm Sorry!"" Trusting in her new self, that's what she did.

The man standing there completely transfixed was, of course, Robin McJeffers, whom had been experiencing thought problems, or what he perceived as thought problems, all of his life. He wondered why he kept dreaming of what he dreamt, and thinking the thoughts he thought. Oh how he wished for the qualifications and experience of, say an architect or a rocket scientist, so he would be able to build these dreams that populated his head.

Uncannily, like the young girl his eyes were currently fixed on across the Library aisle, Robin McJeffers was also shy. Although he loved these designs and thoughts that were in his head, he was concerned that maybe it wasn't what a "NORMAL" person should be thinking of. He was unable to talk to his parents about this issue, as they tended to laugh off anything he questioned about himself, and so had given up on the idea of confronting them. Hence, his attendance at the Library that day and his choice of book "Am I mad? What the hell do my dreams mean?"

Elizabeth put her book back on the shelf and, almost on autopilot, made her way across the aisle, towards the man that she couldn't take her eyes off of. Robin thought to himself, "Wow, she's coming over! Look calm, relax and smile nicely!" and with that he smiled a smile that felt like a toothless one, although he knew that he had a full set. Right there and then, in that moment, he craved for a mirror so he could check and make sure he still had his teeth because the smile that he was pulling felt pretty bad.

To Elizabeth, the smile on the man's face was

anything but toothless. It was breath taking and she was hooked one hundred per cent. She glided over and made her apologies for the giggle. She was the only thing, he thought to himself, which could take him away from this book, as it had truly enlightened him and made him believe that the creative thoughts that he'd been having were in fact related to his past life.

If he was to believe the book, written by a certain Professor Koppenhurten from Munich, then he had been a fourteenth century architect who was now using his fourteenth century skills combined with twenty first century materials to create the ideal designs. He looked at the woman standing with him, put the book back on the shelf, took her by the hand and quickly led her out of the library.

The remainder of that Saturday morning was spent in a teashop in the high street. Unfortunately, they both had plans that night but swapped details and, on leaving the shop mid afternoon found that, not only did they have lots in common, but also that they were very fond of each other. The morals and courting etiquette of modern day society weren't going to feature in their new found romance for they both knew they would conduct it whatever way they wished.

Inseparable, their romance blossomed as it spread through weeks, into months and on into years. As they approached the third anniversary of their fateful meeting that Saturday, they booked a restaurant to celebrate. Nothing fancy, but merely cosy, as indeed the last three years had been. Elizabeth went shopping for something nice to wear; Robin went shopping, also for something for Elizabeth to wear, on her finger.

As the evening wore on he produced the ring and "popped the question." Elizabeth was stunned to tears and accepted straight away. A resounding cheer went up around the restaurant for Robin and Elizabeth, the type of cheer that would be repeated many years later, but in a different setting. They were married six months later at St Johns Church in Beckenham and honeymooned in Scotland, near Ben Nevis.

On their return to Beckenham, they set up house together and both returned to work. It wasn't long before Robin's respect for Elizabeth and his overwhelming desire to be the wage earner, persuaded Elizabeth that she should give up work and become the "housewife that they both wanted her to be." And that's the way it would stay in their marriage for all those years to come.

Although they weren't exactly rich, they were happy and never ever lived beyond their financial means, as Robin went from one job to another, just to earn enough money to support him and his beloved Elizabeth. Over the coming twenty years, both sets of parents would die and they would inherit money from these sad circumstances and so, by the time Robin started at the Houses of Parliament, they were slightly more than financially stable.

So there she sat, on the bottom of the stairs, dazed and listening to her husband re-assure her. Everything was going to be all right. He was a Lord and she was, according to him a "Lordess," and they had a chauffeur, whose name was Eric and who would be here in an hour. Elizabeth regained her faculties and stood up. This pleased Robin no end, although his half hour or so of enthusiasm had just about burnt him out and now he felt awful and sat himself down.

"Robin! Would you like some breakfast?"

"Oh God!"

"Is that a Lord's way of saying 'yes' or 'no'?"

Elizabeth rarely mocked her husband. The last time, probably being the business card incident and her attitude then had been crushed promptly, but this time, boy! Would she make up for it! Right now, the shell that sat before her, the shell that usually resembled her husband, was in no fit state to claim the 'man of the house' award and she was going in for the kill. But only, you understand, because she'd been kept up all night by this drunken bum.

"I don't think I will be eating for sometime yet,

45

Darling. Thank-you anyway."

"Oh, but surely my Lord must desire some eggs, bacon, sausages and toast? Mmm, Surely, my Lord?"

"Erm, Elizabeth, are you taking the.... are you mocking me?"

"Oh no, my Lord, not I!"

"Oh God...I feel ill"

"Maybe you'd like to ascend the "Lords stairs" to the "Lords bathroom" where you can take a "Lords shower" and remove that "Lords stink" from my hallway!"

"Oh...erm...yes dear!"

And with that, he was despatched upstairs for a shower. Once again, it was left to Elizabeth to clear up the paint, brush and stepladder that seemed to be strewn all around the hall. She wondered how four items, five if you included the lid to the paint and the newspaper, could make the hallway seem like a bombsite. Pondering done, she cleared the hall.

On entering the dining room she was pleasantly surprised to see that there was, in fact, no vomit in attendance and that the cat had survived the night without being crushed by her husband. Amazingly, there was no mess at all. She smiled a smile of satisfaction to herself and, on folding the blankets and stroking the cat, she returned the blankets and pillow to the airing cupboard on the upstairs landing. She could hear the sound of running water in the shower cubicle and also the repeated "Oh God's" coming from her severely hung over "Lord" of a husband.

Again, a smile of satisfaction appeared on her face and down the stairs she went. She thought to herself that, although her husband didn't fancy a cooked breakfast, she surely did. There was also the possibility of getting another one over on her husband for the smell would surely turn him green again. By the time that her husband appeared downstairs in the dining room, she had cooked her breakfast and was sitting at the dining room table eating. He looked clean, she thought, but only marginally more alive than dead. And the smell! The smell was turning his stomach and she loved every minute of it!

"Cup of tea, dear?"

Elizabeth pointed to the cup in front of her husband that sat opposite her on a drinks mat. She was enjoying this. Talk about kicking someone while they're down! Her husband was desperately trying to not breathe in and lasted for about ten seconds before the smell of his wife's cooked breakfast filled his nostrils.

"Just, just going to the bathroom dear"

"Oh, don't be long darling. Eric will be here soon!"

She was beginning to hope that her husband would

come home drunk more often. It was almost perfect timing that she opened the front door to Eric and her husband appeared from his twenty-five minute stint in the bathroom. Robin was heading to the armchair for a recovery period when he walked into the hall and saw Elizabeth conversing with the chauffeur. He noticed his wife holding his briefcase at the door and motioning to him to leave the house, now!

"Good bye, darling, and have a nice day!"

"Oh, erm, yes...morning Eric! Goodbye, darling...and thanks!"

With her husband gone, Elizabeth returned to the kitchen to take in that cup of tea that still sat on the table. Sitting down, she felt a warm glow of contentment engulf her soul and began to smile, thinking about what lay in store today for her husband. Whilst she had been subject to an early hours, drunken, rowdy and, at times, desperate explanation as to the very reason why her husband had returned home in the state that he clearly had, there was still a strong sense of disbelief in her mind. Something was not quite right. She thought to herself that this sort of stuff just doesn't happen to anyone! She comforted herself that only time would tell and she'd best get on with her day. Inwardly, she couldn't wait for Robin to come home.

Chapter Four – The next day

For a few steps there on that path, following Eric the chauffeur, Robin felt fully recovered but, as he glanced next door, he noticed the postman, clearly still drunk from the night before and realised that he must surely have taken on the same appearance. He felt ill once again. Eric opened the rear door to the Mercedes and ushered his new boss inside. He shut the door, took his seat and, on starting the car, headed for Parliament and Robin's first full day as a Lord of the House. Hung-over and feeling dreadful.

However, once he'd arrived at the Main Chamber he decided to take a quick peek, just to recollect the events of a few hours before that had radically changed his life forever. A sort of "pinch me," just to make sure he wasn't dreaming. He was surprised to find the main doors open and the smell of brandy made him recoil for a moment. It was true, "no dream going on here," he thought to himself. Once inside, he was shocked, but highly amused, to find the chamber stacked to the gunnels with unconscious Lords and one barman. He now felt strong, fit and well. Well almost, and afforded himself a burst of laughter at their expense as, it appeared that, he was the only one who'd actually made it home.

He realised that the car park must have looked like a

truck stop last night as more than forty chauffeurs had more than likely fallen asleep at the wheels of their respective cars, awaiting the appearance of their respective Lords, all to no avail. Eventually, even the most stubborn and strong willed driver must have fallen asleep; only to awake this morning, probably with a stiff back and aching muscles.

So there he stood, surveying the scene or, at least, the remains of the scene of his finest hour to date. Snoring to the heavens, again over in the far corner, were Lords Charrington, Briars and Nelson, the architect of his newfound fame. Over to his right stood the drinks trolley, complete with Harry the Barman, curled up like a lap dog on the top shelf and, what looked like, Lord Hooey. A secondary glance confirmed that the bottom shelf was indeed supporting the unconscious body of his new found mentor, legs stretched out one end, head flopped out the other and resting on the floor, supported by his crossed arms.

McJeffers felt low, almost lost, in fact. He'd started yesterday as a messenger and finished the day as a Lord. If he'd finished the day as a messenger like he'd started the day then he wouldn't have got drunk and would've been home in bed with his beloved wife right now. Instead, he had finished the day as a Lord and he had got drunk. He had been asked what he thought and he had told them. Was it his fault that they'd passed it as an Act?

He thought for a moment, surely that's not how it works? Surely the Government has more control than this over the Lords, surely? This deep thinking made him feel ill again so, without hesitation, he made for the nearest bench, occupied by a snoring body that vaguely resembled Lord Rothschild. He brushed Lord Rothschild's outstretched arm aside and sat down.

Robin McJeffers was a sound and reasonable man, or so he thought. He knew his country was in a state, a bad state. Brought on, he believed, by mis-guidance and bad leadership for most of the years since the war. He knew that most of his fellow countrymen hated the way their beloved England had been turned into an "International Squat," as he'd heard a colleague describe it as earlier on in the week, but surely, surely all these happenings hadn't happened as a result of these drinking sessions by these Lords?

If they're running the country then what are the Government there for? Then it clicked. It's a front! A young, respectable looking cabinet to take the flak from the population and act as though they're in control and command, when really they're taking orders and policies from these old guys who lay around him snoring!

Robin McJeffers sat there shocked, as it slowly

dawned on him that, if his assessment of the situation were accurate, then he was effectively now leading the country, seeing as all his fellow Lords had worshipped the ground that he walked on the previous night. He, Robin McJeffers, or Lord Robin McJeffers of Beckenham, as he was now to be addressed, was head of the secret and exceptionally irrational and also very aged, but very REAL Government.

He thought to himself, all of those years of being sacked, being escorted from buildings and now the Prime Minister was HIS puppet! He'd never had any time for Blair, Brown or any of the others that had passed through number 10. He wasn't a political person in the slightest, just patriotic. England wasn't England anymore. It had lost its identity and it's national standing. The toughness that it had displayed during the war years had been left in the dust bin as the new breed had become more concerned with not upsetting any other population in the world than actually attending to the needs of it's own. These drunken idiots coming up with more ridiculous ideas, all fuelled by alcohol, McJeffers thought to himself, had no doubt caused the mess that the country was in.

"Well, I can't change that, too late, but I can simplify the things that I don't understand," he thought to himself as he sat there that Saturday morning, amongst his colleagues.

Only minimal levels of staff were in and they were mostly security personnel, so he couldn't even go and see Tone. He took a deep breath and exhaled, puffing his cheeks out. "Better get down to business," he thought, so he stood up and went in search of a computer. Walking into one of the offices, to be found along the corridors, he was pleased to see that there were a couple of people waiting to greet him.

"Good morning, Lord McJeffers!"

Robin was shocked and surprised.

"Excuse my French, but bloody hell! News travels fast in this place! Good

Morning!"

A pretty administration assistant, by the name of Michelle Riley explained.

"It's the computer system, Sir. When you became a Lord last night, stroke this morning, you had a chauffeur automatically assigned to you by security. We administer that system so, when we arrived this morning, the data supplied in the daily report showed this."

"Oh, erm, bloody good show!"

This wasn't the way McJeffers usually spoke, but seeing as he was a Lord and none of his colleagues were conscious, he thought he'd try it.

"Sorry, I don't know your name, my dear?"

"It's Michelle, Sir. Michelle Riley."

"Well, Michelle, I'd really like to use one of your computers to type up a report. Can you help?"

"Yes, Sir, not a problem."

With that, the nineteen year old was on the case. Switching on monitors and P.C's, making sure the printer had paper and loading up the software for him.

"There you go, Sir. Any problems then just let me know."

"Thank you, my dear."

Robin sat down and realised that the aftermath of last night's drunken debacle was now down to him and the future of The Royal Navy was at his fingertips. He'd joined in on a conversation, reluctantly at first, but those magical four words, that had bothered him in the past and caused him distress and that had, years ago, caused him to read a book called "Am I mad??… what the hell do my dreams mean?" by a Professor Koppenhurten had now, or last night at least, elevated him to the most powerful man in the country, although the country didn't know it. Robin now felt a full recovery knocking on the door and the constant refilling of his coffee cup, by Michelle, enabled him to sit for close on six hours and create on paper The McJeffers Act.

Everything from rankings to ships names was included. A "total thorough job," he thought to himself. He'd long since sent Michelle home and now felt that he wanted to do the same thing. The printer had been printing the report off for forty minutes or so and, when it finally stopped, Robin was packed and ready to go. He gathered the print out, put it in his briefcase, shut down the P.C and made for the car park. There, he met Eric who opened the rear door and ushered McJeffers in, closing it behind him.

As they pulled out into the late afternoon traffic around Westminster, the two men chatted about their budding relationship. Eric, the Chauffeur, explained his role and also that of McJeffers. McJeffers, for his part, explained that he wasn't normally in the condition that Eric had first met him in earlier that morning. Eric explained that, all the way home McJeffers had sat singing "Harry, make mine a double!" at the top of his voice and that he had created a very "Interesting piece of artwork down the side of the car in the Crystal Palace area," due mostly to the seventeen brandy's. Eric had had to remove this at seven o'clock this morning. Robin apologised and reiterated that he wasn't usually like that and that he wasn't an artist of any particular kind.

Within the hour they were home, or at least at Robin's home. Eric lived in Bromley and turned down the invite of lunch with McJeffers, as he "wanted to get home to the wife and kids." As Eric drove off, Robin walked down the garden path and opened the front door. Elizabeth was in the kitchen making dinner and was pleasantly surprised to see her husband appear in such fine fettle.

"Hello, darling!"

"Robin, you've finally come home! How do you feel dear and how was your first day as a Lord?"

Robin checked himself for a moment. He was in the middle of gunning for a kiss, but his wife's reaction and reply had reminded him that earlier that morning she'd mocked him on a grand scale. Now the man of the house, the chief Baboon, the head honcho, was back and he hadn't forgotten this display of contempt.

"You still don't believe me, do you my darling, eh?"

Elizabeth was shaking her head and about to plead her innocence when Robin produced, in one swift movement, The Act from his briefcase. Ok, it was loose leaf still, but he motioned for her to follow him into the dining room and take a seat at the table. He then offered her the manuscript. As she sat down, she took hold of the bundle of papers and looked at her husband who seemed to be pulling the facial expression of someone in pain, just for a moment anyway.

What had actually just happened was that Robin had been so impressed with his own manly behaviour that he'd suddenly thought of following it up with a manly facial expression, but Elizabeth had looked at him before he'd been able to choose what one to use. He'd only got as far as the "Tough Cowboy" look, before being rumbled and was in-between expressions when she'd looked up. This kind of dented his morale slightly, but he swiftly put that right with a firm and distinctive "Read!"

Elizabeth started reading, as instructed, and was amazed to find that the name on the front page was that of her husband. In fact the name of the report was that of her husband. What an earth was happening? As she read on, deeper and deeper into the report, she realised that it was all true. Her husband was now a Lord and she was now a Lordess or whatever her title would be. She looked up at her husband for re-assurance, but he wasn't there. He'd crept into the kitchen to make a cup of tea and, while the kettle had been boiling, had been secretly and silently jumping around, punching the air in triumph and the knowledge that, as far as this house was concerned, he was 'The Man.'

Chapter Five – Sir Douglas Squires

"Sir Douglas Squires has been installed as Number One in her Majesty's Navy with immediate effect," came the announcement from the Whitehall spokesman, on behalf of Her Majesty, The Queen and her most senior (Level A) Navy representatives. The announcement was cast out through the damp London air to the hordes of bustling reporters from around the world, who had gathered outside the souvenir shop of H.M.S. Belfast.

The cold, hard fact was that the Navy had gained a reputation as an organisation with a lack of imagination over the past decade and it had been this image that had driven the various Lords and people with "Lord" in their name to get carried away in a tidal wave of emotion, resulting in the creation of a monster, the ludicrous McJeffers Act.

With the aim of, as the Whitehall spokesman declared, "Showing the world that the Royal Navy will no longer be a Navy of simpletons and no imagination. The McJeffers Act, Ladies and Gentleman, will simplify our Navy structure and install it at the top of its professional ladder!" Not quite sure of just how high this "professional ladder" reached, the great unwashed, who had gathered there, accepted this nonsense, for now, at least.

Having declared the changing of the times, the Whitehall spokesman was off, speeding down the road in his limo, dust and everyday debris circulating in the air behind him. The intelligence and perceptiveness of the worlds' press, now left floundering outside the souvenir shop, was being severely challenged by the token briefs being issued by the Government concerning the incoming Act.

They knew, for instance, who Robin McJeffers was and they knew, for instance, that Sir Douglas Squires was now "Number One, Level B" in the Royal Navy, to give him his official title. But, what they didn't know, or at least, hadn't been told, was the "why's," "what's" and "when's" that would complete their jigsaw. For now, at least, all they could report on to their respective editors around the globe were the facts that they had been given or had acquired. Those being the releases concerning The McJeffers Act itself, the gentleman it was named after and the "Number One, Level B" of the new Royal Navy.

Sir Douglas Squires, official title "Number One, Level B," entered the secret Navy operations room at Greenwich Maritime Museum, situated, to be exact, under a blue whale in the Main Exhibition Hall, via a staircase, hidden by its lower jaw. The original whale was situated in another museum but, having a connection with the sea, had been copied and installed in the Maritime Museum under the McJeffers Act. This whale had been suspended in mid-air for a few weeks, but with the changing attitudes of the new "Thinking Man's" Navy, the whale had been lowered to just above the ground, with enough room to allow for an opening in the floor, just beneath the lower, and now severely distorted jaw.

The jaw hadn't started life as a distorted one, but had become so primarily because of a slight oversight when being mounted. On standing back to admire their handy work, the men responsible for positioning it had found that they were actually a couple of feet away from where they should've been. As with everything to do with the new Act, the limited plans available were rather sketchy, to say the least, and thus offered no real clear or precise figure work to position against.

Weighing up the options, they decided that it was far easier to break and thus distort the lower jaw than to re-hang the monstrous lump of fiberglass and so life began in earnest for the copy of the blue whale with the severely distorted lower jaw. The plan had been and was always to cover a staircase that sank downwards into a seemingly thankless dark pit and, after the workmen had distorted the jaw, this was indeed what it did.

Progressing along the lines of "No-one will expect that staircase to lead to a room as important as the Royal Navy Operations Centre," the daily flocks of tourists had stared in amazement from day one, as senior looking Navy dignitaries were to be seen crawling under the lower jaw of a blue whale but, as with everything to do with the new navy, deception was the name of the game.

A directive had been issued by the most senior Navy man, a certain "Number One, Level A" that all personnel entering the operations establishment, for it was a huge underground complex by now, had to carry a cleaning cloth with them which "could be visibly seen by the tourists" to ensure that the "aforementioned personnel" would appear to the "naked eye" as nothing more than a "cleaner inspecting the underside of the blue whale." With the issuing of this directive, the deceptively ignorant arm of the armed forces settled down to a period of, well, ignorance.

"Aaaagh, Douglas, glad you could make it. Come in, take a seat."

"Thank you for the invite, Sir."

Sir Douglas Squires, Number One, Level B, took up residence in the standard, Government Issue, wooden chair offered him by his superior, Sir Horace Hargraves, Number One, Level A. Middle aged, but still slim and athletic in build, with a full head of neatly combed dark brown hair, Sir Douglas cut quite a dashing figure as he sat awaiting the address from his superior.

Since the "Men in the suits and wigs" had passed the Act, as Hargraves himself had declared, the Navy had been split into two levels. Level A being the "desk bound" elder statesman of the service, whilst "Level B" represented the service men and women. The "Hands on" section, so to speak. Of all the many weird and wonderful situations afforded the Navy by the enactment of the McJeffers Act, possibly the most straight forward to understand, although hard to comprehend, was the abolition of all the different levels of rank and the installation of a straight forward numbering system.

Top of the tree was, of course, number one, or his absolute official title, Number One, Level B. From number one downwards, both in the chain of command and what would've been, in the old system, rank, came number two, three etc. Now just when the service men and women reading the new briefing instructions, issued by the Navy on this situation, began to think that they were getting the hang of this new "system," along came the realisation that any number of service men or women previously ranked the same would, in all probability, have different numbers. Thus, a common situation of say, two cooks, one is number two hundred, the other is two hundred and one. Whereas under the old system they would both be the same rank, the new system created the problem that one was technically ranked higher than the other.

Once this problem had been brought to the attention of the gentlemen whose title ended with "Level A," it was decided, remarkably quickly, to keep the numbering system and for all personnel of the same rank…. issue them the same number. Thus, under the Act, it was possible, although, in reality, it was never going to happen, for a ship of, say, four hundred men to have number six hundred, Level B in command with three hundred and ninety nine six hundred and one, Level B's below him/her. Once the realisation of this ludicrous situation hit home to the service men and women they began to wonder just how long it would be before the words "Royal Navy" were replaced with "The Royal Boat People" or "The Floaty Boat Brigade."

"Douglas."

"Sir!"

"Whatever you might think of the new Navy."

"You mean since the Act, Sir?"

"Yes, that's exactly what I mean…The Act"

"It's given us great moral standing, Sir!"

"Really? I mean, Yes! You're right there, Douglas!"

"Is there a problem, Sir?"

"Problem. No! No, no, no, God forbid! Well, Yes!"

"Sir?"

"Well, you see, Douglas. It's like this…"

Sir Douglas Squires motioned to rise up out of his chair and follow his superior across to a small, spot light-emblazoned table on the other side of the "Ops Room."

"No, no, no stay there, Douglas. I'll put what I've got for you on the overhead projector thing."

Sir Douglas found himself, just for a short moment, in an awkward situation, as his superior was obviously having one hell of a fight with the "overhead projector thing," positioned across the other side of the room. First there was light, then there was darkness, mumbled swearing and lots of fidgeting then finally, there it was, now burning its own image into the wall of the operations room.

"You see Douglas, it's like this. The powers that be, I mean…"

"The suits and wigs, Sir?"

"Yes indeed, Douglas, the suits and wigs, well, they feel that, as part of the Navy's new image, we ought to put a new vessel to sea and…"

"That's not it, is it? Sir? Is it?"

64

"Erm, well, yes, Douglas it is or at least, will be."

Sir Douglas now sat there staring at the image, burning bright before him, in horror. He'd gone a kind of pale green-grey colour now and was seemingly struggling to deal with any bodily function other than breathing. Sir Horace, seeing the impending physical and mental collapse of his man, now attempted to snap him out of his approaching demise.

"Douglas! Douglas!"

"Sir, I'm here, but…"

"Now Douglas, Douglas! She's not that bad! Please allow me to show you the plans and go through her features."

"Sir, may I say…"

"Save it, Douglas!"

"But, Sir!"

"Douglas, look at it this way, you'll be at the helm of the newest ship in the fleet, the pride of the nation, and the…"

"But she's half battleship and half…"

"Douglas, listen to me man!"

"Sir!"

"Ok, good man! Right, where was I? Oh yes, the most deceptive piece of ordinance that the country's ever produced."

Sir Horace moved to switch on the Ops Room lights

65

and turn off the overhead projector thing. Moving from there back to the small table, now free from the glare of spot lights, to gather a few rolls of plans and return to where Sir Douglas sat motionless, and in what looked like a state of shock. The rolls of paper he had just collected were, in fact, the plans for this brand new vessel. As he approached Sir Douglas he did, in fact, continue past him, gesturing for him to follow as he did so. Sir Horace, although concerned that his "Number One, Level B" had suffered a breakdown in front of his very own eyes, was relieved to see that Sir Douglas had responded to the 'follow me' gesture and had entered the adjoining room after his superior.

Sir Horace carefully spread the plans out across the table and tacked each corner using pins provided in a bowl for that very purpose.

"Right Douglas, as the American chaps might say "Lookey-here cowboy!""

Sir Douglas approached the table, where his boss had just laid out the plans, with a cold stare in his eyes. As he looked at them he felt a shiver race up and down his spine. The first thing he noticed was the name of the "artist," who'd created these nightmares that he could not avert his eyes from. There, in the bottom left hand corner of each individual plan was the name of both artist and his company. There, before his very eyes, was the legend "D.C Postlethwaite, Model Boats Ltd."

Sir Douglas Squires had served in the Navy for twenty-seven years and had sailed the world's waters in just about every type of vessel afloat. It was this experience that, he felt, justified this nigh-on, full-blown breakdown that he'd just suffered as a result of seeing the artist's impression of his next "ship."

"D.C Postlethwaite, Model Boats Ltd?"

"Aagh, erm, yes, Douglas."

"Sir?"

"Erm, as it turns out, Douglas, ma boy, two reasons really."

"Sir, there are actually two reasons for this?"

"Well, kind of! You see, my friend, the first is, or was, a case of security. We couldn't really let anyone know what we we're creating, not even the designers!"

Sir Douglas felt weak again.

"And the second?"

"No-one in their right mind would design something so unstable and put their name to it!"

Sir Douglas felt weaker still.

"The only way round it was to ask a model boat designer to draw up our plans. That way we can't hold them responsible and they've got no idea that we intend to build a full scale version."

It was the memories, now flooding his brain, which caused the panic currently setting in, in a pale green-grey fashion. The memories of sailing the world in some of the most technically-advanced craft of their day, using systems so clever that he'd, even to this day, never managed to comprehend that microchips and wire could do things and make decisions that those systems had. And now, he was looking at this, thinking to himself that the navy had just slipped back in time by about a thousand years or so.

As he cast his eyes over these plans he knew what the immediate future would bring, not the future weeks, just the next few minutes in the way of what his superior, who stood at his side, silent and observing, would do and say. He knew, for instance, that he was going to get "given" this "ship" and that what he was looking at was the result of cutbacks.

"You see, Douglas, it's like this. Due to cutbacks…"

"We need to produce a new craft, but at a drastically reduced cost!"

"You've hit the nail on the head, my friend!"

"But Sir, this won't float, let alone be stable enough to fight! The minute she fires a round from any of those turrets she'll spin and capsize!"

"Aaagh, that's where you're wrong, my friend!"

"Sir! I must protest! In my judgement, the minute she fires

her guns she'll…."

"She doesn't have any guns, Douglas."

"WHAT!"

"They're just for show, to make it look like she's armed to the hilt. Good God man, if she had guns, she wouldn't be able to float, and if she did, and she fired them, she'd spin and capsize! They, my friend, will be the stripped out shells of VW beetles with telegraph poles mounted through the windows to look like guns. Clever, eh?"

Sir Douglas felt "nervous breakdown number two," waiting just around the corner. In all the years that he'd served in his beloved Navy, he never thought that he'd see the day when she willingly stepped back into the dark ages. "Can, can I have a glass of water please, Sir?"

"No problemmo, my friend. You study ya boat, I'll get the drinks."

That last sentence confirmed to Sir Douglas what he already knew. He was being placed in charge of this new, all singing, all dancing, well, new at least, craft. Sir Horace returned a few minutes later with a glass of water and a pint of lager for himself. As he offered the glass of water to Sir Douglas, he noticed a look of surprise coming from him, but this time aimed at himself and his pint of lager.

"Here you go my friend. What? Oh, the lager! Well, you see,

it's the new Navy! Rum's "outta here!" Lager's the drink for me now!"

Sir Douglas wondered if he'd ever see the lower jaw of the blue whale again or, indeed, daylight. He felt nervous breakdowns three through to fifty queuing around his body. He hoped and prayed that he'd wake up from this nightmare any second now. Instead, he found himself in an operations room below the lower jaw of a fibreglass blue whale, in the Main Exhibition Hall of the Greenwich Maritime Museum, looking at the plans for his next command. This new command was apparently wooden in construction, with a thin covering of sheet metal, although, on closer inspection, this sheet metal appeared to be fridge and freezer doors.

As if this wasn't bad enough, his superior had taken on the persona of someone fuelled by drugs and both American mannerisms and confidence. With this in mind, he rallied himself and thought he'd better take a look across the table at Sir Horace. This he did and was met by a rather chirpy man, gesturing at him with his half-empty pint glass, in a way as to toast him. This action, although bad enough, was accompanied by a ridiculous smile complete with a white froth covering the top lip.

Sir Douglas accepted that it was going to be a long day. What he was essentially looking at, there on the table before him, spread out and tacked down at each corner were the plans to a ship which, when built, would, for all intents and purposes, be half battleship and half Greek Trireme ship. It appeared to be an extended Viking-esque vessel with a flat and enclosed upper surface, much akin to the Triremes ships of old. This surface was where the VW's were sited – fore and aft. Although, he thought to himself, would "fore" and "aft" or, indeed, "port" and "starboard" actually exist anymore under the new Act?

Mortified by what lay there on the table, Sir Douglas Squires began to accept the principle and decided that, obviously, the "serious years" of his naval service had passed and the "comical years" were here to stay. Along with this acceptance came the willingness to study the plans more closely. Sir Horace, seeing his man begin to take to the idea, thought that it was time for the next stage of the briefing.

"It's purely a situation of "New Image, No money," Douglas. They want a new vessel, but don't really have the funds, so they've come up with this. It's, as you can see, a wooden structure with sheet metal covering her from just above the water line upwards. It's effectively a very large Trireme boat, covered in metal sheeting with some fake guns and radar bits added for good measure. She'll have several decks and you'll have walkie-talkie communication with the shore when you're near enough and carrier pigeons for when you're not."

"You'll run the ship as though she were a complete Battleship and the name of the game is deception. No one will expect us to produce such a craft and therefore they'll all be thinking that we've got something on board that they haven't. That is the overriding point of the exercise. We've got to turn the situation around to our advantage, is that clear?"

"Yes, Sir!"

"Very good, Douglas. Now, before we adjourn for lunch, any questions?"

"Power, Sir. What'll power her?"

"Aaagh, an excellent question Douglas! Really very good thinking, erm, Six hundred accountants will power her!"

"Accountants, Sir?"

"Yes Douglas. I'd like to refer you to that plan there. Look, just above the water line…"

Sir Horace guided Sir Douglas' attention to one of the plans that focused on the subject at hand. There, as if completely natural, were hundreds of oars, piercing their way out of the hull of the vessel.

"Oars, Sir?"

"Yep. Three hundred either side. Again, no-one will believe

we're powering her with oars due to lack of money!"

"Sir, two questions, if I may!"

"Proceed!"

"Firstly, do you think this whole project is wise and, secondly, why accountants?"

"Again, Douglas, excellent questions. Firstly, yes, I do. The McJeffers Act has, essentially, sunk the Navy, as we knew her, without a trace. So this is the dawn, so to speak, of the new era. Secondly, they're methodical, reliable and even-paced!"

With questions answered, Sir Horace reached for the Government Issue, black telephone, on the end of the table and, lifting the receiver to his ear, awaited the voice at the other end.

"Aaagh, yes. It's Sir Horace, please have my car ready in two minutes...the usual destination."

The usual destination was a gentleman's club, recently installed beneath the famous Cutty Sark, a short journey down the road from their present location. Like so many things in the "New Navy," the powers that be had shown a fondness for "installing things underground where no-one would think of looking for them." Hence the Operations Room beneath the lower jaw of the blue whale in the Main Exhibition Hall of the Maritime Museum etc, etc.

Sir Horace un-tacked the plans which, when released, rolled themselves up loosely. Gathering them up, he walked over to the safe in the corner of the room. Bending over, he placed them in the already-open safe, snapped the door shut, and stood up straight. He motioned to Sir Douglas to follow him and both men headed for the stairs leading up to the lower jaw of the blue whale.

As they climbed the stairs, both men reached into their respective pockets for their yellow dusters and, as they reached the opening at the top, they naturally began to fake-dust everything around them, as they climbed out into the Main Hall from beneath the lower jaw of the blue monster, suspended not so high above them.

Again, as happened every time this spectacle appeared, the public milling about in the main hall knew that something was hidden below their feet. The concept of cleaning staff dressed as Naval dignitaries hadn't fooled them and although they appeared to accept the situation, they were aware of something happening at the bottom of the steps below the disfigured lower jaw.

However, this couldn't be said of the Naval dignitaries and, in turn, everyone entering or leaving the secretive establishment. Indeed, as if brain washed, everyone involved with the new project believed that fake dusting him or her self and all around, every time they entered into the main hall or disappeared from view, was the "perfect deception." As the two men left the main hall and walked out into the sunshine, that was warming the country for the fifth day in succession, Sir Horace turned to Sir Douglas and stopped him in his tracks.

"You'll be free to pick your own crew and the honour of naming the ship's yours as well, my friend. The only thing the navy want "in on" is the selection of the six hundred accountants. God only knows why, but there it is!"

This brief address from Sir Horace was met by an accepting nod from Sir Douglas. Both men entered the back of the waiting car, which sped off towards their lunch appointment at the "Cutty Club." Once there, both men settled into their respective leather chairs and, whilst perusing their menus, sipped from their respective pints of chilled lager, the "New Navy man's drink." Sir Douglas, now away from the nightmare he'd witnessed in the Operations Room a short while before, was steadily relaxing in these new surroundings and began to smile and make conversation with his boss. Sir Horace, enjoying the sight of his "favourite underling" recovering from several breakdowns, thought that now was the time to ask some questions for himself.

"So Douglas, what do you think you'll call her?"

"Well, Sir. I think I'll be naming her after someone famous. Someone who's displayed certain characteristics that can be found to be similar to the characteristics of the boat."

"Excellent man! Really, that is quite fabulous thinking. Got anything in mind?"

"Well, Sir. If we're looking to deceive the world's populace then we'll need a name that says to them everything that we want them to believe."

"Douglas! That's brilliant! I knew you were the right man for the job! Go on, please, go on!"

"Well, Sir. If you look at what she'll be in real terms, slow, un-manoeuvrable, un-sophisticated, a basic death trap, then you've got to be looking along the lines of "H.M.S. Dead In The Water," but if you want to deceive the punters, so to speak, then she'll have to have a name that says fast, awesome powered, a sort of "Don't Mess With Me" type of name."

"Go on man, spit it out! What'll you be calling her?"

"Sir, after great thought, I've decided to call her...."

"Yes, yes, I'm waiting."

"H.M.S. Osvaldo Ardilles."

"H.M.S. what?"

"Osvaldo Ardilles, Sir. He played for Tottenham Hotspur...and Argentina!"

"Let me get this right. You're intending to name the newest and most important ship the Navy's ever produced after an Argentine footballer?"

"Yes, Sir! Sir, think about it, I know we've had our troubles with the Argies, but this'll show us as being the new "forgive and forget" Navy. Besides, he was fast, nimble, deadly accurate and quite an all-round, erm, superstar, Sir!"

Sir Horace pondered and pouted and pouted and pondered before answering with a heavy bout of realisation. "Right, yes, right, right, I see where ya coming from Douglas, ma boy!"

"Also, Sir, just a suggestion. "The Royal Navy"...sounds a bit, pompous and stuck up, Sir. Do you not think?"

"Hmmm, what are you suggesting, Douglas? Changing the name of our beloved service?"

"Yes, Sir! To "The Floaty Boat Brigade!""

"And what would this achieve, Douglas, eh?"

This response from Sir Horace was bordering on aggrieved.

"Well, Sir, It would distance the style of thinking and behaviour from the old to the new, Sir."

Suddenly, and leaning less towards "aggrieved" and more towards "warming to," Sir Horace seemed to switch on to his favourite underling with a previously unheard of speed and clarity.

"Do you mean, new structure, new craft, new thinking, and new name?"

"Yes, Sir. That's exactly what I mean!"

And with that, the conversation came to an abrupt halt as an immaculate waiter approached their table and served up two meals fit for a king. Both men had chosen the same from the menu, the "Chef's Special" of the day. This turned out to be a sort of beef dish in which many unrecognisable items had obviously met with death and had reappeared as a sort of beef dish. Along with two of the "Chef's Specials" came two more pints of Lager, for two of the Navy's thinking men.

Both men acknowledged the delivery of their meal with a cordial and polite nod to the waiter and then began to tuck in. During the meal the conversation between the two had concentrated on sport, in particular football, and had ventured for limited periods onto women, the arts and motor racing but, with the finishing of their meals, came the stark realisation that they had a new boat to build and crew. Sir Horace gestured for the waiter and then asked for the bill. This was swiftly brought to the table and equally swiftly paid for with his new 'Level A Visa Card,' courtesy of The Act. Both men rose from the table and left the establishment via the door, which led them out into the Souvenir shop on board the Cutty Sark.

Once outside the boat itself, Sir Horace motioned at his driver who immediately started the car and drove up onto the pavement to where the two men stood. Once settled inside, the car sped off towards the Maritime museum. Having been softened up by the lavish "Chef's Special" and a couple of pints of lager, Sir Douglas Squires thought to himself that he was ready for a long afternoon nap.

"I'm ready to get back to the task in hand now, Sir!"

"Excellent Douglas! I, myself, am ready for a long afternoon nap, so I'll drop you off at the Museum, give you the keys to the safe and see you tomorrow morning at ten, OK?"

Having summarily shot himself in the proverbial foot, Sir Douglas climbed out of the car and, turning to collect the keys from Sir Horace, clumsily saluted him then shut the door and watched as the car sped towards and out of the main gates. "Bugger," he thought to himself, and came to the rapid conclusion that his task wasn't going to go away and so he might as well get on with it.

With this realisation in mind, he shrugged his shoulders, entered the museum and proceeded towards the Main Exhibition Hall. On the way down the corridor he happened to glance to his left and notice a painting on the wall. He stopped and studied the oil on canvas piece hung before him. It was of the inside of an old Spanish galleon and centred on the efforts of the oarsman. There were the usual scenes of whippings, blood, sweat and pain, but it was the characters in the centre, and at the far end of the aisle, that caught his attention. There, keeping the beat, was a drummer of some kind, seemingly pounding away with such precision and timing that it would appear to have been nigh on impossible for the oarsmen not to keep in time.

"How, the hell," he thought to himself, "do you employ someone like that?" Then his self-questioning advanced to the next level. "Who, the hell, do I employ as beat-keeper for six hundred accountants?" These questions were causing him great concern as he approached the distorted lower jaw of the blue whale. Without stopping to see if there was anyone around, he naturally reached inside his pocket for his yellow duster and began to fake-dust all around him, as he crawled under the jaw and stepped downwards into the darkness, turning right at the bottom of the stairs, into the Operations Room.

The Operations Room was a fairly cold and basic room. It resembled something in size, colour and ambience of an old cabinet war room. There were no lavish fittings and there was still the smell of concrete paint in the air. Basic furnishings included the obligatory tables, chairs, telephones, an overhead projector thing and an acceptable level of lighting. There was a small kitchen off to one side that had cupboards and a fridge and a kettle but, overall, the whole image of this room and, in fact, the whole under jaw complex was that of a prison without the cells.

Every single footstep, regardless of footwear, regardless of corridor or room, produced a cold grey echo that resonated throughout. No matter from whom or from where the steps originated, the echo was always as loud, as cold and as present. It was, quite simply, home.

He approached the locked safe in the corner and, after fumbling around in his other jacket pocket to which he kept his yellow duster, found the key he was looking for and unlocked the safe. Gathering up all the rolls of plans, at this stage five in all, he set about pinning them out on the display table in a similar fashion to what Sir Horace had done only hours before. Once he'd completed this task, he stood back to grasp exactly what he was to take to sea within a year.

There were various views and diagrams contained on each sheet, from full-blown colour efforts to cut-away drawings of each deck and the mock-up guns and radar stations. As his eyes wandered wearily over the plans he came across the cut-away section showing the rowing deck and, in particular, the six hundred positions that would be filled by the accountants that the Navy explicitly wanted to select. His mind wandered to the painting, that he'd only recently studied in the corridor above, and his attention focused back on the plans to the point where he'd expect to see the character from the painting sat. He wasn't disappointed. There, in all its cut-away glory, was not one, but five chairs positioned along the centre aisle, the length of the ship. Awaiting five of the best timekeepers the country had to offer.

"Now, what type of person would be best suited to one of those chairs? Drummers! Perfect! I'll raid the music industry and find five brilliant young drummers and strike a deal with them to sit in those chairs! No, no, that wouldn't work! Accountants are old people; boring types, who mostly lead quiet, grey lives. Five young drummers would wind them up! I'd be forever receiving noise complaints from them. No, that wouldn't do, we'd never get anywhere with five young drummers."

Sir Douglas cast his mind back to the proverbial drawing board, whilst he continued to scan the five separate sheets of plans laid out before him, all the while trying to come up with the solution to his first crewing problem. "Accountants; drab, boring, grey, methodical, reliable. Who or what would they need to be accompanied by in order to attain their high levels of consistency?" He pondered the question for several minutes, all the while staring at, and sometimes through the plans, until he stepped away from the table and walked towards the kitchen. There, with the question still swirling around inside his head, he filled the kettle, standard Government Issue, with water, boiled it and made himself a black coffee. On returning to the table the answer hit him with the force of someone striking him from behind.

"Book-keepers! I'll enrol five steady-as-you-like middle aged book-keepers to accompany my six hundred accountants."

Oh, the joy that Sir Douglas now felt was overwhelming and he punched the air, Government Issue, with glee before composing himself and attending to the plans once more. His first problem had been overcome. His first big test as Number One, Level B had been set by himself and passed by himself, with flying colours, even if he did say so himself. For the next three hours Sir Douglas Squires sat at the table making notes on a pad, non Government Issue, W.H Smiths, relating to the ship resting before his eyes.

Black coffee followed black coffee before, finally, he un-tacked the plans and returned them to the sanctuary of the safe in the corner of the room. After checking that all electrical appliances were unplugged, he switched off the lights and, picking up his notepad, started up the stairs towards the lower jaw. As it was approaching nine o'clock in the evening he knew that the Museum had long since shut to the public for the day and so felt no need to "fake-dust" his way out from under the lower jaw of the blue whale that dominated the space above his head. To this day he'd never quite fathomed why the powers that be had requested a copy of the blue whale, which had stood for so long in the Natural History Museum. Why copy it? Why not just move the bloody thing? He shook his head and made for the exit.

He walked down the corridor, past the inspirational painting of the galleon, to the museum reception where the night watchman rose from his chair and unlocked the front doors.

"Goodnight, Sir."

"Goodnight, my friend."

With those parting words came the sensation of fresh air storming up and into his nostrils. He was outside and free, but only for a couple of hours. Reality dealt him a slap on the face and with it the awareness that his driver was standing beside the open rear door of his car. Driving home he felt a warm glow of comfort come over him as he reviewed in his mind what had happened that day.

He'd started it with several mental breakdowns and had ended it triumphantly with his first report to Sir Horace, albeit a collection of notes, ready to deliver, currently sliding around on the back seat next to him. He'd, at first, been mortified by the sight of the beast from the dark ages that lay spread out on the table, but had conquered this fear and loathing and, by the time he'd switched off the Operations Room lights, he had become emotionally attached to the wooden creation he was destined to sail.

On reaching home Sir Douglas stepped out of the car and, turning to shut the door, declared "See you at about nine thirty, Peter." A muffled "Yes, Sir" could be heard coming from the front of the car as the slamming of the door signalled to his driver that he could pull away. He headed down the garden path with report under his arm and into the sanctuary of his home knowing that, once inside, the madness that he'd encountered at the Museum would be no more. As the door slammed shut, Sir Douglas relaxed. He instinctively went to call for his wife, Susan, but she was away visiting her sister in Devon, so he was home alone. Just as the thought of his impending evening of loneliness was settling on his mind, he was startled back to reality by the sound of the telephone ringing.

"Bexley two, six, four, nine, one...hello?"

"Douglas, is that you?"

"Sir Horace?"

"Yes, yes, it's me. One thing I forgot to mention, ma boy!"

"Yes, Sir?"

"Varnish."

"Excuse me?"

"You know, Douglas. Varnish...and wood stain!"

"Erm, excuse me for sounding thick Sir, but I don't understand. What varnish and wood stain, exactly?"

"For the ship. Y'know, H.M.S. Osvaldo Ardilles. It's another of the privileges bestowed upon you for being the 'Skipper,' so to speak!"

"Nope, nope, still not with you, Sir."

"Oh for God's sake, Douglas! You get to choose the colour and finish that will be applied to the wood on the ship. Bloody hell, man, wake up will you!"

"Oh, erm, fantastic news, Sir, erm, thanks. Thank you very much, Sir!"

"Not a problem, ma boy. Not a problem at all. You'll, of course, have to attend the carpentry course for a complete understanding and realisation of what varnish and stains do to different woods, but you'll be able to cope with that. See you at ten tomorrow, Douglas."

Before he could reply he became aware that he was

holding the receiver to his ear and listening to a dead line. He replaced the receiver on the phone and headed for the kitchen to rustle up some food and drink. It had been a long day.

Chapter Six – The morning after

When he woke the following morning he found, to his total dismay that he was still fully clothed, bar his officer's peak cap, which had fallen from his head and lay on the floor beside the armchair that he was currently slumped in. His eyes were hurting from, what appeared to be, the brightness of the sunshine that was piercing through the net curtains, but then his head also hurt and, wait a minute, his stomach! Oh, his stomach! It felt as though a blender-wielding maniac had attacked it. "Damn it!" he thought, "bloody hangover!"

The Television was still on and was now blurting out some kind of breakfast programme. One of those which always saw untalented, un-funny presenters trying to be, "wacky," for the sake of the cornflake-eating generation. "Why, oh why," he thought, "would anybody want to face this kind of assault on their humour at any stage of their day, let alone over breakfast?" "And who," he thought to himself, "employed these people…and, and who," he challenged himself to answer, "who was the Talent Scout who 'spotted' these people?" He realised at once that he was questioning himself over something he didn't really care about, except on the rare occasions where he found himself watching these people, whilst nursing a hangover.

Squinting at the clock, showing in the bottom left hand corner of the T.V, he noticed it showed '08:47.' Suddenly, as clear as if the man was actually there in the front room with him, the voice of his boss, Sir Horace Hargraves, broke the silence with "See you at ten, Douglas!" This gentle, but almost sadistic, reminder prompted a panic stricken outcry of "Oh, Bloody Nora!" and, with that, he was out of the chair and making for the upstairs bathroom. All the while he was undressing and reaching for his electric shaver, he was mentally working out just how little time he had to spare.

"Ten o'clock appointment, half hour journey, that means the car will be here at about twenty past, ten minutes for a shave, better make that two minutes for a shave, ten minutes for a shower." However he worked his calculations, he knew it would be tight, but he had a master plan. He'd just managed to make it downstairs when the doorbell rang. He opened it and wasn't surprised to see his driver, Peter, standing there.

"Two minutes, my friend."

This declaration was met by an understanding nod that, in turn, was followed by the man at the door, Peter, retreating to the driver's seat in the car. Sir Douglas pulled himself away from watching his driver and rushed into the front room. Sitting himself down on the sofa, he hurriedly put on his socks and shoes. Next stop was the bookcase where his master plan sat, or rather his lame attempt at creating an excuse for himself being late, sat. He scanned the spines of the books on the shelves. "Where are you, where are you?" Suddenly, there it was. The answer, he hoped, to his "Oh God, give me an excuse for being late" prayer. Its spine almost glowed to him as it distinguished itself from the other books, rising from the flames, or so it appeared, to save his bacon.

Sir Douglas Squires, Number One, Level B of the Royal Navy, or soon to be, The Floaty Boat Brigade, plucked his saviour from the shelf with a smile and a huge sense of relief. It was this book that would save his reputation and standing at this early stage of his new "career." This one book, he thought, would probably be enough to, not only serve as an excuse for being late, but also, he reasoned, probably come across to his boss as "Supreme Thinking."

Indeed, 'The Readers Digest Home Improvements - Volume One...Dealing with wood," would surely serve him well over the coming days. And so, with this 'Holy Grail' and his report tucked safely under his arm, Sir Douglas Squires shut his front door and walked happily, if not slightly wearily, to the car that sat outside. Heading into Greenwich, in the back of the car, he sat there planning his opening exchanges with his boss.

"Look, I've got this!" or "Morning, Sir, sorry I'm late, I've got this!" or "Got reading this book, Sir." That was the one for him, sorted! Sir Douglas Squires, Number One, Level B of The "New Navy" or soon to be "The Floaty Boat Brigade," sat there in the back of the car and scanned the pages, like a naughty school boy writing a fake sick note from his mum, just in case his boss wished to test him on it. On arrival at Greenwich, Sir Douglas despatched Peter for the day, which to Peter and all the other drivers, meant sitting behind the museum at a special driver's assembly point. There they could relax, watch TV, read papers etc. There was a canteen and a rest room for them and it really was, very nearly, home from home.

So, as Sir Douglas entered the museum, Peter drove around the side of the museum, towards the assembly point at the rear, to begin his day of relaxation. Walking down the corridor to the Main Hall, Sir Douglas looked up and smiled at the painting, that had caught his attention the night before, as he passed by. He gripped the report, which had been inspired by it, slightly tighter under his arm. On entering the Main Hall, he whisked out his duster and began to fake dust everything around him. As he manoeuvred himself under the severely distorted lower jaw of the giant blue whale and onto the stairwell, which led down to the Operations Centre where his boss stood waiting, he thought to himself "now for the moment of truth."

"Morning, Douglas, run into any trouble?"

"Morning Sir, I'm sorry I'm late. I got reading this here book and, well, the time just flew. I'm very sorry for my..."

"Book eh? Give it here man. What ya reading, me shipmate?"

Douglas handed him the book, "The Readers Digest Home Improvements – Volume One...Dealing with wood" and was very concerned that his boss had already taken on the persona of Captain Birdseye at twenty past ten in the morning.

"Douglas."

"Sir?"

"What bloody supreme thinking, me boy!"

"Thank you, Sir. I thought that the more information I can take on board, erm, excuse the pun, then the more beneficial I'll be and, more importantly, my crew and our ship will be, Sir!"

"I knew you were the right man for the job. I know I keep saying it, Douglas, but you are the only person who has the imagination and adaptability to sail this thing."

"Thank you, Sir!"

"Do you know, do you know who they actually wanted? I mean, For God's sake Douglas! The men in suits and wigs actually wanted the guy who plays the part of Captain Birdseye in those TV commercials to command the Ardilles because "he looked the part!""

"Captain Birdseye, Sir?"

"I know, I know, but you, with that sort of thinking and initiative, are the man for the job."

"Thank you, Sir."

"I mean, if we'd accepted their proposals for the crew, we'd have one extremely old actor re-living his experiences of fighting the armada rather than progressing with the plans for the modern Navy. They actually wanted Captain Pugwash as well! For crying out loud Douglas! They actually wanted a bloody cartoon as the co-Captain of this ship!!!"

"I'm, I'm honoured to have beaten such famous and esteemed competition for this, placement, Sir!"

"Oh Douglas! Come, come! You're "Da Man!""

Sir Douglas was now concerned that his boss had become a "Vanilla Ice" style rapper in front of his eyes, as he followed him into the room where the plans were already laid out and tacked to the table exactly the way they had been the previous day."

"Ok, Douglas. How do we approach the crewing problem

and all the other problems that we have to overcome?"

"Well, Sir. Six hundred accountants will need time keepers with the same qualities as themselves."

"Drummers?"

"No, Sir! The last thing you want when you're bobbing about at sea, trying to keep the thing upright, is noise complaints from your engine room!"

"Aagh yes, noise complaints, very good thinking. So what do you suggest, Gardeners?"

"Gardeners, Sir?"

"Erm, well, I thought they might be very neat and tidy and be able to give the lads some gardening tips while they're rowing."

"Oh, yes, I do see where you're coming from, Sir, I really do. But, I was thinking more along the lines of Book-keepers."

"Oh, yes, they were actually my second choice, you know!"

Sir Douglas motioned for his boss to join him at the table where he could demonstrate his theory on bookkeepers being the ideal partners for the accountants. He proceeded to point out, on the plans, where they would sit for optimum performance. He explained that, as far as he felt, a total of five would be most beneficial, and then he thought of a question.

"Sir, you know these accountants of ours? The ones that'll be rowing the Ardilles..."

"Yes, Douglas, I know of them!"

"Well, will they be dressed as accountants? I mean, will they be wearing suits, Sir?"

"Oh, yes, Douglas, they'll be sitting down there looking like they've just got off of the seven-eighteen at Cannon Street."

"And the reason they'll be wearing suits, Sir, is? If you don't mind me asking that is?"

"Navy, I mean "The Floaty Boat Brigade" efficiency and image, Douglas!"

"Excuse me, Sir?"

"The aforementioned men in suits and wigs have decided that these accountant fellows will perform better if they're dressed as they would be if they were performing their every day accountant duties."

"But, they'll be down below in a hot environment, rowing a ship, Sir!"

"I know, Douglas, I know, but we'll just have to keep telling them that the air conditioning has failed. They'll be hot, sweaty, thoroughly irritable, but they're professionals so they'll continue to get the job done. Maybe, maybe you can allow them to take their jackets off, or, or even loosen their ties, but that bit will be down to your discretion. You know, for a job well done!"

Douglas was now a bit concerned. After yesterdays initial introduction to this barely floating death trap, he thought he'd recovered sufficiently to overcome any more 'surprises' that Sir Horace, or anyone else for that matter, might throw at him. But he was wrong. He felt weak.

"Now Douglas, tell me about these book-keepers of yours. Age, recruitment angle, tell me my friend, what's ya vision?"

"Well, Sir, I think that they need to be as closely tied to the accountants as possible for the benefit of a good working relationship. So whatever segments of the accounting industry the Navy, sorry, "The Floaty Boat Brigade" recruit from, these guys or girls should come from the same offices, where possible."

"So we save on recruitment costs. Bloody good thinking, Douglas!"

"I was actually thinking of the existence of a good working relationship between the accountant and the bookkeeper, Sir."

"Oh, erm, yes, Bloody good thinking, Douglas!"

"You see, Sir, by bringing over an accountant and a bookkeeper that might know each other and work closely together, there'll already be in existence a trust and camaraderie."

Sir Douglas was, again, concerned as his superior slipped

into his 'Vanilla Ice' guise again and started to laugh and moonwalk around the room.

"A-ha, gotcha, gotcha, gotcha....GOT YOU...let's do lunch!"

Sir Horace stopped walking backwards when he reached the small, Government Issue, table in the corner of the room on which sat the Government Issue telephone, in Government Issue black. While he was calling for his driver, Sir Douglas was un-tacking the plans and placing them back in the safe at the far end of the room. With that done he joined his boss at the base of the stairs. Again, as they climbed the stairs into the natural daylight, that shone in through the large windows above the blue whale, they both took out their yellow dusters and began to fake dust anything and everything that lay around them. And, again, to each and every member of the paying public in the Hall at that moment, deception was the biggest loser as each and every person knew that the men they were observing crawling out from under the big blue whale with the severely distorted lower jaw definitely weren't cleaners.

Once both men had left the Hall and replaced their yellow dusters in their respective pockets, they walked down the corridor and out into the sunshine to where the car and driver stood. Destination for lunch was, again, "The Cutty Club" and, once there, they again settled into the cosy chairs to examine the menu. As per the previous day, Sir Horace ordered two pints of lager, the new "Floaty Boat Brigade" man's drink. Sir Horace decided that the two men would have the same as the previous day, a "Chef's Special."

Douglas was very sceptical of this choice but, as his boss was paying for it, he thought he'd best keep quiet. After about twenty minutes of idle chit-chat between them, the waiter approached the table and served up the two "Chef's Specials." With both eyes half shut through the sheer terror of what lay on his plate, he was pleasantly surprised when he opened them to find that what had met death today wasn't loosely described as beef, but appeared to the naked eye to be fish, of various shapes and sizes.

Having sailed the oceans for many years in the service of Her Majesty, The Queen, Douglas had grown fond of fish and so found what was on his plate to be of liking to him. It was only when he was about half way through his meal, conversing with his boss, who sat opposite, and who had recently ordered two more pints of lager for them both, that Sir Douglas noticed what the "Chef's Special," that he was eating his way through, was called. He felt his stomach tighten slightly as he read the chalkboard menu over Sir Horace's shoulder. Today's "Chef's Special" is "Death to all those who would whimper and cry!"

He sat there for a minute, oblivious to the conversation, and thought that the name of the fish dish that he had been enjoying up to that point conjured up images of trout beatings and haddock torture, all of which had probably taken place in the kitchen, to provide him with the meal that sat before him on the table. He felt ill.

"Now Douglas...Douglas! I want you to report to Chatham Dockyards in the morning and then Portsmouth in the afternoon."

"And the purpose of my visit, Sir?"

"Oh, erm, officially, I mean, as far as the men in suits and wigs are concerned, it's a 'Fact finding' visit."

"Sir?"

"The official reason for your visits is to gather information. Now, how did they put it to me on the phone this morning? Oh yes, "To gather information relevant to the successful building and sailing of this, our most important vessel to date!""

"Information, Sir?"

"Douglas, what they want you to do is attend the museums at both, Chatham Dockyards and Portsmouth and simply get ideas that'll help improve the ship. Pure and simple! On the other hand, what I want you to do, is to steal any good bits of wood or fittings you deem as appropriate, no matter how historically important they are!"

"Sir, is that wise?"

"Now, Douglas! Look, I'll give you an example. Now, I've heard from my sources that the leading edge bit of the Mary Rose is still quite strong and sturdy. If you get that front section then that's money saved on wood, which probably equates to another carrier pigeon or even a walkie-talkie!"

"Sir! Are you actually giving me authority to go into our maritime museums and steal our history?"

"Oh, Douglas, stop being so stuffy. All I'm saying officially is, "Go and get some ideas!" All I'm saying unofficially is "Go and steal to your hearts content!""

To Douglas, this was rapidly turning into "Bad day, number two," as he'd awoken with a hangover, found the "Chef's Special" to his liking, only to realise the name of the dish was "Death to all those who would whimper and cry," and then had been told to go and steal whatever of his country's nautical history he found fit to. He realised that there was no way of getting out of the situation that he found himself in. Then it sank in. If it all blew up then it would be his face it all blew up into, as he'd be the face identified as having looted the museums and historical institutions.

"Sir, I have a question."

At this point Sir Horace Hargraves, sat opposite the man with the question on his lips, felt very smug. He believed himself to be one step ahead in this conversation and put all of his imaginary chips on the table for this question as, he felt sure, he knew what was coming. And so, with elbows on the table and head resting on hands, he invited Douglas to proceed.

"Sir, if this all goes horribly wrong..."

"Pete Tong, I believe the youngsters call it! Proceed!"

"Well Sir, it's just that if it all goes wrong, in whatever way that it might, well, Sir, it'll be my face on the front page, Sir!"

Sir Horace was delighted. If this had been "It's a Knock-Out" then he'd have played his joker on this one. If the chips on the table were real then he'd have made a lot of money because he'd guessed right and was prepared for it. He wanted to punch the air and act like he'd scored a goal. He pictured himself sliding across the floor of the "Cutty Club" on his knees, fists clenched, then being mobbed by the centre forward of a waiter. Then, reality struck, and he had to act dignified again. He smiled at Douglas and, from one of his inside jacket pockets, produced a fake identification card and a pair of glasses. He handed them across the table to the confused looking man who sat before him.

"All sorted, Douglas. Here, take these and use them when you enter a museum or place of nautical interest!"

Douglas accepted the identification card and the pair of glasses. He then set about studying the card. It was then, at that point, that he finally gave in and accepted that his Navy career had just fallen through the trap door. What he sat there looking at, lying flat in his hand, was a copy of his own pass. The amendments to it, he thought, weren't exactly professionally done. For his surname had been crudely changed from "Squires" to "Squits" and his photograph now had an added pair of, again, crudely drawn in spectacles. He felt weak again. He looked up at his, still smug looking, superior.

"Sir!"

"All sorted, Douglas ma boy!"

"Sir!"

"When you get out of your car, you'll still be "Sir Douglas Squires, Number One, Level B," but, when you enter the museum, you'll be "Sir Douglas Squits, intelligent looking bod-type person!""

"Sir! Is this wise?"

"I don't know, bloody clever if you ask me! Those deception lads were up half the night working on your alias. Oh come, come Douglas. 'course it's wise!"

"Oh, ok, Sir!"

"Right then! Best get back to business eh! Come on Douglas, let's "Ship outta here!""

And that was that. With a quick chuckle at his own joke, Sir Horace was up and asking the waiter for the bill. Once outside, Douglas felt an overwhelming hatred for the 'Cutty Club' growing inside him as he'd visited the place twice and had had nothing but bad experiences both times. Sir Horace followed him outside and summoned the car. Driving along back towards the Maritime Museum, Sir Douglas Squires felt an overwhelming urge to "Liberate" his first piece of nautical history. "Hell" he thought, "it's true, it's really true. If you can't beat 'em, join 'em!"

"Sir, I've just had a thought."

"Douglas, how pleasing! Go on."

"Well, manning requirements, recruitment etc aside, the bridge, Sir"

"Go on.

"Well, as I see it, and please correct me if I'm wrong, Sir, but as I see it, the interior of the Ardilles is going to resemble, quite closely, the interior of an alpine ski lodge. All the varnished wood and that..."

"That's fair to say, yes!"

"Well Sir, I just thought that maybe the bridge should be the one place that is different. I mean, apart from it being the one place on board where there's any hint of modern nautical technology, shouldn't it say something along the lines of, "Our most cherished room on board, the heart of the ship?"""

"And what do you propose, Douglas, eh?"

Sir Horace was glad that he wasn't in a position where he'd have to gamble with some of his imaginary chips because he was lost on this one. He had absolutely no idea where the man that shared the backseat of his car was going with this.

"Sir, with your permission and, and taking full advantage of my alias, "Sir Douglas Squits," I'd like to obtain from the Imperial War Museum, the bell from the "Lusitania" and mount it, upside down, on my bridge as a giant plant pot. Thus, being in a position to bring some colour to the bridge, Sir!"

"Erm."

"It'd be our trophy, Sir!"

"But Douglas, you can't re-write history. No-one will believe that you sank the "Lusitania!""

"But we can pretend we sank The Imperial War Museum and recovered the bell!"

"Douglas! For once, just once, I have to question your thinking!"

"Sir! I want that bell on my ship. Just think, Sir, we're building a craft so technically retarded that we have to recruit six hundred accountants and five bookkeepers to power the thing. It's so un-seaworthy that we're creating the biggest deception plan since the Second World War, just to get by. At least during the war they had a good, valid and sensible reason!"

"What! Surely they didn't have Trireme ships as well?"

"No Sir, They had General Patton in the South of England and aimed at Calais!"

"Oh erm, yes, I, I know that, really I do! Ok, ok I'll ask it, Douglas you win, I'll ask it! WHY? Why do you want that bell on your ship as an upturned flower pot?"

"You see Sir, It's as I was saying. This ship of ours, The H.M.S. Ardilles, well, Sir, it's as technologically advanced as a cocktail stick and as useful as a crushed ant. Every 'system' that we have designed or 'laid our hands on' is still years behind all of our other ships systems. Our most advanced features at the moment appear to be walkie-talkies and carrier pigeons!"

"The whole ship is a massive two-finger salute to naval technology and advancement. By having the bell of the Lusitania on our bridge, upturned, with flowers in it, we're essentially continuing that theme by saying to the rest of the world, who incidentally, will probably be mocking us at this time, "we do not recognise the importance of this bell as we are the new breed and that's all that matters and that's all that's important!""

"Bloody Hell!"

"Sir!"

"Bloody Hell, Douglas. Go get that bell!"

"Thank you, Sir!"

If it were at all possible at that moment then there would've been a deep and warm glow emanating from the back of the car as both men sat back grinning stupid grins which told quite different stories. On one side sat Sir Horace, grinning a grin that said "I knew I was right, this man's a genius. A natural at adapting to the challenges set before him. I'm such a good judge of character! Captain Birdseye! huh!" Beside him on the back seat of the car, now pulling up outside the Maritime Museum, sat Sir Douglas, grinning a grin that said "I'm gonna have the biggest plant pot in "The Floaty Boat Brigade!""

And so, with the smug smile of satisfaction emblazoned on their faces, they emerged from the back of the car and into the sunshine that covered Greenwich. After a quick approving squint at the sunshine, they headed into the museum and along the corridor towards the Main Hall. With dusters at the ready, they entered the Main Hall and carried out the standard procedure of fake dusting everything within reach.

The sight of these two uniformed, and apparently very respectable men, waving and flicking the air and surfaces around them with their bright yellow dusters, would've probably taken on a more religious meaning if they were dressed in sacred hula skirts in the middle of an ancient ritual on some Hawaiian Island. Instead they were in the Main Exhibition Hall of the Greenwich Maritime Museum, England, and looked nothing other than stupid.

Having flicked their way to, and under, the distorted lower jaw of the blue whale, they descended the stairs beneath it with an even bigger sense of smugness. And they were smug all right. This enlarged smugness being the result of having just fooled "Joe public" again. "Oh those paying punters," thought Sir Horace, "how little do they know!"

Chapter Seven – Thomas

Thomas Jackson, twenty four years old and enthusiastic maritime student, had just watched in disbelief as two apparently high ranking Navy dignitaries had just dusted their way under, what appeared to be, the severely distorted lower jaw of the main exhibit, a large blue whale or, at least, a model of one. "Something's going on down there!" he thought to himself, as he watched the two men crawl under the jaw and then down into the darkness below it.

"This, I've got to check out!" he told himself and, with the decision made, he was under the red rope and silver upright post barrier, that looped it's way around the whale, and walking swiftly towards the distorted lower jaw. Hoping beyond hope that, neither security nor any of the tour guides were alerted to this intrusion. Now that he was close up alongside the gigantic model, Thomas could clearly see the reason why the jaw of this blue monster was so distorted.

Stairs! Not just stairs, but badly concealed stairs at that. He peered down into the darkness, but failed to recognise anything at all. As he strained his eyes for just that one, slight, discernible object, he began to pick up the faintest sounds of voices coming from the darkness down below. Taking that as an invite to investigate further, he descended the stairs with an inquisitive air.

As he reached the bottom of the darkened stairway, he noticed that the voices, that he'd previously heard whilst up above, were coming from a room to his right. As he looked towards the room he noticed that a beam of light was escaping from the door and emphasising its presence across the blackened surroundings, indicating to him that the door was slightly ajar.

Thomas approached the doorway with cautious excitement. The voices he could hear grew clearer with every footstep. Four semi-silent strides were all it took to take the inquisitive young man to the doorway. Listening, as he strode, he peered through the small gap, from where the light was escaping, for even the briefest sight of the men that he could now hear quite clearly. Annoyingly for Thomas, no matter how he manoeuvred and angled himself, he just couldn't get a clear line of sight. The voices from within continued.

"So, let me get this straight, Sir."
"Go on, Douglas."
"Apart from the intended plant pot that I've requested for my bridge..."
"Yes, proceed."
"You are, shall we say, hinting in strong, Government Issue,

language, that I steal the front bit, the bow, of the Mary Rose?"

"Well, Douglas, if you put it like that…"

"By way of chainsaw!"

"Well, Douglas, by any means really!"

"Sir, I must protest!"

"Douglas! Come, come! We are building, what will be the most famous boat in the world. What publicity do you think The Floaty Boat Brigade and, indeed you, will get when it becomes public knowledge that The Ardilles' bow is actually the bow of the Mary Rose eh?"

"But, Sir!"

"Oh come, come Douglas. Think of it in terms of, erm…"

Sir Douglas noticed a gleam appear in the eyes of his senior. He also noticed that Sir Horace now appeared to take on a type of "Gene Kelly on a Broadway stage" character as he continued with his address, but using his hands to emphasise his description of the future and it's possibilities.

"…the new Navy. "The Floaty Boat Brigade," producing the most important and eagerly awaited ship in it's history and what's more, celebrating the link between "the old and the new" by using the front bit of the Mary Rose!"

"But, Sir, I must protest!"

To Thomas Jackson, twenty-four, painfully thin and

annoyingly inquisitive, this was criminal talk. He'd joined the conversation, or at least, had first started to listen to the conversation, midway through, but what he'd overheard was criminal and treacherous. Especially to those like-minded folk, who studied, nay worshipped, maritime history. For those people in question, who devoured every fact and figure and absorbed every minute morsel or crumb, relating to the subject of nautical history, would shudder on hearing what he'd stumbled across.

He felt his anger and frustration build up inside. How could two, seemingly high ranking men in the Royal Navy, be talking in such a treacherous manner? How could they even be thinking of raping the nation's maritime history, let alone recycling it? Thomas couldn't take it any longer. Forgetting where he was and the minor issue that he was trespassing, he burst through the door, ready to savage the treasonous blaggards he'd been listening to.

"You can't do that, you traitors!"
"What the bloody!.....who the bloody hell are you?" declared a startled and concerned Sir Douglas. Not so much concern because of the unwelcome guest, or the potential security threat he posed, but concern that someone had interrupted his protest and derailed him, so to speak.

Now, it was Sir Douglas who felt angry and

aggrieved. How dare this young upstart burst into the room in the middle of his "Anti-cut-up-the-Mary-Rose-and-rape-and-pillage-the-nations'-naval-history" campaign and launch into an "Anti-cut-up-the-Mary-Rose-and-rape-and-pillage-the-nations'-naval-history" campaign of his own!

The three men suddenly found themselves standing still and silently staring at each other. Just for a moment, but what an awkward moment it was. Thomas, who could feel regret was about to pay him a visit, Sir Horace, who'd already spotted the opportunity that the intrusion had brought with it and Sir Douglas Squires, cut down in his prime, mid rant. Awkwardly, Thomas winced, as he realised that the last move he'd made wasn't particularly too good.

A cold and rather clammy sensation was now spreading all over his body. He was wrong, for it wasn't just regret that came calling but also fear. Silence held court until Sir Horace took control of the situation. Whilst his favourite "underling" stood staring at the intruder, who'd stopped him in his prime, he himself, moved stealth-like towards the Government Issue kettle in the corner of the kitchen, which stood on a small, Government Issue table. Without looking once at the stranger, he enquired…

"Tea or coffee, my man?"

Jackson crumbled.

"Oooh, erm, argh…yes!"

Sir Horace was now King of the Hill and he knew it. "In for the kill," he thought. Sir Douglas stood motionless, knowing he was about to see his Lord and Master demonstrate the ingenious mind that had made him "Number One, Level A."

"I think you need a strong, black coffee, my friend. Perhaps with a little bit of sugar?"

"Oooogh, erm…"

Sir Horace poured the contents of the kettle, that he'd previously boiled, whilst discussing the finer points of chain sawing the Mary Rose, into a black enamel, Government Issue, mug to which he added coffee and sugar. After a quick stir, he picked up the mug and, turning round, walked to the nearby table where he placed it on a placemat. Pulling one of the standard, Government Issue, chairs from under the table he played his trump card.

"You see, my friend, whoever you are…."

Sir Douglas stood watching this turn of events silently and statuesque from the middle of the room, exactly where he'd been standing when Thomas Jackson, twenty-four and now wishing he was somewhere else, had burst in. Sir Horace continued.

"By descending that stairway out there, you probably didn't

know it, but you were taking the top off of our barrel and dropping your trousers."

Both, Jackson and Sir Douglas, were taken aback by this statement. Sir Douglas, in particular, having got used to his bosses' various new personas, was now feeling quite disturbed as he was struggling to guess just whom Sir Horace was now portraying with this latest address to the young and most unwelcome visitor.

"Then, by bursting into this room...do you have any idea what you were doing?"

"Erm, well…"

"You don't, do you!"

"Well, erm…"

"Think you'd better sit down, son!"

Right at that moment, the sight of the chair being offered to him by this unknown man, who was obviously the superior of the two he'd interrupted, was just what the doctor ordered because, right at that very moment, Thomas Jackson, twenty four, maritime student, felt very small and almost defenceless. As, seemingly, every word leaving this Naval man's lips landed with a heavy blow on his being. Just for that few moments, Thomas afforded himself the momentary get away by likening these blows to being in the ring with a heavyweight boxer. Suddenly, moments later, he was back to reality. He ghosted forward and slid onto the chair that Sir Horace was offering him.

"Erm....Th...Th...Thank you!"

"Your welcome, young man. Now, Y'see my friend, by bursting in like that on Douglas here and myself, you have, how can I put it, well you've basically put your young nuts in our very secret barrel!"

Jackson sat there stunned. If the chair hadn't been offered to him moments before then he knew his legs would've given way by now. He felt faint. Sir Douglas, on the other hand, still felt confused by what he was witnessing. "Barrels, nuts, nope, lost on that one!"

Thomas, confused as well as scared, responded.

"I, I don't understand."

All his anger and desperate urges to protest had drained away. Now he sat there like a young schoolboy, who'd just been caught doing wrong. Sir Horace continued, secretly loving his now obvious dominant position.

"Well, lets see, what's your name, my friend?"

"Erm, Jackson, Thomas Jackson."

"Oh right, pleased to meet you, Thomas. My name is Sir Horace Hargraves and that there is Sir Douglas Squires."

Sir Douglas nodded as the young intruders eyes followed the outstretched arm and pointed finger of Sir

Horace, as it directed his attention to the still confused Number One, Level B.

"Ok, Thomas. You were upstairs, minding your own business, yes? Maybe studying the historical artefacts gathered therein, yes? I bet you're a student of Naval history, yes?"

"Erm, yes, yes and, erm, yes!"

"Good, whilst Sir Douglas and I were doing the same down here, that is, minding our own business. Now, lets think back to who interrupted whose world eh? Mmm, your up there, we're down here, now your down here with us!"

Now, Sir Douglas was beginning to smile inside. He still didn't have a clue what his superior was on about, but he liked the sarcasm being fired at the, now very pale youngster, sat at the table in the middle of the room.

"Tell me, Thomas, what does that suggest to you eh?"

"Erm, I don't know."

"Oh come, come, Thomas! Your world, our world. You up there then, suddenly, you're in here with us. That must mean that you've crossed the boundary and entered our world? Now, I know that Sir Douglas, over there, and I haven't actually invited anyone into our world, and yet, here you are! So what does that mean eh?"

"Erm...."

"Correct! You're absolutely correct, young man! If "ERM" means that you've entered into our world, without an invitation, that you've entered an area that is strictly off limits, out of bounds and that you recognise the fact that you're trespassing and that you are now in the sticky stuff way over your head then, yes, "ERM," is correct!"

A definite, and most unwelcome, feeling of paralysis crept over Thomas, as he realised that his rash decision to follow the duster waving dignitaries down the mysterious stairway, under the distorted lower jaw of the gigantic blue whale, was now proving to be possibly the worst decision of his life. He was being questioned, he knew and understood that much. He reasoned with himself that it could easily have been torture of the physical kind and, with that thought in his mind, decided that things could've been worse at this moment in time. At the precise moment that Thomas was mentally encouraging himself, Sir Horace continued with his summary of events and Thomas Jackson's paralysis returned.

"So, young Thomas, it appears that we have quite a situation here. One thing you have to realise is that I can call security at anytime. Right now, at this very moment, there are no guards present. That means that, should you choose to do so, you could make a break for it and run out of this room and up them stairs but, and this is the crux of what options

117

I'm about to give you, should you decide to do that, or should you decide that you cannot agree to or abide by these options, then my security team would apprehend you within seconds and I do mean seconds!"

"So, young Thomas, your first decision was to enter our world. Your decision as to whether that was wise or stupid will probably come later."

"But..."

"No "but's" and definitely "no erm's," my young friend. Douglas!"

"Sir!"

"Would you be so kind as to open the door and then come and stand at my side please?"

"Yes, Sir."

Sir Douglas moved towards the door, which had slammed shut, from the force with which the young student had burst through it. He leant forward, opened the large, stained wood structure and returned to the far side of the room where his superior stood. Thomas had swivelled in his chair and watched this and now sat facing the two naval men once more.

"Your next, immediate choice or decision, my friend, is whether to take the first option that I am giving you. Are you going to make a run for it or are you going to sit there

118

like a good gringo and listen to my offer?"

"Erm, I....I don't think I want to leave right now. Thank you both all the same!"

"Good man! Now, I'll set another scene for you, paint you another picture."

"The only reason," the young intruder thought to himself, "That I didn't bloody make a run for it, you swine, is that I have a paralysis in my legs!"

Once again, Sir Horace continued. He motioned for Sir Douglas to shut the door. Sir Douglas carried out the request and then returned to his boss' side.

"Now, Thomas, unfortunately for you, walking uninvited into our world now means that you leave your world behind, for good!"

"What!"

"No "what's," Thomas! I know I said no "buts" and no "erms," but please consider "what's?" to be on that list from now on in! Now, with you here, in this room, are two men who have a very, very important and very, very secret mission or task, if you like. Do you row, Thomas? Or, let me re-phrase that question. Do you like to row, Thomas?"

"R...r...row...no!"

"Oh, I see. I ask because, now you're in our world, one false move and you'll find yourself rowing for the rest of your life! And, do you know what, Thomas?"

"W...what?"

"No-one will ever know where you are, except the other rowers!"

"I, I don't understand."

"You see, young Thomas, you've entered into our world. A world that contains much secret, erm, stuff. And because it contains so much stuff, there's no way we could possibly allow you to return to your world. What with you knowing that our world has secrets and all. Because, no matter how much we like you, and we do like you, we can't let you go back to your world because, well, you might tell on us, you might tell some porky pies!"

Sir Douglas, having tuned in rather late to his bosses' direction of thought, had enjoyed several minutes of knowing just what was going on and being "up with play," but now, with Sir Horace's' latest "our world, your world" declaration, he had effectively tripped over his own laces and been left behind on the conversation. He felt stupid and annoyed with himself for losing the plot. "Our world, your world, it can't be that difficult to follow!" he thought to himself.

Thomas was stuck for an answer. He wished his brain could assess the situation quicker than it currently was able to. He was unsure of what way to play the situation. Run?

Nope, clearly not an option, not with his legs still paralysed. Get aggressive and defend his actions and the reasons why these men can't be allowed to continue? Nope, too damn tongue-tied! He wanted to ask Sir Horace for a couple of minutes, but knew that wasn't a good idea. He continued to search inwardly for his next move, just as Sir Horace opened up with another salvo.

"Y'see, Thomas, Sir Douglas here and my good self were discussing the finer points of something we've been asked to do by some very important and very influential people. You've walked in on us, un-invited mind, and so have joined our team. There, Thomas! I've said it in plain English; you've joined our team! Like it or not, you're in!"

The young intruder sat stunned. Sir Douglas, still stood at his bosses' side, felt warmth within. Warmth, that indicated that, at long last, he finally knew what his boss had been prattling on about all this time. He felt pleased that he hadn't allowed his stupidity to shine through and alert the young intruder, sat before him and, more importantly, that he wasn't the only one in the room who didn't understand what was being said. Sir Horace, knowing he was on a roll, continued.

"….see, if I had my way, you'd be shot. Problem is, we're not allowed to do that and so, because there's no way that I can let you go, or even imprison you, I'm lumbered with you. Now, young Thomas, as I've already said, if you choose to betray me or refuse to sign your services over to me then, I'm afraid, you'll be handling an oar for the rest of your life. However, if you're a good gringo and help me and Sir Douglas here, out with our little venture then, I'm sure you'll find your new life to be very rewarding and most enjoyable."

Sir Douglas' warmth drained from him, in a moment, as he recalled that, having had numerous breakdowns recently, he'd be hard pushed to think of a single moment within the last couple of days that he could describe as being "very rewarding and most enjoyable." He felt cheated, as though someone had shown him the wrong careers video. Thomas, realising that he was very much outmanoeuvred at present, summoned the strength for a very slight fight back.

"But, the Mary Rose!" he began to squeal, as though pleading for the ancient crafts' life.
"Now, now, young Thomas. Sir Douglas and myself are more than willing to discuss her with you. More than willing."
"No we're bloody not!" Sir Douglas thought to himself.
"Aren't we, Douglas!"
"Yes, Sir, absolutely! Just say the word, give the nod, and I'll

quite happily update Mr Jackson, Sir!"

"Y'see, Thomas, we're both happy to discuss it all with you, but we'll need to see ya squiggles first!"

"Squiggles?"

Sir Douglas, not for the first time, had been left totally confused by his superior. He was desperately trying to work out what he meant when he had just proclaimed, "we'll need to see ya squiggles first." He wasn't alone, although he didn't know it, as Thomas was feeling rather confused as well. It was the younger man who broke first and saved Sir Douglas, yet again.

"W...w..what do you mean squiggles?"

"Ya signatures ma boy! We'll be needing you to sign some bits of paper firstly, before Sir Douglas and I even think of telling you what we're up to."

"Bits of paper?"

"Erm, yes! We need you, Thomas, to sign a few bits of paper to show to us that you're going to be a good boy, a good gringo, and that you promise not to tell anyone anything about what we, and that WILL mean you as well, Thomas, do. By signing these bits of paper you will be agreeing to the rules and conditions set down, and in use, in our world."

"There you go again," thought Sir Douglas. "How the hell can I be expected to follow what's going on if you keep bloody slipping into this "our world, your world" nonsense? This morning, and, and yesterday as well, it was you and me. Nothing was said of any "world's" coming into play! Everything was fine and dandy. I knew where we both stood, although thinking about it…"

"We like our world, don't we, Douglas!"

"Erm, yes, Sir! Our world's great!"

"There, you see, Thomas! Sir Douglas and myself really enjoy our world. It's really interesting and above all, fulfilling! Now, if you sign whatever we put in front of you, we'll gladly show you around our pad."

Thomas Jackson, twenty-four year old maritime student and currently residing in Mire Street, had regained some strength and feeling in his legs and body as a whole. At first he'd been fooled and taken in by these two uniformed men who stood before him, but now he felt that he had them sussed. The man on the left, as he looked at them, was quite obviously the senior of the two.

He appeared to be in his late fifties, early sixties. He didn't have a fat face, usual for a man of his years, but with his tall, medium built frame he appeared to Thomas to cut a rather "dashing" presence. The second "officer" appeared to be mid-fifties and very stocky in appearance. Thomas could not help but be impressed by the physique of this man and thought to himself that he hoped he looked that good when he was that age.

"Now, Thomas, any questions?"

"If I sign these papers, to whom am I answerable to and what powers do I have? Also, are there any people under me, that I'll be in charge of?"

"Woh there, erm…Silver! Recovered a bit have we, my friend? You'll answer to Sir Douglas and myself only. Except if we get visited by anyone I'm answerable to, but I'll let you know who, should that circumstance arise. As for who's answerable to you, well, just about everyone you come into contact with in the, erm, Navy, will be answerable to you, although they may not know it, as the work you'll be doing will be top secret."

"And what will I be doing? If I sign, of course!"

"Oh, of course, Thomas!"

"Well?"

"Give us your squiggles and we'll tell you! If you don't feel that you'd like to sign our bits of paper then the only choice you'll have left in your life to make is whether to choose a lifetime of solitary confinement or a lifetime with an oar in your hand!"

As much as he tried to fight it, he couldn't. The weakness that had prevented him from making a break for it, as soon as he'd realised that barging in on these two men stood before him had been a mistake, had returned.

"Ok, ok. I'll sign!"

"Oh that's wonderful news, really wonderful! Isn't it, Douglas!"

"Oh yes, Sir! Really made my day. It's strengthened the team! I'm over the moon!"

"Exactly! You see, Thomas. You've not even signed anything yet and we're happy!"

Thomas sat there nodding and smiling in agreement at the two men he'd now condemned himself to work with for the rest of his life and whom, he thought to himself, were becoming increasingly unstable in the mental department. He was beginning to think that he'd get out of this mess quicker if he humoured them, hence the nodding and smiling.

"Now, my friend, there's a slight problem with regards to the bit of paper we'd like you to sign."

"There is?"

"Erm, yes! Y'see, Thomas, we've never had someone trespass before and didn't really expect to have someone trespass at all, really."

"And...."

"Well, my friend, money is, as they say, far too tight to mention."

"Which means?"

"Which means we're not going to waste money printing up hundreds of "I promise not to trespass anymore and will work for you and be a good gringo" forms are we?"

"And so?"

"And so my friend, Douglas here, will leave the room and visit our admin team down the corridor. He'll find something for you to sign and then when you've done the deed and put pen to paper, we'll amend the wording. Ok?"

Thomas felt awkward. Just what would he be signing? He didn't want to think about it as it scared him. Instead, he watched Sir Horace nod to Sir Douglas who then walked towards the door and out of the room into the corridor.

"Now, my young friend, you seem to have let your coffee go cold."

Sir Horace stuck his finger in his own cup. Pulling it out and sucking it dry, he continued.

"In fact, it would seem that we've all let our drinks go cold. Would you like another?"

"Erm, yes please, Sir Horace. That would be very welcome!"

"In fact, give or take a couple of squiggles, you're a navy man now, or attached to the navy at least, and us navy chaps have taken to drinking lager y'know. It's the new navy man's drink! How about the three of us start celebrating the birth of our new partnership with three pints of the navy's finest. Sound good?"

"Erm..."

Still wishing to humour them, Jackson agreed.

"Why not!"

"Right then, through that door, over my shoulder, is a small kitchen. You'll find some cans in the fridge and some glasses in the cupboard above it."

"What, you want me to get the drinks?"

"Yes!"

"But I've not signed anything yet! Can I be trusted?"

"Of course you can, Thomas. Call it a goodwill gesture! And besides, what are you going to steal? A few cans of lager, some glasses and our kettle! Or are you after the sink cleaner?"

Thomas, not sure if his legs had sufficiently recovered, accepted defeat and put all his reserves of strength and concentration into standing up. Once on his feet he walked nonchalantly towards the kitchen. Sir Horace sat down and pondered the recent events, smiling a smile to himself that suggested he was happy with the outcome, whilst the sounds of cupboards and cans being opened and that of lager being poured, permeated the air around him.

Within minutes, Thomas had returned with three pints worth of lager, the new navy man's drink.

Placing them on the table, he offered one to Sir Horace, before sliding one across to where he sat. He moved the third across the table to a vacant position that he anticipated would be filled by the soon-to-be returning Sir Douglas, before finally taking his seat. Sir Horace took the lead, as he felt a man in his position should.

"We can't wait for Douglas, so I'd like to propose a toast..." Raising his glass upwards and towards Thomas, he felt the moment gain the upper hand. He felt a tear that, as far as he was concerned, represented pride, run down his cheek.

"To us!.....and our new team!"

Thomas, rather amused at this, raised his glass for the toast as well.

"I've found this Sir! Thought we could amend the text to suit our needs..."

Both men, seated at the table, looked up at the figure of Sir Douglas entering the room.

"Aagh Douglas, my man, what've ya got there?"

"It's all I could find, Sir!"

"That's ok, my friend. I'm sure it'll do. Erm, what is it?"

"It was just laying on the desk, Sir. Everybody's gone home, so all the filing cabinet's were locked!"

"That's ok, Douglas. I'm sure it's just fine. Now, be a good fellow and hand it to me!"

Sir Douglas handed his superior the document, which he'd just acquired from the office down the hall. It had been found on the desk of an administrative assistant, left there by the owner/occupier of the desk with a view to it being processed in the morning. The fact that it was now in the hands of the Number One, Level A meant that it would never get processed, at least in it's original form. Sir Horace noticed that his "favourite underling" looked troubled, almost nervous. With this observation came the sharp realisation that it may be a good idea to actually cast an eye over the document he now held in his hand. For Thomas Jackson, the scene wasn't quite farcical, but near enough.

Silence. Sir Horace came to his senses first and slowly glanced down at the piece of paper, stiff in his hand. "It's a..."

"Purchase order for four hundred tea bags, Sir!"

"You have brought me a purchase order for...."

"Sir! There are two key points, that I'd like to bring to your attention, regarding the said purchase order for four hundred tea bags."

"Oh please, Douglas, do continue!"

"Sir! Number one centres around the fact that there was no

other documents to be found in the whole establishment."

"Ok, I'm listening. I'm dying to hear number two!"

"Sir! Think about it, it's the perfect document to use!"

"Don't tell me you expect me to...."

"Oh no, Sir! There is no disguising staff as tea bags in our service! No Sir, what I was about to say, was not to think of it as a purchase order for four hundred tea bags, more as a 'requisition order' for one new team member. I'm sure with a little re-wording here and a slight amendment there, we can get it to say what we want."

Now, it was Sir Horace who heard a breakdown knocking at his door. He studied the situation and was feeling at a loss for just what to do. At the very same moment that defeat stared him in the face, inspiration slapped him on the back. The answer to his over-loaded brain hung in an official manner in the middle of the wall to his left. Rubbing his eyes, through sheer exhaustion, he spoke as though he was Eisenhower, pondering whether to take a trip to Normandy in rough seas.

"Gentleman, it's late and I'm tired. We've all got busy days ahead. Thomas...."

"Yes, erm, Sir?"

"Why don't you just be a good chap, a good gringo and sign the bloody form? We'll amend all the wording later!"

"Erm, ok then."

And with that, Thomas Jackson took the pen being offered him by Sir Horace and signed and dated the purchase order for four hundred tea bags.

"Good man! Welcome on board!"

"Thank you, Sir."

"Now, Douglas."

"Sir!"

"Your wife's away, yes?"

A concerned Douglas answered tentatively, knowing what was coming next.

"Yes, Sir."

"Good. Excellent! Thomas, you can stay with Sir Douglas tonight."

"Sir?"

"Douglas! You and Thomas will be working together until the project is completed. He can't get home and there really is no point, seeing as you both have to leave early in the morning for a couple of busy days, so it makes sense for him to stay with you."

"But, Sir!"

Sir Horace addressed his man again. Knowing that he was close to pushing the deal through, he was sympathetic to his man's ear.

"Douglas!"

This tone of address clearly worked as any ramifications from Sir Douglas quickly changed on hearing the soft tone of voice from his superior. As if under a spell, the potentially aggressive stance changed to one of calculated thought.

"There is a point to it. I guess you are right, Sir!"

Sir Douglas had forced himself to say those words and he hated himself for it. For the first time in hours he could see what was occurring. He was being placed in charge of this young upstart, who'd stole his thunder earlier on in the proceedings. "Yes," he thought to himself, "it all made sense now." By having this youngster stay at his home he was in charge of him. If the boy escaped, then it would be his responsibility and more importantly, his head on the block.

"Now Douglas, it's twenty past twelve, I'll arrange the cars and you assign the first bit of kit to our new colleague!"

"Sir?"

"The duster, Douglas, the bloody duster! Sod the beer, gentlemen, lets go home!"

Chapter Eight – Coming to terms

Sir Douglas Squires, not so much "International Man of Mystery," but more an "International Man of Mockery." Or, that's how he felt, when he woke the next morning. He reasoned with himself that he'd done well to get upstairs to bed the night before. This sort of reasoning, he thought, would stand him in good stead for the next couple of days.

Positive, in a realistic kind of way, and with his young, inquisitive apprentice asleep in the spare room, Sir Douglas lay there on his bed for a moment, staring at his clock radio, which was showing seven twenty-two. He lay there a while longer, in his very creased uniform, trying to think up a way, an easy way, of explaining to Thomas Jackson, former maritime student, just exactly what mess, and the size of said mess, that they now both found themselves in.

He hadn't attempted to go there last night, as the journey home had beaten them and left them weary and unable to communicate above a level of grunts and the occasional slice of "so where are you from?" and "so, how long have you been married?" It had continued, briefly, once inside Sir Douglas' home, but had come to an abrupt halt as a rather dishevelled Sir Douglas had stood in the doorway of the spare room at the Squires' residence, pointing to the bed and summoning his last reserves of strength to mumble, in real caveman style, "you sleep there, good night." This primitive instruction had been met by an equally limited response from Jackson, as it was as much as he could do to keep his eyes open and reply, "thank you, good night."

After that brief exchange of caveman English, Sir Douglas had shut the door to the spare room. On the other side of the door and within the sanctuary of the spare room, Jackson had waited for the latch to click shut and, when it did after what felt like a couple of minutes, but, in reality was only a second or two, he had fallen forwards onto the bed. He was asleep by the time his head had crashed down into the pillow. Sir Douglas had fared only marginally better, barely making it to his room, let alone his bed. The results, however, were the same. Two exhausted men asleep on their respective beds, both fully clothed.

Sir Douglas had reached the stage of a snoring, and soon-to-be dribbling wreck, due to waking up that morning with a hangover. He'd been late for his appointment with his chief, had had to endure another "Cutty Club" lunch and had then found himself standing on his psychological doorstep inviting in any mental breakdown that happened to be passing. All the while fighting to establish any reason in his mind why on earth he should be expected to put on a fake pair of glasses and enter a museum in broad daylight under the alias "Sir Douglas Squits." If that wasn't bad enough, he was also expected to remove a five hundred odd year old ship. Then, to top all that, just as he'd begun to take to the whole idea, in had stormed Thomas Jackson, maritime student, to wreak further havoc with his mind.

For Thomas, on the other hand, the reasons for the now uncontrolled chattering, currently emanating from the young student, were that he too had also started that day with a hangover. He had left the room, that he rented in East Dulwich, to travel the short distance to Greenwich. By bus, this only took about twenty minutes, but he'd felt it would be wiser to walk that day. All morning he had fought his rather large desire to stay in bed as he had, at first, visited the library and then had wandered around the local high street in search of some drawing pencils, a sketchpad and a good book to read.

He'd picked up his pencils and his sketchpad with ease but the reading material he so desperately longed for had eluded him in all the bookshops the high street could offer. On this realisation, Thomas had given up his search and returned to the local library. An hour or two of painstakingly frustrating combing of the shelves again had lead him to the realisation that, if he was going to buy a book then it might as well be at the Maritime Museum where he was heading in the afternoon anyway.

After a relaxing lunch in the park, situated behind the impressive building that housed the museum's collections, Thomas had entered the building and had instantly changed his mind. Instead of just going to the museum shop, he had decided to actually take a walk around the museum. After all, he'd not been there since his dad had taken him a few years previous when he was in awe of just about every exhibit. He'd paid his money and wandered down the first of the corridors, taking in the large paintings depicting scenes of battle and hardship from an age long since gone.

He'd stopped for some time at one particular painting, depicting a scene inside a Spanish galleon of oarsmen battling against hardships of indescribable proportions, before heading into the Main Hall, whereupon he set eyes on the Museum's life-size model of a blue whale, copied from another museum. At that moment, passing down the side of the blue monster suspended only just above the floor, he noticed the remnants of the afternoon tour, with the stragglers at the back, getting their last eyeful of the Main Hall whilst their fellow tour-ees had moved on down the connecting corridor with their guide.

Just as he thought to himself that he'd join the back of the tour, he noticed two very smart Naval dignitaries enter the Hall, step over the looped rope barrier and head for the front of the whale. Mystified by this strange sight, Thomas Jackson, twenty-four, maritime student, stood still, watching with intrigue. The two men approached the lower jaw of the whale which, to think of it, seemed to be severely disjointed. As if this wasn't enough, what he saw next convinced him that he'd stumbled upon something much more interesting than the back of the afternoon tour.

There he had stood, that sunny afternoon, in the Main Hall of the Greenwich Maritime Museum with the sun shining down through the glass roof, watching intensely as two smart looking Naval dignitaries approached the severely disjointed lower jaw. This vision, in itself, struck him dumb. Being dumb struck was quickly surpassed when they both broke out the yellow dusters and started to, what appeared to him, fake dust everything around them. At this point, the force of the fast developing situation hit home.

Before any sense could even begin to assemble in his inquisitive mind, he found himself heading past the rope barrier and towards the path the two uniformed men had just taken. As he lay there in bed, chattering in his sleep, going through these events in his mind, this, this, he realised now, was one heck of a nosey mistake to make.

Having laid there assessing just what 'a fine mess' he was in, yet again, Sir Douglas rose from his bed and, after taking off his creased uniform, made straight for the shower. The water felt great as it pummelled his weary body. A ten-minute soak, with a quick scrub added for good measure, ensured that he left the bathroom draped in towels, but in good spirits. He thought to himself that he felt surprisingly good considering what he'd been through and the situation he was now embroiled in.

Once he was dry, he donned a dressing gown and headed downstairs to the kitchen. The morning sun shone bright through the open windows. As he walked down the hall he shielded his eyes from the brightness illuminating everything around him. The thought entered his head that he would've been ok right now if he'd only managed to draw the curtains last night "bloody curtains!"

Entering the kitchen with another stretch-come-yawn signalled the next phase of his personal wake up plan. Checking the water level in the kettle, Sir Douglas switched it on, having decided that there was enough in there to make two cups of tea. Once this was done, out came the cups and tea bags. This in-depth preparation of kettle, then toaster and grill continued for the next ten minutes or so. By the time

Thomas appeared at the bottom of the stairs at the opposite end of the hall, the scene in the kitchen resembled a military operation. Although the more he studied the trance-like movements of his host, the more he realised that the scene in the kitchen actually resembled the famous "kitchen routine," expertly performed by Morecombe and Wise in one of their shows.

By now, everything was on the go. There was the smell of everything associated with a cooked breakfast wafting down the hall and into the nostrils of the young guest. Sir Douglas finally noticed Thomas by the front door taking in deep, wonderful breaths of the fry-up taking place a few feet away.

"aaagh Thomas, my friend. Good morning!"

"Erm, good morning, Sir Douglas."

"Right, let me guess. Full English breakfast? Tea, toast, bla-de-bla, yes?"

"That would be most welcome, Sir Douglas."

"Lets dispense with all of that, shall we, Thomas? You can call me Sir or Douglas and what should I be calling you, Thomas?"

"Erm, either Thomas or Tom, Sir."

"Right then, Thomas. Breakfast will be a few minutes more so either grab a shower, towels in the cupboard, or make yourself at home in the front room. Put the telly on, if you wish!"

"I'll grab a shower, I think. Don't smell too good! Can I borrow...."

"Some smelly stuff? Top shelf in the cabinet, my friend, but don't be long!"

Thomas motioned towards the first step of the stairs; all the while his nostrils were full of breakfast smells. "Better hurry up," he thought to himself, as the hunger pangs began to take up residence in his stomach.

"...and Thomas! Wear the clothes you have again today and you can do some shopping this afternoon, on my visa card, ok?"

The reply was distant, as Thomas was by now nearing the top of the stairs, but it was an "ok," all the same.

When he appeared downstairs ten minutes later, he noticed that the back room, the room that Sir Douglas referred to as "The eating room," had become the site of the soon-to-be-had morning feast. Everything that he could wish for was on the table. Sir Douglas, who had just sat down at the table and who was rapidly warming to his young guest, motioned for him to join him at the table.

"Thomas, come, come. Sit down, dive in!"

"Thank you, Sir. Most kind of you!"

"Oh nonsense, my friend. You're part of the team now. Besides, what would you have me doing eh, starving you?"

"Oh no, Sir! It's just that…"

"I don't know you from "Adam" and that I've taken you in and fed and watered you etc, etc?"

"Exactly! And I just feel, well, awkward. But don't get me wrong, very grateful."

"aaagh, but there, you see Thomas, is the connection."

"Connection?"

"You, don't forget, have had this new life dumped in your lap. You've had no choice in the whole thing. I know you didn't want to get involved but…"

"I'm actually warming to the task ahead now, Sir!"

"Bloody good show! Lets eat. Got to be at Bromley South for the train as soon as we can because after Chatham we've got to get to Portsmouth."

As the two men tucked into the feast, that Sir Douglas had prepared, their respective thoughts were both, strangely, centring on the impending visits to Chatham Dockyards and to the Naval docks at Portsmouth that lay before them. Thomas was quickly assembling a list of questions that he wanted to put to his boss, but felt that the train journey would provide a more suitable setting in which to do so. There was one question, however, that he felt he should ask right now.

He looked up from his plate and towards Sir Douglas who was having a battle royale with a piece of bacon on his.

"Sir Douglas?"

"Thomas, my friend?"

"Why are we going by train and not by car?"

"A great and worthy question, my dear Thomas. Basically, a car would be too "High Profile" for us, in this instance, so I decided to go by train. Also, I'd already given my driver the day off!"

"Oh, I see."

With the immediate questioning over, the two men sat through the rest of breakfast in silence. Sir Douglas had resumed his fight with a particularly stubborn piece of bacon, before overwhelming it with the 'assault from behind the sausage' tactic, which he'd heard, had been widely used at breakfast during World War One. On overwhelming his bacon foe, Douglas had come close to punching the air in a victorious manner, but had realised that it was just a piece of bacon and that he had a guest across the table from himself just in time. Instead, he allowed his mind to bathe in victorious glory for a few seconds before snapping out of it and hoping that Thomas hadn't noticed anything un-to-ward.

Thomas, sitting across the table, had watched in amazement as his boss had nigh on assaulted a piece of bacon on his plate. From what he could see, it appeared that the piece of bacon in question was not submitting to Sir Douglas' desire to cut it into two or three pieces. He'd continued to sit there and not believe what he was watching as Sir Douglas had turned his plate around so a sausage lay on the plate between himself and the piece of stubborn bacon.

That would've been bad enough, but to then actually watch Sir Douglas crouch down in his seat and attack the piece of bacon from low level, and from the cover of the sausage, seemed very surreal. There he'd sat, unable to close his mouth around the food that he'd just placed in it, as he continued to watch Sir Douglas take the piece of bacon prisoner between knife and fork and with wrestling-like moves, produce a folded little bundle that he'd popped into his mouth in one go.

Having successfully eaten his prisoner of breakfast, Sir Douglas checked his watch and then tried to work out a mental timetable for the day's schedule.

"mmm, just gone eight thirty, we'll leave here in, say, ten minutes. Get a cab to Bromley, train to Chatham. Be there by ten thirty, Portsmouth by three, home by eleven. How's that sound?"

"Sounds ok. I'll get my coat. Left it upstairs."

"Guess I'd better get changed too! Ten minutes, by the front door. Forget this lot, I'll do it tonight or tomorrow."

And with that, both men rose from the table and rushed upstairs to their respective rooms. Thomas merely leant inside the spare room and grabbed his coat before returning downstairs. Sir Douglas entered his bedroom and reached for another uniform he already had prepared in the wardrobe. Of all of his wife's attributes, that he so greatly admired, probably the most pleasing of them all was the fact that she was always preparing spare sets of uniforms for her husband and hanging them in the wardrobe and it was one of these spare sets that Sir Douglas reached for and put on within minutes, after a liberal dosing of "smelly stuff" that he had left on his wife's dressing table. Next, he sat on the bed and reached for a pair of socks from the drawer that held multiple pairs.

It wasn't long before Thomas looked up the stairs to see a very smart looking Sir Douglas descending them towards him. Sir Douglas looked at his watch and was pleased to see that they were both by the front door within the agreed ten-minute time frame.

"Ok. Ready?"

"Of course!"

"Good. Lets go then! There's a cab office around the corner."

With that, Sir Douglas opened the front door and invited Thomas to leave first. Following him out the door he turned around, shut, and then locked it. Both men then walked down the path and out into the morning sun. As they walked to the cab office there was much 'small talk' regarding the day ahead. Both men were anxious to say what they wanted to say, but both withheld for now. Thomas had many questions, the main one being "why?" Sir Douglas just wanted to explain everything so this mess he was in was then not his alone.

They soon arrived at the cab office and found a driver ready to go, which pleased Sir Douglas. Within minutes they were at Bromley South station and it was inside, once Sir Douglas had paid the driver, that he had an idea. Whilst Thomas was off getting the tickets, he saw them and marvelled at his own genius. "Instead of accountants, maybe we could use them," he thought to himself. "Although, someone would have to feed tickets in at a fair old pace for the ship to actually go anywhere." On his return from the automated ticket machine, Thomas found his boss staring at the mechanical ticket barriers and grew concerned. Sir Douglas was, by now in his mind, adding huge forty-foot oars to these barriers to see what they could do.

"Got the tickets, boss!"

"Oh, erm, right..."

"That platform in three minutes..."

"Oh good, Tom, perfect timing!"

Seeing that a certain someone's mind wasn't really dialled into the conversation, Thomas felt a little icebreaker was needed.

"Why were you staring at the barriers, Sir?"

The question seemed to work and bring an urgent and much needed focus back to Sir Douglas.

"What? Oh, erm, no reason!"

Feeling that he'd caught his superior on fragile ground, Thomas felt it best to side step the issue rather than push for answers.

"Oh, ok. Shall we go?"

"Why yes, Thomas. Not much time, you know!"

They walked down the steps and about half way along the platform before stopping, just as the train came lumbering into the station. As it came to a halt the announcement confirmed to them that this was their train. After waiting to allow the passengers to get off, they boarded and quickly found an empty First Class compartment. Sir Douglas felt that he needed to get the whole 'fine mess' thing out of his system. It hadn't quite been eating away at him, but it had been bothering him somewhat. As they took their seats, he couldn't wait any longer.

"You see, Thomas. It's like this...."

As the train began to jerk and shudder away from
Bromley South Station, Sir Douglas began the unenviable
task of explaining to Thomas Jackson, maritime student and
newfound inquisitive lamb to the slaughter, just what a 'fine
mess' he'd gotten into. This, he'd decided, would take an
official stance with the emphasis on not letting himself
descend into depression or let his voice reveal the farcical
situation that he too found himself sinking into.

"Sir Horace and myself have been selected by the,
erm, the "Men In Power," or, erm, as they are known within
our close-knit community, "The Men In Suits and Wigs," to
build a ship which, although not necessarily at the cutting
edge of technology, is, erm, how can I put this? Designed to
"serve a tactical purpose."

"That," he thought to himself, "had been a hard thing to do!"

The young maritime student sat looking and listening
to his new boss with an expression of alertness and attention
to detail, which, as Sir Douglas continued, slowly began to
change to an expression of disbelief and disillusion, as the
details of the H.M.S Osvaldo Ardilles were passed from the
elder to the younger man. As these details were revealed,
both men were thinking vastly different thoughts, although

Sir Douglas truly believed he was pulling off a masterstroke of a sales pitch to the youngster sat beside him.

"I think he's hooked! I really think the boy's sold on the idea! What a stroke of luck! Good job, Douglas!" The naval man thought to himself.

"What, the hell, is this guy on?" Thought the young maritime student.

"Sir, may I ask just what the Mary Rose has to do with the O.V?"

"The what?"

"The Osvaldo Ardilles, Sir!"

"My dear Thomas, she is soon to be the most important vessel afloat in the Floaty Boat Brigade. She is, and always will be, "The H.M.S Osvaldo Ardilles." The one thing she will never be is "The O.V." Understand? NEVER! She may, however, be referred to as "The Ardilles. Ok?"

"Oh right! Sure thing, Sir! So?"

"So, what?"

"Sir, may I ask just what the Mary Rose has to do with the Ardilles?"

"You may my friend, and I shall answer your very astute and clinical question as best as I can. The Mary Rose is one of the focal points of British Maritime history. She's looked upon as graceful and important, revered by all who are interested in ships and their construction."

"That may be so, Sir, but I do not understand the reasoning behind her forthcoming donation to the Ardilles cause?"

"The reasoning, my dear Thomas, is pure and simple. Due to the fact that a lot of old men who know nothing about everything, got drunk one night, we are required to put together a ship and sail it, mind, to their specifications and new "laws." Although, we are actually talking about an "Act." The fact that the whole idea is farcical and dangerous to all those on-board is neither here nor there. They want a boat to show off to the world."

"...a kind of new boat for the new order?"

"Exactly!"

"The fact that it all came about through the thoughts of alcohol is clearly visible throughout the whole Act."

"So, we are very much lambs to the slaughter then?"

"Yes, Thomas. I'm afraid so. But, there is a way out!"

"Please, Douglas, do tell!"

"Well, Sir Horace, as you know is, erm, "well hooked" on the idea of this ship. The overall Act, I'm not too sure about but, this ship, absolutely. Now, all he wants is a ship and a crew he can show off to the waiting world. So far, every suggestion I've made has been met with complete approval. Yet, between you and me, Thomas, every suggestion I've made has been as farcical and stupid as I can think up."

"So what you're saying is that you're ..."

"What I'm saying is that by working this way we have nothing to lose. The men at the top want a boat that they can show to the world. As you said, "new regime etc," but, they can't understand or accept that the rest of the world is not governed by The McJeffers Act, and so still has technology. If we try and stumble through this then when it all falls apart in front of everyone, we're going to look as stupid as our boat. Whereas, if we follow the orders and guidelines to the 'T,' and that means more stupid ideas, then, at the end of the day, we'll not be scapegoats because we were "just following orders!"

"Ok. I accept your rationale but, where is the connection between The Mary Rose and The Osvaldo Ardilles?"

"The connection is this. They realise that, for this to work in the eyes of the world, they have to pull a masterstroke. If they put to sea in a steptoe-like floating scrap yard then, in order for them not to get laughed off the planet, they need an ingredient that stirs the mind, makes those watching wonder why they've put such a wreck to sea. Reverse psychology, if you like. By making the spine of this ship out of the nation's most famous piece of nautical history...."

"It'll make people wonder why they've done it!"

"Exactly! The natural reaction to it will be for everyone to laugh, but when they see us still straight faced and operating her like any other ship, they'll start wondering and soon they'll be desperate to get on board!"

"So, the reasons behind her are that of no money, but needing to be on the world stage?"

"Yes! But, the only way you have a chance of surviving the launch of one of the most technically retarded ships ever, is by smothering her and everyone around her in a bluff...for want of another word!"

"So you're saying, off the record, of course! That the only way we, as in the two of us, can survive with our respective careers in tact, is to..."

"...be as bloody farcical as we can!"

"OH JESUS!"

"Thomas, even Jesus would probably laugh at The Ardilles!"

Having brutally stripped the situation to the bone, both men sat silent for a while as the train rattled along the tracks. Both men, assessing their respective parts in this tragic play, sat deep in thought. A few miles down the line, Sir Douglas, who had thought of some more information that he'd missed on his initial brief to Thomas, broke the silence.

"Of course we or I, actually, get to choose what colour wood stain or varnish is used for the interior!"

"Oh, erm, great! No, I mean it! Actually a large "woo-pee-doo" on that one!"

"Oh come, come Thomas! It's not so bad!"

Sir Douglas found himself saying the words, "Oh come, come, Thomas" again. He realised that they were the correct and appropriate words, but they lowered him, he felt, towards some dark naval abyss every time he heard himself say them. He quickly found new words of wisdom that he assured himself would raise the spirits of his young aide. "Close range communications will be walkie-talkie's..." Thomas' repeat of the words was a less than subtle salvo of sarcasm aimed at his chief. Sir Douglas felt obliged to continue.

"...long range will see the use of..."

"...oh...oh....let me guess....carrier pigeons?"

"Why, YES, Thomas! That's exactly what we'll be using!"

It was now the turn of the young student to receive a broadside of sarcasm and it was one, which hit him hard and sank him, dejectedly, deeper into his seat. Sir Douglas, on the other hand, now wanted to leap around the carriage punching the air in triumph, but felt better of it. He made a mental note to himself that he must try and curb these boyish desires to celebrate even the smallest of victories. He felt that, to continue now would be best, and proceeded to brief Thomas on all the remaining issues, not yet discussed.

So, as the train rattled and jerked it's way along the tracks towards Chatham, both men sat calmly discussing the finer details of the ship that they were to build. Having listened to Sir Douglas explain how he was mentally approaching this mission, Thomas had himself prepared thoroughly for the brief and so, when it came, took it in his stride. The fact that it was to be made of wood, old, famous wood, and had some kind of steel sheeting as its skin, could not dent his confidence. The subject of accountants and bookkeepers caused a slight irregularity in his breathing, but once that returned to normal, so did the levels of enthusiasm and disbelief.

What he found hardest to take, this student of maritime history, was that a nation with such a history, such a proud pedigree of nautical craft and exploits, could think up something so sinkable, and then commission it's building. The hours and hours he, Thomas Jackson, had spent reading and learning about actions past, all the famous figures, both sailors and designers, were now to be consigned to assisting his knowledge in the theft of famous artefacts for the building of a craft so unseaworthy that, according to Sir

Douglas, once built and in harbour, all other harbour movement/traffic may well have to be stopped to allow safe passage of this craft. How was it put to him? "Any wake or water movement could be catastrophic for her..."

Closing in on Chatham now at a high speed, young Thomas was brought up to speed on the events that would change or maybe even scar his life forever. He was told the "why's," "what's," "if's" and "buts" of the project. He was given all of the technical data that was known at that stage. That there'd be two types of carrier pigeon used, for example. This particular statistic had concerned him greatly. Not so much the actual use of pigeons, but more the fact that there were to be fat "Trafalgar" birds for "non-urgent" messages and pigeons of the racing variety for more pressing issues.

Thinking about it, Thomas decided that it wasn't even the actual pigeons that bothered him. No, it was the thought that someone must've actually been hired and briefed to catch the pigeons in Trafalgar Square that concerned him. "How the hell," he thought, "do you advertise that job? And what type of person would have the necessary experience to apply?" Agitated by these thoughts, he felt that he'd be best served by asking the man he was travelling with.
"Douglas."
"Yes, my friend."

"About the pigeons..."

"Oh."

"Why "Oh!"?"

"Oh, no reason really. Not a big fan of the crapping little blighters. That's all..."

"No, me neither but, I have a question, well several questions actually, about the pigeons."

"Ok, Thomas. I wasn't going to touch on the pigeons, because they're such trivial little things, but here's the full story."

Thomas sat up from his slumber, ready to pay attention to the up and coming brief. His eagerness resembled a five year old readying himself for a bedtime story.

"Sir Horace had the idea for pigeons as a way of communicating when at sea, heaven forbid. If we ever get to sea, the first and only time they're used will be when we are sinking and they're carrying a plea for help! Anyway, after the initial idea of using them, no more was said for a while. Then another alleged idea from our boss was sprung after or while he was on business up North somewhere. Now HE says that he found this place on purpose, but I've heard the message he left on their answer phone!"

Thomas sat, steadily growing more animated, as Sir Douglas continued.

"The official line is that Sir Horace found a bird farm or something like that. A breeder, of racing pigeons, but the expense of each bird meant limited amounts for the project, hence someone being hired to coax the pigeons at Trafalgar Square, with the aid of a tranquilliser sub-machine gun, into the back of a van. Now the place he found is called "Fast Glamour Birds," which means that, in normal working hours, any enquiries are for racing pigeons, but, when you leave a recorded message at half eleven at night requesting the company of "several very fast and very glamorous birds" for "some after dinner company," you're not looking for the fastest flying crap machine in the west to sit on you're pillow and coo at you!"

"Aagh. So our boss was after some late night entertainment and stumbled upon the answer to the long-range urgent communication and short range, low priority issues. How convenient!"

"Yes, Thomas. Convenient, it was. For both him and us!"

"But..."

"Yes, Thomas?"

"It was a bit drastic, wasn't it?"

"And what is it that was a bit drastic, my friend?"

"A tranquilliser sub-machine gun? Are you telling me that a man, hired by us, walked into Trafalgar Square and let loose with a Tranquilliser Sub-Machine gun?"

"Aagh, Yes! You see, once Sir Horace had realised his mistake, and the cost of fast racing pigeons, he briefed one of the young admin lads and set him packing late one night to Trafalgar Square in a van. With this rapid, erm, stun gun. The gun itself fired five hundred darts a minute and so it really only took him a couple of minutes to have the place asleep.

Once he'd fired his last dart, he and a friend began loading the sleeping crap-meisters into the van. It really was a clinical job. Much cheaper than hiring someone who knew what they were doing..."

"And that was allowed, was it?"

"Oh yes! The police were fine with it. We told them we were removing the pigeons from the statue of one of our heroes!"

"And all was fine, eh?"

"Well no, not really, not quite. It turned out that our young chap had not only taken out two thousand pigeons, but he'd also taken out a bus queue that was seventeen people long. There were a few casualties on the pigeon side of things too. It seems that when the gun was first fired they began to scatter, which caused a few mis-placed shots."

"Mis-placed? Please, go on!"

"Well a few of the pigeons lost eyes and a few have lost legs, but we've not left them out. Oh, no! We've put them through a pigeon disability and rehabilitation scheme and they're as fully trained and valuable as the rest, who weren't shot in the eye or leg."

"So, would it be a stupid question if I asked how you overcome their new found disabilities?"

"No, it certainly would not be! For your information, Thomas, our chaps in the disability section created wonderful little eye patches and tiny wooden stumps."

"Oh, my God!"

"A pigeon can still serve his country, Thomas!"

Chapter Nine – Becoming Douglas Squits

The train began to slow and, after a minute or so, was juddering to a stop. Both men looked out of the window to see Chatham Station loom into view. That sign ended the conversation, as both men quickly gathered their belongings and made their way out onto the platform, via the side corridor. Sir Douglas led the way towards the exit, stopping to hand their tickets to the man on the gate. Once outside, he motioned for a cab, which was parked in the rank across the road.

On seeing the gesturing hand of Sir Douglas, the cab driver started his car and proceeded across the small driveway outside the station to where the two men stood. The driver wound down the passenger window and leant across. "Where to my friend?"

"The Dockyards please."

With an accepting nod from the driver, both men climbed into the back of the car, where they sat in silence for the whole journey. For Sir Douglas it was bliss, a time to gather one's thoughts and prepare for the impending adventure. For young Thomas Jackson, it was through total and utter shock. He was still thinking through what he'd just been told about the pigeons and their peg legs when the driver announced that they had reached their destination.

Thomas was first out of the car and, after a brief stretch, turned to see that Sir Douglas had followed him, but had already turned around to pay the driver. With the transaction completed and the car door shut, the car sped off whilst Sir Douglas turned to address his young assistant. Thomas was amazed to see Sir Douglas produce two pairs of thick-rimmed glasses from within the leather briefcase he'd been carrying along with, what looked like two plastic identity cards. On offering a pair of glasses and a card to Thomas, Sir Douglas began to explain.

"Here you go, my friend! Under the terms laid down by the McJeffers Act, we are to assume new identities for our research work connected to the Osvaldo Ardilles."

Thomas looked closely at what he was accepting then looked up to see that Sir Douglas had already donned his pair.

"I am "Sir Douglas Squits," and you are..."

"According to this, I am Thomas Jerkson!"

"Yes, that's right! Thomas Jerkson!"

"But…"

"Aagh, no buts, Thomas! Just put the glasses on and lets go about our work!"

Both men proceeded to walk through the main gate wearing their respective pairs of fake glasses. Both of these strange looking characters walked proud and tall, almost statesmen like, but beneath those facades laid two bundles of nerves. Neither could let the nerves show because the other was there. On reaching the reception they entered and it was the senior man who approached the window. A middle aged, bespectacled woman stood on the other side ready to greet him.

"Can I help you, Sir?"

"Yes, good morning my love, Sir Douglas Squits and Thomas Jerkson here on Whitehall business."

Thomas stood, bemused by the term, 'Whitehall business,' as did Sir Douglas, the more he thought about it.

"Oh, right Sir. Will you be needing a guide or…?"

"No, that won't be necessary, we'll be fine thanks."

"Oh, ok then, Sir. If you Gentlemen would like to proceed through the double doors over there then you'll find signposts for all displays, buildings and exhibits."

"Why, thank you very much."

Both men picked up their belongings and were gone, through the double doors and out into the courtyard. Thomas, following Sir Douglas like an obedient dog, was still feeling troubled by what had just been said by his elder colleague. Whilst walking across the courtyard he moved for some clarification.

162

"Can you explain, "Whitehall business," please?"

"Not really. It was once a place of power and respect and the war was effectively run from there years ago, but now it's just a shell, a parody of its former self. But, for some strange reason the word "Whitehall" still projects power and Government strength. Since the war, everything's either been moved to cheaper premises or closed down, due to the thieving Governments this country keeps producing."

"So, "Whitehall business?""

"Thomas! Think about it! It still sounds powerful. Two men turn up wearing fake glasses and carrying fake i.d's. Okay, what's the more likely scenario for them getting past reception? "Hello, we're here on "Whitehall business," or "Hello, we're here on Gondola Suite, nineteenth floor, Docklands Business Centre business?"

"And people still fall for that, eh?"

"You've just witnessed it yourself, my friend! Now lets get to work."

The two men agreed on a meeting place and, indeed, a time to meet there. They both worked out who would cover what exhibits and buildings and then they were off, covering the ground as though their lives depended on it. It had been decided that Thomas would cover all indoor exhibits, whilst Sir Douglas would put his years of experience to good use on the actual vessels that lay moored or mounted around the actual Dockyards themselves.

Before splitting up, Sir Douglas had reminded his young assistant that this visit was "purely for observation only," and it was these words that sat heavy on his mind as he wandered up and down and in and out of the exhibits. As he checked rope patterns and types, wood construction methods and everything generally associated with the craft of shipbuilding, he gradually forgot about his hell the previous day and the fact that he'd been a victim of what basically amounted to a press gang.

Indeed, by the time Thomas checked his watch and realised that he was due to meet up with Sir Douglas in under half an hour he felt contented, almost happy to be involved and with few regrets. Although he had made no written notes, he was happy that he had managed to store enough information in his memory to enable him to contribute greatly to the soon-to-be built H.M.S Osvaldo Ardilles. For Thomas now realised that what he had just done had ensured that he would have an influential say in her final design and building.

Sir Douglas, on the other hand, had spent the two hours that had been agreed wandering around ships and submarines, all the time picturing each and every craft with automated ticket barriers fitted. As soon as he'd seen them at Bromley South Station he'd realised that he was hooked and also that they'd probably be in his thoughts for the whole day. And sure enough they were. His train of thought was centred on building a craft that could then be fitted with these machines.

For three days prior to his visit, and for one more after it, her Majesty's ship The Ark Royal was in town on a P.R exercise. Her vast bulk sat awkwardly out in mid river. Getting her there had proved an exercise, so big in logistics and co-ordination that, at one point, it had been too close to call as to whether it would actually be undertaken or cancelled. But, as it had turned out, they had decided to sail her, ever so gingerly, up the river to the museum to sit, larger than life, looming over the site.

For a presence, so obviously out of proportion to it's surroundings, it came as quite a shock to Sir Douglas to see her there, but only after about an hour and a half of wandering around the dock side in her shadow. The reason that he'd been so oblivious to her, automated ticket barriers, and when he did finally notice the rather large aircraft carrier looming many, many feet over him, his mind rapidly began sizing up how many barriers, with oars, would have to be fitted in order to move the bloody thing. He was hooked on the idea. Barriers were the way forward, lots of them! With great big oars but, then there was the matter of the accountants, currently being selected in London and shortly to be commencing training.

He told himself that there was no reason why he couldn't have accountants operating the ticket barriers. Although actual London Underground staff, who were used to dealing with these machines, would be significantly better. His mind began to go round and round in circles, as he came flying back to the accountant's idea at full speed. Having decided that London Underground staff spent all their time leaning on barriers perfecting their "hard man with arrogance" stance so would be of no use at all.

Again, accountants became the number one choice, as their qualities were what would be needed to operate the ticket barrier turned oar machine. For, in order for the boat to move anywhere, thousands of tickets would need to be fed through each machine at a constant rate. Not too fast, and not too slow. Sir Douglas found himself, not for the first time, supporting the recruitment of the accountants for the engine room.

Having stood there for a while, staring up at the colossus that cast a shadow over, what felt like, the whole county, Sir Douglas alerted himself to the fact that he'd better put ticket barriers on hold for a while and check his watch. Realising that the time for ticket barriers was over and the time for meeting Thomas was upon him, he hurried off to their agreed meeting place where he found the young man waiting patiently.

Both men swapped greetings before a suggestive nod from Sir Douglas led to them walking towards the double doors and, once through them and reception, out into the sunlight again where Sir Douglas approached a taxi. Within seconds both were in the back of the car, which began the short journey back to the railway station. A quick "how did you get on?" was followed by an equally quick "Yes ok...not too bad." That brief exchange represented the sum total of conversation all the way to the station.

On arrival at Chatham Station, Sir Douglas paid the driver and then turned to Thomas. As he began to discuss the finer points of train times and platforms, the taxi driver nestled his vehicle into a nearby taxi-rank and, after switching off the engine, settled down for a snooze. Having stood for a few minutes to agree on a strategic plan for "operation how the hell do we get to Portsmouth from here?" Sir Douglas and the now eager Thomas headed for the designated platform.

It wasn't long before the train, that would take them

to London, arrived. Thomas, being the ever-eager recruit, had studied the timetables and charts on display in the station at Chatham and had decided that the easiest route to Portsmouth was via London. Once on-board the train, both men settled down and began to mentally organise and formulate, what they had seen at the dockyards, into some kind of list come report. The silence only occasionally broken by an "I'll get the coffees in then" or a "not long to go now."

This near silence continued all the way through London and then down to the Naval fortress of Portsmouth, which lay waiting for them, courtesy of a secondary train. What both men had realised, not long after departing from Chatham, but which neither wanted to admit, was that their respective memories were not quite up to the task at hand. Both men craved a notebook, but with the task at hand bringing a sub-conscious competitive edge, neither man wanted to accept defeat and go and purchase one.

After a few hours of mental torture, undertaken in an atmosphere of silence and continued posturing, Sir Douglas and the young Thomas Jackson found themselves hailing another cab outside another railway station. The surrounding architecture did nothing to disguise the appearance of a town steeped in historical importance. Both men instantly felt as though they were only the latest in a very long line of Naval personnel to pass through these streets. Along with that thought came the realisation that, because they were only "the latest," meant that what they were here to undertake would shape the thinking and the reasoning for why the men and women of the future would pass through these same streets.

These thoughts suddenly became too heavy for Sir Douglas and it was the weather, which came to his aid. That age old topic, which never failed to save a situation, was now performing it's duty again, as he sat with his young assistant in the back of the taxi that was now making it's way through the local traffic towards the Naval Base. The relief was clear for all to see, as both men had become so heavily bogged down in their own personal bog of thoughts, that it had become harder with every passing second for them to declare their need of a notebook. Now that most mundane of conversations had saved the situation the pressure was suddenly gone.

In an instant, the driver had been paid and both men stood at the gates to the dockyards, staring out at the impressive sights that greeted them. Sir Douglas took a deep breath of fresh air and, in an instant, became revitalised and ready for this next stage of his mission. In an almost over enthusiastic voice, reminiscent of Sir Horace, he launched into a kind of tour guide speech.

"Here, Thomas, here is the very heart of English Heritage. The very essence of what we, the English, are about!"

Thomas followed the line of Sir Douglas's outstretched arm and was left a little bit confused at the vision, which lay beyond the pointed finger.

"Brittany Ferries?"

"What? Erm, no, Thomas! THE FLEET! I'm talking about the bloody English Fleet!"

"Oh, I see. I didn't think you meant the ferry company, although that's what you pointed at."

"I can assure you, Thomas that, had I actually pointed at the ferry, it wouldn't of been in conjunction with my declaration of what I see as the heart of the English people. If I HAD pointed at the ferry, I would've said something along the lines of "That ferry will take you to Normandy," but, you see, I didn't…did I!"

"Well, no, you didn't. Which is why I asked, but it certainly looked as though you did."

The expressions on both men's faces seemed to indicate that a neutrality factor had come into play. An area of common ground had been reached, for both men shrugged and accepted that it had been a case of cross wires and, therefore, a situation that was best forgotten and that they'd best get on with the task at hand. An agreeing nod at each other and they were off. Through the gates as their alter egos, "Sir Douglas Squits" and "Thomas Jerkson."

Over the coming hours they were to see everything that they were required to by their senior, Sir Horace. Instructed to take in "The ships, the theories, the designs and the disasters," it was satisfying to be able to tick these off of the list one by one. Most important of all was the Mary Rose herself. It was while they stood in awe of this famous lady that the younger man had glanced across at the elder man and noticed a rather strong gleam in his eyes.

Not wanting to bring attention to, or focus on, this gleam, Thomas decided that it was either through sheer terror or the result of being immensely proud. Terror, as he knew Sir Douglas would feel responsible and also guilty for being the man that pulled the Mary Rose apart. The thought of being that man would clearly cause physiological problems to a man of his standing. On the other hand, the gleam could be the result of seeing the terrific work being done to the historic craft and the sense of being so proud. Either way, he felt it was best not to address the situation and just let the man have his moment, whatever the reason for it.

The two of them stood for, what felt to Thomas, quite

a long while, staring at the mass of scaffolding and planks that seem to almost encase the 'Rose.' Having spent a fair, but sufficient, amount of time perusing the other vessels and artefacts around the site, this detailed and prolonged studying of the elderly relic seemed somewhat disproportionate to the rest of the "to do list." Eventually, however, Sir Douglas seemed to snap out of whatever concentrated stare he was in and, satisfied that he'd seen enough, quickly looked at his wrist watch before addressing the younger man.

"Time, as they say, Thomas, is marching on! Unless you have any last minute requests, I think we should hail a cab and get on that nice warm train back home! What say you?"

Thomas, not wishing to overstate his desire to go home, pondered a suitably reserved reply.

"I believe that I have seen everything that I need to and that I have enough information, Douglas, so I think catching that train is a good thing to do! Although, if it's ok with you, I would like to make a brief stop on the way back to the station?"

A slightly quizzical, but accepting nod, from Sir Douglas meant that the cab would take a slight diversion on its way back to the station. In no time at all they had flagged down a cab, taken the diversion Thomas had requested and reached the station. As they stood on the platform, waiting patiently for their train, Thomas thought of another part of the process that he needed clarification for.

"Douglas?"

"Yes, Thomas, my friend."

"About what we've just done, I don't understand what happens next!"

"Oh, well, that bit's easy. We both go home and sleep. Then, when we're ready, we evaluate everything that we've seen, in a kind of de-brief sort of way. From that, we will submit a list of "recommended parts" to Sir Horace and, before you can say "HMS Osvaldo Ardilles," the required parts will be acquired by plain looking gentlemen in white coats for "Scientific Evaluation." They will be delivered to a secret destination where our beloved craft will be built and they will then form a kind of historical scrap heap, just waiting to be used by our boat builders."

Once on board the train, Thomas and Sir Douglas settled down for a bit of rest after what had been an exhausting day. As Thomas sat staring out of the window, he suddenly felt the cold for the first time since he'd been in this mess. He realised that, for the first time in the last twelve odd hours, he was in control of everything about his person and that a sense of returning to the norm was about him. He'd only been staring blind into the darkness, outside the train, for a couple of minutes before a loud snore emanated from the heap that sat beside him.

A quick, intense glance, at Sir Douglas and he was back from staring out of the window and focused on the job at hand. He smiled to himself. Not so much a smile of relief, but more one of realisation. Realisation that both Sir Douglas and himself had been far too stubborn, on the way down to Portsmouth, to actually buy a notebook to record their respective thoughts in. Now this situation had been resolved, courtesy of the souvenir shop in the D-Day museum, all was well in young Thomas' world as he jotted down thought after thought on line after line.

After what seemed like only twenty or thirty minutes they came shuddering to a halt at Waterloo. The final bone breaking jolt was accompanied by a huge snore come throat clearance, by the senior Naval man, as he finally succumbed to consciousness and sat up straight before adjusting his peak cap, that he'd used to sublime affect as a snoring muffler.

"Here already?" The rather obvious answer to this stupid question was delivered in a very courteous way by the ex-maritime student, as he understood the mind numbing affects that sleep can have on an older man. He trod carefully.

"Erm, why yes. Doesn't time fly!"

Sir Douglas took this at face value and felt that it was time to play the elder statesman.

"Why yes, it certainly does young Thomas! Shall we get a cab? I think that may be more beneficial to the project, seeing as we need to report to Sir Horace at ten in the morning."

A silent but very agreeing nod from Thomas met Sir Douglas' eyes and, with that, both men were off of the train and walking down the platform. Once through the barriers, they found themselves a black cab and settled back in the bench like black seats, as their charge cut a swathe through the busy late night London traffic, heading for Bexley, and a quick cup of tea for both men before retiring to their respective bedrooms for the evening.

Before finally shutting his bedroom door for a well-earned sleep, Thomas smelt himself and made a desperate plea to his host.

"Douglas, I'll need to get some new clothes tomorrow, as I am now beginning to stink even more than I thought possible!"

Forgetting the promise that he had made the night before, Sir Douglas humbly replied

"Oh, erm, yes, Thomas. We'll shop on the way in tomorrow. Good night!"

Before closing his eyes, Sir Douglas made a mental note that shopping tomorrow would be a good thing to do, if not for the sake of their nostrils. Note made, he switched out the light and fell, fully clothed, onto his bed.

Chapter Ten – Preparing for Sir Horace

On returning from their exhausting trip, both Sir Douglas and Thomas had taken a day off to rest and compose their thoughts, to assess what they had seen and what they thought they had seen and to do some shopping. The original plan was to report to Sir Horace at ten the next morning, but an early morning call from Sir Douglas to Sir Horace to explain that there was too many notes to organise, had ended with an agreement that an extra day was needed.

Travelling into Greenwich, the next working day, had seen both men sat silently in the back of Sir Douglas' car, seemingly stuck on one issue. In fact one issue, but two different angles. One sat there thinking to himself just how, indeed why his boss had taken so lovingly to those ticket barriers. The other sat there starry eyed in wonder of the same machinery.

So, as the car cut a path through the London traffic that morning, its occupants in the back sat staring out of the side windows, Thomas on the left, Sir Douglas on the right. After what seemed like only a few minutes, they arrived outside the main entrance to The Maritime Museum and were startled back to the present by the rear door being opened by Peter, the driver.

"Bloody hell! Here already?"

"Yes, Sir Douglas. It was a good run in this morning."

Sir Douglas exited the car via the open door whilst Thomas, on the other side of the car, felt very humbled as he opened his door himself. Once outside the car, Sir Douglas nodded to his driver a nod that said a thousand words, abbreviated to "Thanks Peter, see you later," on this occasion. Both men watched the car slide off around the corner and then turned and entered the building. Striding down the corridors and into the Main Hall, their postures became more purposeful with every stride.

With note pads and folders tucked menacingly under their respective arms, their confidence was high as they approached the blue whale. They felt confident and assured with the information that they had gathered and very sure that the marathon museum trip had been a success. With dusters at the ready, they descended the stairs under the distorted lower jaw. The two men entered the Operations Room to find Sir Horace pouring three lagers in anticipation of their arrival.

Both men accepted their leader's invitation and took their places at the table, where a cold glass of amber liquid sat waiting for them. They accepted that it was exceptionally early for alcohol but, in the "Floaty Boat Brigade," anytime is seemingly a good time. On being asked by Sir Horace to "show me whatcha got!" both men produced identical notebooks, previously purchased from the D-Day museum shop in Portsmouth.

"Aagh, Gentlemen!"

Both Sir Douglas and Thomas responded at the same time. "Sir Horace."

"Let us discuss your little adventure."

"OK, tell me, just how did you two get on? I mean, "Sir Douglas Squits" and, and, "Thomas Jerkson," were they fooled? Did it work?"

Thomas looked at Sir Douglas in an inviting way. Sir Douglas understood and thought it best to humour the old man.

"Oh YES, Sir! Can I take this opportunity to congratulate you, on behalf of Thomas and myself, for the masterful disguises? They worked a treat, an absolute treat!"

"Really?"

"Oh yes, Sir, we could wear them all day and no-one would ever guess that we're up to something!"

"They didn't work, did they?"

"Erm, no, not really. At least, as far as our undercover work goes, no!"

"Oh. Please explain."

"Well, Sir, if you're approaching this from the "I'd-like-to-look-like-an-idiot-and-hear-laughter-everywhere-I-go" angle then you'd be spot on with your creation. If that is, indeed, the reason for the creation of "Sir Douglas Squits" and "Thomas Jerkson," then you, Sir, are a genius! If, however, you were hoping to send the two of us undercover, so we could assess the situation and the needs of our beloved Ardilles, then report back to your good self with our findings without the outside world knowing, then you've, erm, failed, Sir."

"That bad, eh?"

"I'm afraid so, yes!"

"Not a hint of secrecy at all?"

"Not at all. We could've been dressed as one of the Ardilles' pigeons and achieved a higher level of cover…of the under variety!"

"Oh! Thomas? Are you of the same opinion?"

"Oh yes Sir! I'm of the same opinion alright."

"Was it the names?"

"I don't think the…"

"What about "Sir Dougal Squirt?""

"Erm…"

"And "Timmy Jacksoff"?"

"As I was about to say, Sir, the name's aren't the whole

problem. Its the "groucho" style fake glasses, Sir, they don't exactly give us a James Bond-esque edge when we're undercover."

"They don't?"

Thomas looked at Sir Horace, and then looked at Sir Douglas. Sir Horace looked at Sir Douglas, having looked at Thomas. Sir Douglas noted all these different looks and felt disheartened that his superior genuinely did not have an inkling that these disguises would fail.

"Are you sure that it's the disguises and not the names alone?"

"No! Erm, Sir!"

"How about pencils, pads, raincoats and, and maybe, "Doug Squirch, reporter"?"

"Sir Douglas!!!"

Thomas could take no more and cried aloud for Douglas to step in and stop this senseless onslaught on his intelligence. Once was farcical, twice was alarming, but repeated suggestions! He could take no more. Sir Douglas realised that his young aids' stress levels had just risen to defcon twenty-something and so he felt it was time to bring his superiors' frantic search for a suitable alias to an end.

"Sir Horace. I think that we need to take the aliases back to the drawing board and, maybe, leave them there, erm, Sir!"

"Oh, Bugger me. Well, best get on with your reports then…"

Sir Horace noted immediately strange comparisons and yet, at the same time, some glaringly obvious differences between them. Whilst both men sat admiring their notebooks with an obvious glow of pride, Sir Horace couldn't help but notice the difference in the condition of the respective notebooks. Opposite him, to the left, sat Sir Douglas whom, he noted, had an immaculate notebook. The kind of notebook that, if it could talk, would proudly declare "my owner's a Naval man!" or, rather, "my owner's a Floaty man!"

Thomas, on the other hand, had what appeared to Sir Horace to be a notebook that had walked a different path. Again if it could speak, it would've probably declared that "my owner's a student who has become bored on the train journey home and doodled all over me!" Pictures of boats with huge flags of skulls and crossbones bore evidence to the fact that boredom had come the way of this young man over a few hours. If the pictures didn't give the game away then the words "The Smiths" and "The Velvet Underground," scrawled all over both covers, certainly did.

Thomas looked at Sir Douglas. Sir Douglas looked at Thomas. Thomas made an "after you" gesture with his hand. To which Sir Douglas nodded and preceded to begin his de-brief. Thomas lifted his glass of ice-cold lager to his lips as his immediate superior began.

"Well, Sir. On arrival at Chatham I began to assess the physical aspects of our mission. What I mean by that is the designs, difficulties, features and overall performances of said issues. I realised that if I could obtain an overall assessment of all of these, the plus and minus factors, if you like, then the Osvaldo Ardilles could only benefit from it."

Sir Horace felt overwhelmed. He felt as though he wanted to rush into the "I knew you were the man for the job" speech, but realised that, over the past few days, he'd used that one a bit too much. He felt proud, immensely proud. Proud to see that his "favourite underling" had shaken off the threat of complete and utter nervous exhaustion and now sat before him with a thorough and oh-so-professional assessment. He knew that 'his' man had come home with the true beginnings of The Osvaldo Ardilles in his little D-Day Museum notebook. At last, he felt, things were taking shape. Professionalism was the name of the game.
"...And I also saw something that I think could be an improvement on the accountants, Sir."

Sir Horace felt overwhelmed, again. But, this time, totally overwhelmed. What had he done to deserve this genius? This last statement had put him on the brink and he felt that he had to find out what kind of person or 'thing' could possibly improve on accountants. He felt like the mouse that was about to get caught in the most obvious trap in mouse history. Even though he knew it was a trap, he just couldn't help himself. Even if the cheese had sat on the trap with a huge banner saying "Attention all mice, this is a bloody great trap!" he would've felt obliged to have a nibble. And so he did.

"An improvement, Douglas?"

"What could possibly improve on accountants, Douglas?" Sir Douglas felt empowered, whilst Thomas almost choked on his mouthful of lager, as he realised what Sir Douglas was about to say. His young mind was pleading inwardly "Oh no, not the ticket barriers! Please, not the ticket barriers!"

"Ticket barriers, Sir!"

"I...I beg your pardon!"

"Ticket barriers, Sir!"

"Ticket barriers, Douglas?"

"Oh yes, Sir. Really, I do mean, "yes!""

"You really mean, "yes," do you?"

"Oh yes, Sir. I mean, "yes!""

"Oh. Better compose yourself and explain this one to me, but slowly, Douglas, very slowly."

All the while this exchange was developing, Thomas sat back in his black, Government Issue chair, quietly listening. In what felt like several weeks, but in reality was only a few days, he'd long since acclimatised to the absurd task at hand, the 'mission.' And whilst he knew what was about to be explained, he thought he'd just stay silent, play dumb. Become part of the furniture, Government Issue.

The more he thought about what he was hearing; the better that plan appeared to be. And so he was not surprised when he saw Sir Douglas and Sir Horace in mid conversation, seemingly oblivious to his presence and totally ignoring him. Of course, he knew he'd be dragged into the mire with the almost traditional "What do you think?" but, until then, he was a silent witness.

With both men now composed, Sir Douglas began. "Ticket barriers, erm Sir."

"Yes, yes, you've already mentioned what they are, but "how's, why's and what the hell's," if you please!"

"Oh right, Sir. Well. Accountants, methodical, even paced etc etc. Correct, Sir?"

"Oh yes, Douglas, for the sake of all things floaty, you're correct my friend!"

"Well, Sir. I was thinking. What happens if they catch a cold, or develop a fever, toothache, or they all want a bedtime story…or…"

"Yes, yes I get the point. Proceed!"

"Oh, erm, right, Sir! The answer is that you lose power. If any of the above occurred then the Ardilles would suffer as a result. Regardless of where she was in the world or whatever the situation she found herself in, she would lose power. If her engine room wanted a bedtime story or found a particularly interesting article in the Times, then she would lose mobility."

"Douglas. I can see that you're inspired with this one so please carry on!"

"Thank you, Sir. Well, the key factor is this. Think Ardilles, think handicapped. Money, as you said, or that ginger guy said, is far too tight to mention. Therefor, we must make do with what we have or can get. If you employ five hundred accountants and they row as and when you want then you have a very economical and reliable engine bay but, and here's the "but," as I have already said, if an anomaly occurs…"

"You mean a spanner in the works?"

"Yes, Sir Horace, I mean a spanner in the works, a hiccup, then we have a problem. Unless the situation is resolved immediately you'd be faced with meetings, union activities, discussions, votes, improved rowing conditions, news letters, focus groups etc etc."

"Go on…."

"Well why put the Ardilles at risk from these possibilities when you can have ticket barriers?"

"I whole heartedly agree Douglas. In fact, I would go as far as to say you're absolutely right! If only I knew just what the hell you wanted to do with said ticket barriers!"

"aagh, erm, yes…erm Sir! Ticket barriers. Right, erm, picture, if you will, your common British Rail or whatever they're called now, ticket barrier. Honourable, loyal, reliable and always willing to work. Except at Bromley South where they don't seem very willing to work, but anyway, where was I? Aagh yes, willing to work! One ticket is fed in and that generates an action which, I think could improve the Osvaldo Ardilles' performance."

"So you want each accountant to buy a ticket before sitting down to row?"

"Oh no Sir. That's not what I want the barriers for, not at all!"

Sir Horace was intrigued as to how such passion and enthusiasm in a man could make him so unable to actually describe what he was so enthusiastic about in the first place. Here he was, sat there looking at his number one man, who was so full of life at this very moment, that he was just simply unable to say anything about it. The more he smiled and looked at Sir Douglas, the more Sir Douglas just repeated the same few lines. "Swap accountants for ticket barriers, blah, blah, blah," but why?

That was the only question he wanted answered. Oh maybe "how?" would be another good one to ask. He sat there watching and listening for a short while longer before deciding that he had to get his man out of this repetitive rut that he was happily wallowing in. Sir Douglas started another loop.

"You see, Sir, if you take the accountants away and replace them with ticket barriers...."

"Douglas. I bloody know that bit!"

"Oh erm, right, Sir. Well..."

Thomas could stay silent no longer. Even if, just for the sake of his sanity, he could stay silent no more. He was well aware of the implications involved in speaking up, but the risk was worth it. For it was rapidly becoming too painful to sit there in silence, listening to the same half-an-explanation over and over again.

"You see, Sir, if you take the accountants away and replace them with ticket barriers...."

Thomas snapped.

"Oh, for the love of Monty, boss!"

Sir Douglas froze. It was the kind of shock he needed to get himself off the same line that he'd been spouting for a few minutes. Sir Horace was shocked as well, as he'd totally forgotten that Thomas was in the room. But, this verbal reminder had pleased him, as it had saved him a job.

"He wants to strap large oars to the actual barrier bits of the machine so they can row instead of the accounts. There! Was that so hard?"

A sense of relief came over all three men. Sir Horace was the first to smile.

"Aagh, I see. Douglas my boy, it's an interesting idea for sure."

"Thank you, Sir"

Sir Horace was just about to ask Sir Douglas to explain, but realised they'd been stuck on that road for far too long, and so thought better of it. Instead, he directed the question to Thomas.

"Ok Thomas, the stage is yours."

"Well, I think what Sir Douglas is suggesting, is a row of ticket barriers down each side of the boat. Placed there with a rather large oar attached to one of the actual moving barrier parts. Then, when someone feeds a ticket into the machine, the barrier opens and closes thus creating a rowing effect with the large oar. I think that's his idea."

Thomas felt that disassociation was the key to this one and felt that adding, "I think that's his idea," to the end of his explanation was good enough to keep the men in white coats from his door. He reasoned with himself that all had gone pretty well.

Sir Douglas felt pretty relieved that Thomas had actually jumped in and helped him get his wondrous idea across, but was concerned with the complete lack of emotion or reaction coming from Sir Horace.

Sir Horace sat motionless, just kind of starry eyed. Every time Sir Douglas thought he'd caught his eye, he stretched his hands and fingers out in a "well?" kind of way, but all to no avail. There just seemed to be no life in Sir Horace. Well that was a lie, his eyes were open and he was breathing, but not much else was going on as far as Sir Douglas could see.

During this period of silence and expectation, Thomas had returned to his glass of lager. He had momentarily thought to himself that, if his new job was going to be about drinking lots of lager at stupid times of the day, then he was going to build a good career for himself. But, before he could get carried away in his thoughts, the silence and air of awkwardness around him drove him to stand up and grab the bull by the horns.

"Sir Horace, Sir Douglas' idea is to remove the accountants and replace them with ticket barriers. There will of course still be the need for a timekeeper of some description. However I feel that to have bookkeepers mixing with British Rail staff…"

"It's Rail Track, I think…."

"Oh, excuse me, Sir Douglas! As I was saying, to have bookkeepers mixing with Rail Track staff may not be the best policy. If this were to happen then they'd need a sound from the underground, say a busker. That way they'd feel as though they were in their natural environment and happily feed the tickets into the machine in a timely manner."

Enough was enough for Sir Horace. The actions of the young man before him had been just what the doctor ordered. He was back in the real world. Vibrant, alive and in control of things, once more.

"Thank you, Thomas. That is exactly the sort of explanation that I have been wanting. Douglas ma boy, you really need to calm down and compose yourself when you come up with ideas. I know your genius is there for all to see, but you'll be needing to tone the enthusiasm down a bit, in order to tell others just what visions you have come up with in that well groomed cranium of yours. Ok?"

Sir Douglas felt suitably scolded. "Yes, Sir"
Sir Horace, now standing and thinking on his feet spoke up again.

"Ok. I understand where you're coming from, Dougie my man, but I really don't think we can go for that idea. At least on the Osvaldo Ardilles."

A very disappointed Sir Douglas replied quickly.

"Oh! We can't, Sir? May I ask why? As it seems a quite revolutionary idea, even if I do say so myself!"

"Several reasons really. Firstly, the plans are already drawn up for accountants. Whilst we're not under any sort of pressure, completion wise as yet, that can't be far off and so to change to ticket barriers is just a logistical 'no-no.' Secondly, I've had word that the accountants have already been selected and that they are all reporting to South Norwood swimming baths in, erm South Norwood, on Monday. Douglas, you are charged with training them up. They're your men now. Thirdly, and that's the last one for now, I accept that if we changed to ticket barriers then we'd have to change the source of time keeping. I accept that. What I can't accept, at least for this vessel, is the fact that everywhere she went there'd be the acoustic sound of Bob Dylan or some other dodgy busker number emanating from her engine deck. How could she possibly glide stealth like into enemy waters with Stairway to Heaven or Smoke on the Water blasting out? Maybe, maybe even the odd cry of "Big Issue" wouldn't go a miss eh?"

"I see, Sir."

"Oh come, come, Douglas! I'm not trying to pooh-pooh your idea, but it wouldn't work for this vessel, plain and simple. It may, however, work for the next one!"

"The next one?"

Thomas, who had started pint number three whilst all this was going on felt a warmth inside and perked up on this news, as did Sir Douglas.

"Sir Horace, are you telling us that there's going to be another ship?"

"It's not concrete, but I know that the men in suits and wigs are looking into it, should the Osvaldo Ardilles prove successful."

Thomas seized the moment.

"Oooh, can we call her the H.M.S Brian Cant? He's my hero, y'know!"

Sir Douglas rebuffed him, but then thought a bit more about it.

"No we bloody well can't! Although, thinking about it, that's a damn fine name for a potentially damn fine boat. Right! That's it settled then. If we are instructed to build a second ship, even though we haven't actually completed the first yet, we'll call her H.M.S Brian Cant!"

Thomas smiled a smile filled with satisfaction. The

morning was still upon them, he'd had three pints of lager, and his suggestion for the name of the next boat had been accepted. Life felt pretty good for young Mr Jackson. Sir Douglas, on the other hand, felt pretty low. He wanted his ticket barrier idea to be incorporated into the sleek and flowing lines of the Osvaldo Ardilles, but this had been rejected. Instead, from what he could gather, there was likely to be another ship built and it would be this one, which would look at his idea. He felt as though both the other men in the room had stabbed him in the back.

Just then there was a knock on the door. Sir Douglas broke away from his self-pity and opened the door. Waiting to enter was an orderly, from down the corridor, holding a large bag. Sir Horace gestured for him to enter and that's what he did. Walking up to the table, he swung the bag from over his shoulder and landed it in front of Sir Horace. Sir Horace looked at the bag on the table, then at the orderly. He felt compelled to ask.

"And what do we have here, my good man?"

The orderly didn't feel he had to speak at this point, so here merely handed Sir Horace a piece of paper. Sir Horace took it and cast his eye over it, before speaking. "Aagh and indeed an "erm" on this one! I guess we never did actually get round to changing all the wording on that purchase order did we, Douglas!"

The orderly broke his silence before Sir Douglas could answer his boss.

"We didn't have a clue what "Four Hundred Thomas Bags" were, nor did we understand why the name of the form had been changed to "Jackson Purchase," so we just ordered and delivered what we thought you meant, that being four hundred tea bags, Sir"

"Right then! And, "Jolly good" as well! That'll be all, thank you my friend. Could you shut the door on the way out? Thanks awfully!"

With that, the orderly turned and walked out of the room, shutting the door behind him, as requested. A sense of disbelief filled the air. Sir Horace spoke first.

"Four hundred "Thomas bags?""

Sir Douglas thought he had an idea, one that would restore his faith in the world that morning.

"Sir, may I speak?"

"Why yes Douglas, if you think it'll help!"

"Pigeons, Sir!"

Sir Horace sat frowning. He couldn't quite get the connection. Thomas, who was now on his fourth pint, sat back with his with arms folded behind his head. Snuggled into his chair, he felt ready for this one. Sir Horace couldn't place the connection and felt compelled to ask.

"No, Douglas, can't quite get that one. Just what do our little feathered friends have to do with tea bags?"

Sir Douglas was back! Back in the 'ideas' big time and his connection between tea bags and pigeons was just about to be explained.

"Well, Sir. You have already briefed me on the pigeon situation. The case being that the Osvaldo Ardilles will be filled with them. The fact that there will be two types etc etc."

"Yes, yes, Douglas. Go on! Jesus man, what's wrong with you today? You're doing it again, stuttering and stumbling. Blah, blah, blah. Get to the point will you!"

Sir Douglas felt that he'd been brought down a peg or two.

"Oh right, Sir. Not wishing to point out the obvious, the pigeons will be cramped up down below. They'll have very little comfort. So why not use the four hundred tea bags as pigeon pillows? Why not give our feathered friends a little bit of help on the relaxation front?"

A rather disillusioned reply came back at him from Sir Horace.

"Right! Lunchtime. Don't wish to think about pillows for pigeons!"

Thomas, having a quite warm, alcohol-induced

feeling inside, was quite keen to see what lunchtime would bring. As with previous days, it actually meant a phone call, a quick dust and walk, a short car ride and a cosy chair in the "Cutty Club." Sir Douglas and Sir Horace had engaged in, what appeared to be, quite in-depth mumbling, of which he couldn't quite tap in to. Without four pints inside him, he was aware that he may well have taken things personally but, with said alcohol intake, he was quite happily following behind with a smile on his face and not a care in the world.

Ordering and, indeed, the whole lunchtime experience itself had just passed Thomas by and he wasn't that bothered by it. Four pints had pretty much put paid to any concentration for the day. The problem was, he remembered suddenly, after lunch it would be his turn to discuss his findings. A strong coffee and a pint of water quickly set him on the way to recovering some of his senses. All the while, Sir Douglas and Sir Horace continued to mumble. By the time they wrapped things up with a rather loud and out of place, "Ok then, Gentlemen!" Thomas felt ready for the afternoon stint.

As per normal, all the good intentions seemingly fell out of the car window on the short drive back to the museum as, on exiting the car and turning to face Sir Horace, Thomas was met by a rather unexpected declaration.

"Thomas, I'm too exhausted to listen to anymore ideas. Sir Douglas there has worn me out."

A quick look across the roof of the car, to where Sir Douglas stood, showed a man who was inwardly pleading his innocence. Sir Horace continued.

"I'm now handing this project over to you two, bar a few things. I'll be retreating to my little office down the corridor and you two just get on and create your vision. But, remember Douglas! No ticket barriers!"

A begrudging "Yes, Sir!" came back at him from the man stood on the other side of the car. Sir Douglas shut the door that he'd left open and that, as always, was the signal for Sir Horace to be driven away at speed and out of the main gates. Thomas was unimpressed.

"All that work, all that time and effort! All that sobering up!" Douglas came to his rescue.

"Calm it, Tom. We have the project now. We'll get our thoughts on board!"

And with that, both men walked into the museum to start another afternoon's work.

Chapter Eleven – Reporting in

The forecast had been for rain. Not just a little bit, but a bucket load. And, surprisingly, the weather people were right. Bang on the money, in fact. Sir Douglas woke and, for once, there was no hangover tearing through his brain. Awake and alert, a man with a purpose, he got out of bed. He started for the shower, but a tapping on the window outside checked his stride. He walked over to the curtains and peered through them.

Heavy rain was driving at the double-glazing outside. "Bugger," he thought to himself, "but this is the day I have waited for and nothing is going to dampen my spirits." He apologised to himself for the pun and headed to the shower. No head pain, no troubles and no concerns with what the day had in store, Sir Douglas felt great. And the reason he felt great? It was Monday!

Not just any Monday, but the Monday that he had been working towards for weeks and weeks. For today was the day that he would introduce his first real project to Sir Horace. Sure he'd been on the scouting mission to Chatham and Portsmouth, but he'd considered them just that, scouting missions. Having been assigned the task of training the accountants a few weeks ago, he'd really gone to task and put two hundred per cent into his assignment. He'd also put a lot of research into this particular phase of the Osvaldo Ardilles program and had undertaken a lot of the negotiating, regarding this, in secret. It would not have been seen as, "good form," if he'd briefed Sir Horace along the way.

For there were one or two little oddities that would definitely not have been allowed to continue if that had been the case. Sir Horace would not have entertained certain people involved in the discussions. There was the possibility that, even the knowledge of their very existence, could've damaged the health of Sir Horace. No, it'd been the best policy to conduct this part of the program without any interference from the others.

Like a young child on Christmas morning, he was too excited to eat breakfast so, instead, he took a long, refreshing shower and, after towelling himself and dressing, he left for his meeting with the boss. Even Thomas had not been privy to what was going on at first. And that had been the way Sir Douglas had wanted it to be throughout, but the communication channels between him and the accountants had proved to be very problematic. With this being the state of affairs, he'd had to enlighten the young Mr Jackson to the situation.

Thomas, who by now was fully up to speed with

every aspect of the Osvaldo Ardilles program, loved his new career. The weird, almost sick humour of the whole situation amused him greatly. He'd been spending his days since the scouting mission with Sir Douglas, holed up beneath the blue whale with the distorted lower jaw, in the Operations Room. His designated projects included fake guns, pigeons, the outer skin of the vessel, pillows and just about every other aspect of the H.M.S Osvaldo Ardilles that didn't involve accountants or at least the training of.

After the initial fury of the first weeks "do this, do that…go here, go there," everything had settled down. Sir Horace had taken a back seat and was happily monitoring the project from afar. He'd been concerned by the tea bag incident and had set about amending all the paperwork in the service. He also had the little matter of changing the name of the service to deal with. This had concerned him at first, as he foresaw a very large concrete wall in front of him, but felt sure that a few brandies down a few select throats would see the "Floaty Boat Brigade" come into being and that wall crumble to dust.

With Sir Horace in the background, and tucked away in an office down the corridor, Thomas had gained a free hand within the service. Sir Douglas, being the senior of the two of them, had been charged by Sir Horace with the task of setting up a training program for the accountants and had more or less vanished off the face of the earth. When Thomas had seen him around, he'd noticed that Sir Douglas had acted very cagey, as though he was up to no good. Amused, Thomas just continued with his own select tasks and ignored this petty behaviour. He didn't care much for what the others were doing for he had some gems of his own up his sleeve.

He thought to himself that, if anything went wrong, then he, Thomas Jackson, was the first that they turned to. If they needed anything then, again, it was he, Thomas Jackson, who had to arrange or obtain it, and yet, he would grumble to himself, the subject of the accountants, and the training of, seemed above him, as far as Sir Douglas and Sir Horace were concerned.

For the first few weeks of the program he had had not a sniff of information on how things were going. Sir Douglas, it seemed, was handling everything in a very secretive way. This situation hadn't really bothered him as he had masses of work of his own work to deal with which meant that if he wasn't working on the issue of what should be used as the outer skin of the ship, he was working on what the weaponry should look like. And, if he wasn't taking one of these tasks to hand then he could be found formulating a list of questions that he would put to the pigeon keepers as and when he met them.

Again, as with the subject of accountants, the subject of pigeons was a closely guarded secret and he was privy to only certain snippets of information. This subject represented another of the Act's priceless examples of ill-thought-through confusion. For pigeons were on Thomas's priority list, but he was only afforded certain chunks of data. Just how was he supposed to work like this?

He often thought to himself that the best way to deal with this subject was to just plod on, and make lists, of suggestions, recommendations, logistic requirements etc etc. All of it, he realised, would be totally irrelevant, if the information he wasn't privy to suddenly came his way and was completely different to what he guessed it to be.

Both Sir Douglas and Thomas had been briefed regarding a potential building to house and prepare the pigeons. At first, the early indications were that it was to be called "Stoke Pigeon Ville" but, no sooner had this name been mentioned, than it sort of faded away. With no fresh information on the proposed building, it was left to Thomas to assume that somewhere, in England, there would be a building, which, would simply be full of vets and prosthetic specialists trying to create suitable stumps or legs for the pigeons injured in the "Trafalgar Square Massacre."

Then, one day and very much out of the standard, Government Issue, blue, came a call from Sir Douglas who had rung him in the Operations Room and had spoken as if there'd never been a secretive issue. He had spoken for several minutes in order to update Thomas on what was happening with the training schedule and what he was required to do.

This conversation generated phone calls to each accountant assuring them that all would be well and calming their potential first day nerves. One accountant even asked for clarification of the lunch break time and another asked if he'd be allowed to call his wife from the canoe to make sure that her hair appointment had gone smoothly.

Within minutes, the accountants training schedule had gone to the top of the 'To Do' list and Thomas was fully aware of what was happening. For Thomas, this was quite stressful and yet, in a funny sense, enlightening. Here he was communicating with six hundred accountants over varying issues from lunch breaks, to suitable attire, when amongst all these conversations, a clear and vivid picture of innocence was emerging.

Accountants. This methodical breed, so clearly the backbone of working society, so utterly professional and with levels of dedication far above the common man and yet, completely oblivious to the task ahead. They had simply applied for the position advertised, interviewed, been selected and given a start date. Not one of them had any idea what they had got themselves involved in. They were simply following orders. Quite what they would think of these orders after their ordeal was over would be a question for another time but, for now, they were primed and ready for training.

After a couple of weeks of fairly intense communications between himself and the six hundred accountants in question, everything had been tied up, nailed down and finalised. Each man knew where he had to be and at what time. He knew what he should wear and what items he could bring. This latter point was basically the same for every man selected for the final six hundred man crew, umbrella, The Times, a briefcase (complete with apple, sandwiches and flask) and mobile phone. With the calculations completed and the communications ceased for now, Thomas was happy that every detail, regarding the training schedule for the accountants, was sorted. Six hundred of the finest accountants the country had to offer were to be trained over twenty days. Two days per batch of sixty. Thirty canoes each time with two men in each. All seemed fine to him.

For now, at least, he could return to the other

questions asked of him, such as, what the outer skin will be made of? What design could he come up for the turrets? What design could he come up with for the hull of the H.M.S Ardilles? This last question worried him. It was much the same worry that had seen him step into this mess in the first place. He knew that if Sir Douglas or Sir Horace got wind of some piece of wooden nautical history that existed in a strong condition then that would be "acquired" and bolted to the bow of the Mary Rose, which had by now, been acquired and delivered to the boat yard.

A kind of 'writers block' hit Thomas. He sat there staring at his pages of notes on the table before him. There were so many questions to answer, so many angles to approach from. Quite what one to start with was proving to be a bit of a teaser? Guns, skin, varnish, timber frame, just what one should he look at next? They were all beginning to merge into one! He sat back in his chair, Government Issue, and puffed out his cheeks. He gazed at the wall and followed it around the room. Before he knew it, he was staring into the kitchen and in particular at the fridge. BINGO! "That's that one sorted!" he thought to himself.

With one question answered, he put pen to paper and drew up rough guidelines and drawings, while it was still clear and fresh in his mind. A few minutes of silence followed, while he scribbled furiously in his notebook. He realised that the sort of people that he'd been dealing with, the sort of people that he'd be passing these suggestions onto, would really be challenged with what to do with them. With this in mind, he figured that he'd best explain things as clearly and as simply as possible.

He really didn't fancy boat yard personnel contacting him to ask stupid questions while he was working on some other part of the project so, again, with this in mind, he felt that he had to ensure that he detailed clearly just where the materials required for each project could be sourced. For example, looking at the fridge in the kitchen had just made his day worthwhile and it was also where the answer, to a major question posed of him, had just shown itself. Just what could be used or how would they skin the hull of the Ardilles? The answer was fridge and freezer doors. Pure and simple.

Oh, the feeling of power that was now coursing through his veins. From sacred lamb to all-powerful master, Thomas felt good. Realising that, at this very period of his life he was the most influential person in the country, felt good too. For every pen stroke, every doodle and every single note made, he knew that it was highly likely someone somewhere would act on it. If he scrawled a giant pigeon on top of the mast, he knew that there was a good chance that a giant pigeon would be present on top of the mast when the boat was launched. And so, not wishing to get serious or detract from the lunacy of the whole situation, Thomas felt obliged to pen the words 'The outer skin of the H.M.S Osvaldo Ardilles will be formed of fridge and/or freezer doors.'

A smile to himself then onwards with the details… 'It is my recommendation, that the outer skin of the H.M.S Osvaldo Ardilles be formed of full size fridge and or freezer doors. The very construction of these doors will form an insulation and they will also be used to water.' It had started so well. *"It is my recommendation that the outer skin of the H.M.S Osvaldo Ardilles be formed of full size fridge and or freezer doors. The very construction of these doors will form an insulation…"* Professional and almost engineer-esque in its descriptive content, it fell around its ankles with the words "and they will also be used to water." 'What the heck,' he thought, 'Fridge and freezer doors it is!'

Next on the agenda would be pigeons. He didn't really want to think about the vermin, but pigeons seemed to be the most popular word in the entire project. Everyone seemed to be obsessed with the things. Since Sir Douglas had mentioned how they had all come about, what with Sir

Horace calling the wrong number one night, they really had become the must have item. And now, with the addition of four hundred tea bags to their quarters, they really had become as important as the accountants. A sense of belief came over him. If he could crack the whole pigeon issue then he'd be on the home straight as far as this project would be concerned.

He noted his problem, which centred on an unknown quantity of pigeons. Of this number, there would be a quantity of racing pigeons and also a quantity of "Trafalgar Pigeons." This, then, created a class issue within the pigeon community on board, and so the level of comfort had to differentiate between the two classes. There had to be storage facilities for the prosthetic limbs of the disabled 'Trafalgar Pigeons' in the same way, as there had to be miniature exercise bikes and tread or waddle mills for the racing pigeons to train on.

There had to be baths for the racing pigeons in the same way, as there had to be a smoking den for the cigarette sucking Trafalgar Pigeons. Problems! Problems! Problems! For Thomas, it was an enthralling time. The ideas began to flow and soon page after page of script found there way onto the pages of the notebook before him on the desk. First, the pigeon quarters were dealt with. Next came the bathing and smoking requirements. Swiftly followed by the training needs of the feathered crewmembers, so on and so forth.

Thomas Jackson, ex-maritime student, and now interior designer, sat and penned page after page of details that simply flowed from his brain. A masterpiece was in the making. He was looking forward to seeing the looks on the other two's faces when they read what he was documenting. His vision surely had to be created as they had left the finer details to him to complete and he couldn't really see either of them objecting and redesigning things. Nope, the canvas was his and his alone and it was blank and inviting!

He continued to write. Once again it seemed that the word "pigeons" had inspired him. A simple feathered beast. Some had called them "flying rats." Whatever people thought of them, there was no escaping the fact that they were a key and integral part of the H.M.S Osvaldo Ardilles and, whilst the common variety went about their everyday existence, crapping all over whatever place or object happened to be in their vicinity, the selected "few" were in a different location, within the same and, as yet unknown, building, being prepared for their, soon to commence service, in the "Floaty Boat Brigade."

He paused and thought some more, realising that, in years past, animals and birds had often been honoured for their bravery and service to the crown. This latest group of pretenders brought with them much spirit, cigarettes and tea bags but, above all of this, and hanging over these birds like a neon sign, was the anticipation of just what service they might produce and, thus, what honours may be bestowed upon them in the not too distant future. He suddenly felt sorry for these birds as, he thought to himself, they were about to set sail in a vessel whereby their primary function was to carry messages in small containers, written by hand and rolled up tightly.

This method had been used as far back as world war one and, Thomas thought, maybe even earlier, and yet, it was to be used again, in the modern age, on board a vessel that was so technologically backwards, but which would share the world's waters with some of the most advanced Naval killing machines in the world. An alarming image to present to the world. With that horror in his mind, Thomas was startled back to the present, just as the door to the room he was in opened.

Pleasantly surprised to see it was Sir Horace and Sir Douglas, he welcomed them warmly.
"Sir Horace, Sir Douglas, good morning to you both."
Both men nodded an equally warm acknowledgement. Sir Horace stopped short of Thomas' desk while Sir Douglas

211

continued around until he stood next to Thomas, who by now had stood to formally greet the two men before him. Sir Horace addressed both men, standing before him, together.

"Gentlemen, I have a letter to read to you and I shall do so in a moment but, firstly, I would like to thank you both for your efforts to date. Thomas, Sir Douglas will update you shortly on where we are with everything, although, you probably know it already but, in summary, Sir Douglas and I are heading out tomorrow morning to watch the first training session for the first batch of accountants. I'm sure that you will agree, a very big day and, indeed, very big news for our team. Delivered, if I may say so, Douglas, in a very enthusiastic and sprightly manner this very morning!"

A slightly embarrassed Sir Douglas acknowledged his superior and realised that, in hindsight, he was perhaps too excitable for a Monday morning but, before he could put any more thought to the situation, Sir Horace continued.

"Anyway, Gentlemen, I have received a letter, from the men with suits and wigs, and am obviously obliged to read it to you. This, I shall do now, and will field any questions afterwards. So please hear me out as I read to you the official communication from the men in suits and wigs, or the office of Sir Robin McJeffers, if we're going to be all above board!"

Sir Horace then began to read the letter. His tone reminiscent of Neville Chamberlain's declaration of war speech in 1939...

"To Sir Horace Hargraves and all of the team working on "Project New Boat,"

It has come to my attention that we, as an arm of service, are in danger of being left behind in the cold, that we are not "up with the times." I refer, of course, to the rather large and lovely blue whale, which has hung so gracefully above the entrance to your wonderful Head Quarters for a fair while now, and which has also become a symbol for fake dusting throughout the world.

Whilst I am sure that you and your team are very fond of the giant beast, suspended above you, I feel sure that you all understand that the image of the re-born service, that you serve so honourably, is vital if we are to achieve all that I envisage for it.

I refer of course to marketing, the public, and worlds eyes respectively, and also what her Madge the Queen thinks of it all. In short, the whale has fallen from favour and is in the process of being replaced. The reason for its sudden demise is quite straightforward really. I could blurt on about

213

image this and up with the times that but, the plain and simples of the whole thing are as follows...

Queen Elizabeth was apparently watching a documentary on the blue whale last Tuesday night. All was going well until one of the documentary makers entered the water and attempted to fake dust the whale. It would appear that blue whales do not appreciate being fake dusted as the one thus being flicked with a duster took umbrage to this act of cleanliness and ate the diver. As it was a live broadcast it caused her Madge to vomit over two of her corgis and put her off of her tea.

Because of this display of violent tendencies, her Madge has decided that the nations' newest arm of service, currently undertaking such a high-profile project, can not and should not have such a violent beast marking its' Head Quarters.

And so, Ladies and Gentlemen, the blue whale will now be replaced with a model of Nemo, the clown fish. You may ask why...Lord knows I did. Again, the answers are as follows:

Nemo is a gentle fish.
Nemo is too small to eat a diver.
Nemo has a manky fin on one side, perfect for placement

over the entrance.

The Queen likes the fact that Nemo managed to get up through the tube and block the pump in the fish tank with a small stone or pebble.

And so there it is. Your new gate monitor will be Nemo the clown fish. Not quite the imposing figure cut by the blue whale, but that is not up for discussion. Please ensure that you continue the standard security practice of fake dusting for each and every entry and exit from the site.

Pick the bones out of this one if you can....

Yours truly,

Robin McJeffers – of the "Sir" variety

Silence in the room highlighted the concern felt by all three men. Sir Horace laid the letter on the table in front of him and lowered himself into a chair. Sir Douglas by now had his head in his hands and tried in vain to talk, whilst his head was still smothered.

"So, let me get this right."

In no mood for briefings, explanations or anything

else to do with the project, Sir Horace cut his man short again and declared an end to the day's proceedings.

"Gentlemen, our options are to either continue with the briefing, take a journey to Christchurch to visit the Ardilles construction team or, my personal favourite, take a trip to the Cutty Club and get plastered!"

Sir Douglas was about to open his mouth in response, but thought better of it. Having been cut short on every occasion he'd opened his mouth this morning, he felt silence was more appropriate at this time. Instead, Thomas shrugged his shoulders and declared, "I'm up for a beer."

With that, the three men drew a close to that day's proceedings, all one hour, thirteen minutes of it. Out went the lights as they left the room and, after negotiating the turns and corridors, they climbed up and out into the Main Hall and wondered just how long the massive hunk of fibreglass might remain for.

Thomas felt compelled to seek assurances from Sir Horace and felt he'd best get his questions in quick, before the allure of the Cutty Club took a hold.

"Sir Horace, may I ask you something?"

Swiftly walking down the corridor that led to the exit, Sir Horace answered in a somewhat jovial manner. "Why so Jovial?" Thomas thought, seeing as his beloved blue whale

216

was about to get the sack.

"Of course you can, young Thomas. Please proceed!"

"Well, Sir. That letter. The one from Lord McJeffers.."

"About the whale?"

"Yes, that's the one!"

"What about it, Thomas?"

"Well, Sir. Is it likely to happen? I mean, will they remove the whale and bring in Nemo? Can they make that kind of substitution?"

Realising that all was not well with his team, Sir Horace stopped and turned to Thomas, who wasn't ready for this action and had to do some quick side step to avoid collision.

"My dear Thomas. Do I think that they will replace our whale with someone else's Nemo? No, I don't! The Queen obviously has a desire to get it swapped and, probably, imprison it or something daft, but I don't see it happening." Satisfied that the case was closed, Sir Horace resumed his walk towards the exit, fresh air and his favourite club. Within two or three steps, he reluctantly stopped and turned as Thomas quizzed him again. On turning to face Thomas, an expression of dejection, reminiscent of a teenagers sulk, could be seen on Sir Horaces' face. Thomas continued.

"I understand where you are coming from, Sir

217

Horace, but can I just point out that they have passed an Act that has destroyed the Navy. I'm sure that they can remove a blue whale and send it to jail!"

Reluctantly agreeing that he had a point, Sir Horace mumbled a swift "Point taken!" before turning and resuming his walk down the corridor. On seeing and hearing this, Thomas thought that, perhaps, the line would be best drawn at this point so that they could all move on. All the while this stop, question, start, question episode had been happening, Sir Douglas had felt it best to stay out of it, and so merely shadowed his boss, like some playground game. When Sir Horace walked, he walked. When he stopped and turned, he stopped and turned. The timing and efficiency of his efforts was not lost on him and he inwardly smiled at his professionalism.

The three men walked along the corridor, back towards the reception, silent and intense. All three felt the same. All three felt betrayed and confused. They all looked at the paintings and exhibits, which they had done so many times before, but on this occasion they read something different into each one. Outside, in the bright sunshine, all three men squinted momentarily, as they adjusted to the daylight, before climbing into Sir Horace's car and speeding off down the road to the Cutty Sark for a session.

Another busy and proactive day in the life of the Ardilles drew to a close. Sir Douglas thought to himself, as he stared at Greenwich, rushing passed his car window, "what mighty heights of achievement will we ascend to tomorrow with such exertion and commitment to our cause!?!?!"

Chapter Twelve – Eeen Arrrt!

As the two men walked towards the entrance of South Norwood Swimming Baths, Sir Douglas felt that it was time he prepared his boss for the sights and sounds that were about to confront his senses.

"Now, Sir..."

"Yes Douglas, ma boy"

"About the, erm, gentleman that I've recruited to train our chaps."

"Yes, Douglas."

The two men had, by now, entered the building, nodded to the girls on duty at reception and begun to climb the stairs to the viewing area for the main pool.

"Well, Sir, he's not exactly your modern day champion rower, although, strangely enough, that's exactly what he is, a champion, although modern is too strong a term really!"

That famous sense of timing, that always presented itself in these situations, was present in abundance as, just at the precise moment Sir Douglas finished his initial description, "although modern is too strong a term really," they reached the top step and gazed down onto the first batch of thirty or so accountants, crammed into two man canoes and bobbing about on the water.

Sir Horace scanned the men for sight of this champion rower, that had just joined his team. He was looking for a well-defined man of Steve Redgrave-esque build, with arms that could row to the moon and back. As he checked out the men one by one, he mentally checked them off of his list. Then he ran out of men to check. Then he heard him. Then saw him....

"eeen arrrt eeen arrrt....thats how ya bloody do eet....doh want any of yer fancy crap....just eeen arrrt eeen arrrt....you'll soon bloody.....errrrrrrumphhgh.....champiun geezers if yer eeen an arrrt...."

He felt ill and was experiencing a clammy sensation spreading across his skin, as there before him, well, actually there before him, down beside the main pool, stood one Arthur Pounder. Five foot four with greyish-white eyebrows and what appeared to be twenty pounds in weight, eighteen of those being made up of tattoos and ash. The ash, seemingly never ending and miraculously suspended on the end of a roll up, precariously balanced on his lower lip. Well-worn black shoes, baggy tweed trousers, dirty white shirt with rolled up sleeves, complimented by a sublime paisley patterned waistcoat.

Sir Horace took in these details and began to feel much worse. In fact, he had an overwhelming desire to collapse but, with Sir Douglas at his side, rapidly overcome this emotion and regained his composure. Looking up at his man just in time to see him proudly declare with an outstretched arm…

"That, Sir, is Mr Arthur Pounder."

"Oh, my God!"

"Sir?"

"It's Dick Van bloody Dyke!"

"Sir?"

"You've employed Dick Van bloody Dyke to train the accountants!"

"No Sir, begging your pardon, that's not Dick, that's Arthur!"

Sir Horace, feeling numb and knowing that his senses were bordering on full paralysis, just couldn't wait for another verbal salvo from the poolside to attack his nervous system. He didn't have to wait too long.

"Naw.....during the war see, we di ernt av any of this teccernology gubbins so we ad to make do wiv what we could lay our pinkies on....Me, see before that...I errrrrrrumphhgh....made my 1957 championship winning boat outta a barf tub. I set the most record like time see, but I knew that I could've gawn even faster if I ad sealed up the plug ole. The point that I was gonna make escapes me naw as

I have forgotten and carn't fink, so get rowing....eeeen aaart.....eeeen aaart..."

Staring downwards through his hands, unable to summon the motivation required to lift his head to speak, Sir Horace mumbled.

"Oh...Is he really a champion? Can I ask what he won?"

"Oh yes, Sir, he's an actual champion alright. Arthur won the 1957 "London Bridge to Tower Bridge rowing Festival of Speed and Endurance," Sir!"

"London Bridge to Tower Bridge?"

"Yes, Sir! That man's a thoroughbred champion!"

"A champion in a bath, sorry, "barf" tub?"

"Oh yes, Sir, times were hard back then."

"Oh right. Does that account for not sealing the plug?"

"Oh no, Sir, that was just something he forgot because he left the pub later than he'd planned to."

"Oh right."

Sir Horace was just beginning to shed some light on this man with a seemingly battle-hardened but very wrinkly skin, when a voice interrupted him from down below.

"Naw...you gents av done good today....a few more laps and yooz will av the idea. Sorry bout all the ash I dropped in the war-er...never mind eh....they can always drain the fing and send it to some fird world gaff for them to use on their flars.....Anyhows, if any of you gents fancy a swifty wiv yours truly i'll be in the pub darnnn the road...if not then I'll sees yaz tomorrow morning ere... errrrrrrumphhgh.......sorry gents...its me lungs...they're a bit buggered...."

And with that, Arthur Pounder was off. Away, out of the building, turning right and heading for the pub. In the pool sat thirty or so bemused and suit clad accountants in two man canoes. Silence held court until one of the grey looking canoeists suddenly shouted "eeen arrt, eeen arrt" and started rowing again. The rule adhering nature of the accountant beast held firm as the rule of "eeen arrt" was applied and everyone started to follow him around the edge of the pool.

Up above, in the viewing gallery, stood Sir Douglas with Sir Horace seated and slumped in front of him. If Sir Douglas had been clever he would've realised at this point that he was applying a subtle type of revenge to his superior for what he'd gone through those many weeks past when Sir Horace had introduced him to H.M.S Ardilles. Unfortunately, for Sir Douglas, he wasn't clever. He wasn't thinking of revenge, far from it. He was excited and proud.

Sir Horace, on the other hand, was still numb. Unable to say much, he tried desperately to come to terms with the latest member of the team. For a moment he considered

224

rising to his feet but, unsure of just how his lower limbs would function, felt that the better course of action would be to stay seated and address Sir Douglas from there.

"Ok, ok. Let me get this right, Douglas."

"Please, Sir, continue."

"You have recruited, to join our team, to train our men, someone who resembles Dick Van Dyke in every way except that he doesn't have Mary Poppins hanging off of his arm...."

"Yes, Sir."

"Who won the 1957 "London Bridge to Tower Bridge rowing Festival of Speed and Endurance" in a bath?"

"Correct, Sir!"

"Who has dodgy lungs and drops ash everywhere?"

"A minor cold and nervous shakes, I'm sure, Sir!"

"And has more body art than the whole of the civil service put together."

"Yes Sir, that'll be Arthur Pounder you are describing, Sir, but look down there."

Sir Douglas pointed to the pool. Sir Horace was aghast. Down below, on the main pool, bobbed sixty of the nation's finest accountants, all dressed in their normal city attire. All crammed into two man canoes, but all rowing in a line around the outer edge of it. Sir Horace looked down at each and every man as they bobbed past. Much, he thought, resembling the plastic ducks at a fairground that encouraged children to hook them and win a goldfish.

In an instant the realisation struck home that these men, floating past his field of vision, were not ducks of any kind, but were professional men whose desire in life was to achieve and maintain new goals. The goal, that had produced the steely determination in the eyes of those currently bobbing through his field of vision, was pure and oh so simple. They were determined to master their canoes.

"You see, Sir."

"Oh, go on, Douglas, just go on." Replied Sir Horace, shocked, numb and more than a bit confused by it all.

"We tried to get the Olympic team, or at least one of the team, to come down and train the chaps."

"…but let me guess, they were "too busy?"""

"No, Sir. They were, I mean, yes, Sir, they were in training themselves."

"Well, there's a surprise, Douglas!"

"No honestly, they were. And they wanted two hundred thousand pounds if they were to pull out and help us."

"TWO HUNDRED THOU.....two hundred thousand pounds, Douglas!"

"Yes, Sir, and they wanted the pick of the bunch for their boat!"

"Bloody cheek! Douglas. What a bloody cheek!"

"Yes, Sir?"

"But, Douglas, follow my train of thought, will you?"

"Oh, of course, Sir!"

"If the Olympic squad, which is the best we have, right?"

"Oh yes, without a doubt."

"Right, if they cost two hundred thousand pounds to hire, and they're the best..."

"Yes, Sir?"

"....then how much, dare I ask, how much, Douglas, have we spent securing the un-deniable championship winning services of Mr Pounder?"

"Erm, aagh, well, erm, Sir."

"Just tell me, Douglas. Please, I'm too weak to fight!"

"Twenty pounds behind the bar of the pub, up the road there, for every day that he's required, Sir!"

"mmmmm...."

Sir Douglas stood facing Sir Horace, who was still seated. The expression on the face of his superior indicated to him that his boss was thinking. This concerned him, as he generally lost the plot of what was occurring when his boss began to think. There had been too many times whereby a thought had tripped him up. Sir Douglas grew tense and so, leaning backwards slightly, gripped the front rail of the seating area for comfort and support.

"Good job, Douglas!"

"Sir?"

"Good job my man! Thinking about it, it's a favourable comparison of qualities and costing."

Sir Douglas knew this would happen. He had stood and watched as his boss had sat there and thought for a moment and now, not for the first time since this mission had started, he was lost. Just how had he allowed the plot to slip from his grasp in a few mere seconds? "A favourable comparison of qualities and costing?" He found himself asking his own, deepest ounce of intellectual matter; just what the hell does that mean? He realised that he'd do well not to look stupid on this one.

"Erm, well, erm, Sir. We did our research."

"Yes, yes...I can see. The Olympic team, the best in the world, two hundred grand. Arthur Pounder, championship winning, "barf" tub rowing Dick Van Dyke character, twenty quid! Perfect assessment!"

It suddenly clicked for Sir Douglas and he realised that he'd eluded the guards at "stupidity-ville" by the skin of his teeth, once again. Just as he was about to declare his own genius to his boss, a noise interrupted his impending speech as, down below, an immense wall of "eeeen arrrrt's" began to build and rise in volume. The two men peered over the rail and down onto the main pool, where they were greeted by the sight of their accountant rowers thrashing wildly with their oars and screaming "eeeen arrrrrt," as though they had gone mad. Sir Horace looked at Sir Douglas, Sir Douglas looked at Sir Horace and, both with expressions as bemused as each other's, came to the conclusion that something had to be done.

"Douglas, I think they've had enough for today."

"Oh right, Sir."

In a flash, Sir Douglas was off, skipping up the five steps of the viewing gallery and then down the main stairs to the pool area. Sir Horace sat assessing what he had seen. Anyone observing his facial expressions at this point would've noticed that with each point assessed in his mind, an accepting raise of an eyebrow, coupled with an Al Pacino type mouth shape meant that it had been accepted with great thought and that he'd moved onto the next issue. His thoughts were interrupted with the voice of Sir Douglas downstairs.

"eeeen arrrrt, eeeen arrrrt…"

"GENTLEMEN, GENTLEMEN. YOUR ATTENTION, PLEASE!"

With that, the carnage in canoes came to an end. The

main pool at South Norwood Baths no longer looked like a white water rapid as the thrashing, oar-wielding accountants calmed themselves and bobbed down to the end where Sir Douglas stood. As they arrived in one floating mass Sir Douglas began to address them, accompanied by a calming gesture with both arms.

"Gentlemen. May I congratulate you on a job well done? You are the first group to undertake this training and this is the first day of the overall training program so, once again, I congratulate you all on a superb showing. If the remaining groups show the spirit and initiative that you have, then we can only achieve our goals with stunning ease. Now, you're all aware that tomorrow is the second and final day of your training and so, if you have any questions at all, then it'd be wise to catch Mr. Pounder before he leaves the pub. Would I be correct in saying that Thomas has been in contact with you all regarding dates and a job description etc? Is this correct?"

A mumbling gathered slowly and quietly in front of him.

"Ok, I'll take that as a "Yes" then! Wonderful! Okay then, we'll see you all here at nine in the morning then. Thank you and good evening."

Sir Douglas looked up at his superior and caught his attention. In doing so, Sir Horace gestured that he'd meet him downstairs. With that, Sir Douglas nodded and made for the corridor, leaving the suit clad accountants to prise themselves out of the two-man canoes. If he'd turned around, at that point, he would've froze in horror at the scene of mass awkwardness and human movement that was bordering on clumsiness, occurring at the waters edge behind him.

At first, it was one canoe that seemed to empty it's contents on to the edge of the pool. A lunch box and a briefcase appeared from the depths of its' hull, but that seemed to be the signal for all of the other canoeists to jettison their contents onto the side of the pool as well. Lunchboxes, briefcases, waterlogged copies of The Times, rain coats, umbrellas and even laptops all began to appear from inside of them. As Sir Douglas disappeared down the corridor, the last few accountants were stepping onto the poolside, brushing down their slightly damp suits and adjusting their hair, before making for the exit.

Outside, in the corridor, Sir Douglas met Sir Horace at the bottom of the stairs that lead up to the viewing gallery. He wasn't sure what to expect from his boss by way of temperament but, because he had not witnessed Sir Horace's assessment and, indeed, acceptance of the situation, he was surprised to find him distinctly 'chipper' with everything. Sir Horace descended the final step to the waiting Sir Douglas, rubbing his hands and with a smile on his face.

"Excellent, Douglas. Now, shall we go and meet Mr Pounder?"

"Why, yes, Sir, I think we should!"

The two men exited the swimming baths and walked, side by side, up the road to the pub, "The Chattering Gerbil," in which the "barf tub rowing, Dick Van Dyke champion" stood at the bar with a pint of light and bitter. As the two Naval dignitaries walked in, Arthur Pounder turned to look at who was entering the pub. On recognising Sir Douglas, he nodded and gestured for him, and the stranger accompanying him, to join him at the bar.

"Arthur, well done!"

"Fanx, guv'nor! They're crap at the moment, but eyes will be slapping erm into shape…you'll see….ooo are you chap?"

The "ooo are you chap?" had been aimed, with careful precision, across the front of Sir Douglas and at the man stood to his left, Sir Horace. Sir Horace, rather taken aback by this sudden and rather course questioning, stood up straight and aimed his reply with deadly accuracy, before Sir Douglas could introduce him.

"I, chap! Am Sir Horace Hargraves, Number One, Level A of her Majesty's Royal Navy, soon to be known as The Floaty Boat Brigade! I command the whole service and that, in case you hadn't realised, includes YOU! In other words, erm, chap! I am your boss, how do you do?"

Sir Horace felt quite pleased with himself and leant towards Arthur Pounder, offering his hand. Arthur responded and leant forward to greet it with his own. Just as the two hands made contact and grasped each other, a huge piece of ash departed from the end of the roll up, hanging out the mouth of the elderly champion, and landed smack bang on the hand of Sir Horace.

"Pleased to meet you, Guv….oooh…er…sorry bout that Guv….they've put men in the moon, but they ain't designed ash that stays on the fag…bloody disgraceful if you ask me!"

Sir Horace was taken back by the ash falling onto his hand but, before he'd been able to react to it and maybe brush it off or pull his hand away, he'd been even more shocked than he'd ever been before, as the baggy-skinned, skeleton type thing in front of him, whose cigarette the ash had fallen from, had actually held his hand tight and, in trying to rub it away, had actually rubbed it in. Then declared…

"Oh…sorry guv'nor…..ya hand looks like someone's tried to cremate it!…….still, ya gotta larf, ain't ya!"

A mortified Sir Horace let out a faint whimper come chuckle, accompanied by a false and rather weak acknowledging smile.

"...erm Yes! Yes, you have Mr Pounder!"

"Oh craps the meester pander stuff, Guv, yooz can call me "Danglers," like what me mates do..."

Without thinking, Sir Douglas enquired.

"Why "Danglers," Arthur?"

"...well....."

Sir Horace realised the impending situation a fraction too late as, before he could react and withdraw his colleague's question, the answer Sir Douglas craved for, to satisfy his inquisitive mind, was delivered with the force of a ten-ton truck greeting a squirrel.

"...well...me mates always said I ad huge knackers, so one day I stirred me tea with erm as a bet. They were a bit burnt and swollen after that, so me mates called me "danglers."

Sir Douglas felt he was onto something good, but was soon shot down in flames...

"So, do your friends shorten it to "Dan"...erm "Danglers?"

Again Sir Horace was too slow to react.

"...no they bloody don't guv....although sometimes they call me "monster nuts" or "fat sack""

Sir Horace could take no more.

"Ok, Douglas, enough questions!"

"Oh, erm, right, Sir!"

"I've actually potted the black on a snooker table by striking the cue ball with them before...."

"Erm, thank you, Mr Pounder! Can we talk business, please?"

"Ok guv...whatever you want...."

"Now, erm, Arthur."

Sir Douglas felt the need to remind his boss that they were all friends now.

"Danglers, Sir!"

"Thank you, Douglas! I'll address him as Arthur, if it's all the same to you!"

"Oh right, sorry, Sir!"

"Right, Arthur..."

"Yes, guv...."

Sir Horace felt awkward and uneasy being referred to as "Guv" by the Dick Van Dyke-esque elderly gentleman in front of him. He'd believed that he was coping quite well with this strange old man until the comments and referrals to "Danglers" and "Fat Sack" came at him like a salvo from one of his big ships. Sir Douglas, on the other hand, was enjoying this man's company. He was visibly bonding with this champion from a bygone, bathtub age.

"I will be brutally honest with you and say that, when I was briefed by Sir Douglas here on your selection, I was very sceptical and uncertain of your credentials. This continued right up until the moment you left our chaps in the pool and came here, but…"

"They started rowing, di ernt they!"

"Why, yes they did, Arthur!"

"Ya see...they're crap at the moment, but they be wise old buggers who've seen it all...that's probably why you picked em cos they be reliable. If I'd left a load a yungsters in there they'd be spraying paint everywhere right now but, cos they be dissypleened geezers, you shart at em for a while then let erm get on wiv it.....you soon know if ya message sticks..."

Sir Horace suddenly felt very proud. Proud of Arthur, probably due to relief, proud of Sir Douglas for showing the qualities, once again, that made Sir Horace believe he'd chosen the right man for the job and proud of the fact that he was in charge. Sir Douglas, on the other hand, was totally relaxed and was continuing to bond.

"You fink I've dun good then, Guv?"

"Yes, I do Arthur. I was very impressed with your first day."

"Good, cos I wanna rise..."

"What! A rise after one day???"

"Yes, Guv....wanna add somefink to me twenty quid...."

"And let me guess Arthur, If I don't agree to your new demands you'll not work anymore and...."

236

"All I want is a packet of crisps beyind the bar wiv me twenty, guv!"

"What?"

"Saves me wasting me twenty on em...."

"You just want us to change your fees from twenty pounds behind the bar everyday to twenty pounds and a packet of crisps?"

"Oh yes, Sir Guv....dont want anyfink else...."

"Well, bloody Nora! Douglas!"

"Sir!"

"Amend Arthur's contract as appropriate and get this man some crisps..."

"Yes, Sir!"

"Oh fanx, Sir Guvnor...you is a true gent."

"Right then, now that we have that little matter sorted, who would like a drink? Arthur? Douglas?"

A relieved Sir Horace then proceeded to buy his two colleagues a drink and stand talking with them for the next hour and a half before suggesting to Sir Douglas that, impending business else where, meant that they really should be going. Sir Douglas nodded in agreement and finished his drink quickly before turning to Arthur, who was busy picking bits of crisps out of his teeth with a matchstick, much to the horror of Sir Horace.

"Arthur, it's been a pleasure, but Sir Horace and myself must be heading on now."

Silence greeted the naval men as the target of Sir Douglas' address had ignored him due to the fact he was concentrating on dislodging a rather large lump of chewed crisp from behind one of his back teeth.

"ARTHUR!"

"....ugh....eeeeerrrummmpppgh....yes, Guv.....you were saying?"

"I was saying, Arthur, that Sir Horace and myself have to leave now and that it's been a pleasure being in your company."

"Oh right, Guv....fanking yous two....will ya be here tomorrow?"

"Yes, Arthur. Sir Horace and myself will be here at nine a.m to watch your second day of coaching. So, for now, we will bid you goodnight."

"Oh...goodnight guvs....."

This final farewell from Arthur was accompanied by the tipping of the flat cap in the direction of the now departing men.

"Erm, goodnight, Arthur."

Sir Horace had waited until he was a safe distance across the floor, away from the numerous bits of crisps on the ends of matchsticks that lay strewn all over the bar, before saying his farewells. Once outside, relief descended on the two men whilst, inside, Arthur Pounder merely turned back to the bar, replaced his cap on his head, and continued to work at the large lump of soggy crisp remains, stuck behind one of his back teeth.

The two men started to walk back down the road to the swimming baths, where their car and driver awaited them. Another day of turmoil and its various emotions had left both men feeling exhausted. Sir Douglas felt as though he wanted to go home and crash out, but thought he'd better show commitment.

"Think I'll head to the office, Sir, and look a few things over."

"Bloody good show, Douglas! I, myself, was thinking along those lines but have decided to go home and crash out!"

Sir Douglas mentally kicked himself, "Bugger, done it again!" Sir Horace came to his rescue by interrupting the momentary clumsiness of the situation.

"Forget it for today, Douglas, go home and rest."

"Oh, ok then, Sir, thank you!"

Within minutes they had arrived back at the car and entered via the rear door. Once their driver had sat down and started the engine, the car pulled out of the car park and headed back to Greenwich. The journey was mostly in silence, as both men were too emotionally drained to discuss anything. Their meeting with Arthur Pounder had left them shell shocked and weak. They were both of the belief that they had coped, and indeed, were coping with this man quite well, but now as they sat in the back of that car, the experience of the past couple of hours began to hit home. Like a recurring nightmare the words "eeen arrt, eeen arrt" were swirling round in their respective heads, gathering speed like a tornado that destroys everything in its path. These words, indeed these thoughts, would stay with them long into the night.

Chapter Thirteen – Piggs' yard

Having enjoyed peace and quiet in the office for past few days, whilst both Sir Horace and Sir Douglas had been out watching the accountants being trained, Thomas had been rather looking forward to a nice little trip to the sea side but, in all honesty, the three hour journey had been rather boring. The scenery outside had cut a drab and dreary cloth right from the word go and the immensely more picturesque view, once on the motorway, soon blurred into one continuous, monotonous sludge outside his window.

Of course, he'd had the option of joining in with the conversation, being held by his fellow passengers but, when that conversation centred on three hours of Sir Douglas trying to get Sir Horace to say "Aagh Pigsy," in a mock Japanese voice, the monotonous sludge outside became increasingly more interesting.

"Try it again, Sir."

Sir Horace, really not feeling as enthused about learning fake Japanese as maybe he should, tried again. "Oh, Pigsy!"

Sir Douglas felt he was really onto something and was determined to get his training methods across to his somewhat bemused superior.

241

"No, no, no, Sir! You see, the thing is, the man I'm going to introduce you to is called Brian Pigg. He is an outrageously talented boat builder and has taken on the task of converting our model boat plans into something remotely sailable. The joke is obviously in the name. His name is Pigg, the pig in the seventies Japanese show was called "Pig" or "Pigsy," and so it is almost customary to address Brian as "aagh, pigsssssy," just like Monkey would've done in the seventies."

Short on will power, Sir Horace went for the simple plead. "Oh, I see, Douglas, I really do, but I'm not Monkey, and he's not a pig, so can I not just say "Hello Brian?"" A rather aggrieved Sir Douglas responded with an almost hurt tone to his voice. Determined to overcome all obstacles, he approached the task at hand once more.
"No, no, no, Sir! Please try again. It's a classic and we need to get it right. Now try once more. You're so close!"

Thomas momentarily withdrew his stare into the abyss and focused on the absurd conversation alongside him. Sir Douglas sat waving his arms in encouragement, as though he was conducting the London Philharmonic through another classic recital. His actions brought another woeful attempt from Sir Horace.
"Aaaagh Pigsy!"

"Oooh, nearly, but still rather English. C'mon, go again!"
Enough was enough for Thomas and he swiftly returned to
staring at the world speeding past outside. Again, the
conversation's alarming and odd cycle began and Thomas,
trying desperately not to listen, was on tenterhooks by the
time their car rolled into Christchurch, Dorset. In fact, by the
time they stepped out into the mid-day sunshine, Sir Horace
had been so well drilled in the art of Japanese vocal tones
that he felt as though he were Emperor Hirohito himself.

"So, this is Christchurch, eh?"
Sir Douglas, as excited as a child in a sweetshop, felt the
need for accuracy.
"Mudeford Quay, actually, Sir."
Sir Horace looked around and took in his surroundings. As
picturesque a car park as he had seen, it was sandwiched by
the sea to his left and inland waters and boat storage to his
right. A constant rattling of boat masts and associated
objects, designed to keep the birds away, drummed a
constant rhythm in his ears.

In the distance, way across on the far side of the
inland waters, he could just make out the spire of a church.
Turning to look out to sea, the Isle of Wight loomed large, as
if trying to creep up undetected. All of this bathed in
sunshine led Sir Horace to think that this was a good place to

be. Taking in the sights, sounds and a large dose of fresh air led him to declare:

"Well, Mudeford Quay, you are a real slice of beauty!"

Thomas had also exited the car and felt powerless to do anything but soak up the scene. A smile of satisfaction showed itself on his face. From across the car park, on which they stood, came a man walking at a steady pace. Nothing about his appearance or demeanour indicated that he was a boat building genius, although his weathered hands and face seemed to indicate that he worked outside and with hand tools. Jeans, shoes, casual shirt, relaxed expression, no obvious hints towards being a skilled craftsman...or pig.

Sir Douglas caught his eye and a mutual smile from both men preceded a hearty handshake. The warmth of the initial greeting was clearly the result of two old acquaintances meeting again. Time had seemingly not cooled the warmth of this friendship. More smiles and some friendly shoulder slapping and the introductions were upon them. Sir Horace noted that these two appeared to go back a long way, a question, maybe, for later.

"Piggsy, allow me to introduce the boss, Sir Horace Hargraves."

The moment had come. He gave it his best shot.

"Aaaagh, Piggggssssssyyyyy!"

A shake of hands, a mighty roar of laughter later and the three men wandered off across the car park chatting and giggling like schoolgirls. Thomas, amazed at what he'd just seen, decided that he'd just wander over to the edge of the quay and watch the children crabbing for a while.

In, what seemed like a blink of an eye, Thomas was summoned to where the three others stood. Sir Douglas cut short the jovial banter with a quick introduction.

"Piggsy, I want you to meet Thomas Jackson. Thomas, here stands before you a certain Brian Pigg, boat builder extraordinaire."

The two men greeted each other with a friendly handshake and a nod of acceptance. Thomas felt an overwhelming urge not to go Japanese on this occasion. It was "Piggsy" who spoke next, throwing his arms wide at the same time in a rather Gene Kelly-esque manner. Now where had he seen that before?

"Gentlemen, gentlemen! Welcome, welcome...to "Piggs Yard.""

They followed the movement of his arms across to the yard itself. Built on the far edge of the quay next to the channel entrance, it resembled more of a Wild West fort than a boat yard. A massive structure of wood, it cut an oversized and out of place figure in its surroundings. Two very large

245

wooden doors with arched tops were swung open, seemingly straining at the massive hinges mating them to the solid beam doorframe. The perimeter was one continuous line of vertical planks, all standing to attention. In order to stop inquisitive eyes, each plank was sharpened to a point.

Thomas decided that, for all intents and purposes, it was a fort. There weren't any corner look out towers, nor were there any savage Indians attacking it but, it was a fort all the same. And whilst there was a wooden sign hanging above the door and yes, it did swing and creak in the wind, it didn't have "Buzzards Breath" or "Fort Alamo" on it, but merely "Pigg's Yard." Plain and simple, soft and almost understated for the structure it adorned, "Pigg's Yard" was what it said.

Piggsy began to introduce his yard but was politely cut short by Thomas, who had suddenly recalled something, much to his horror.

"Gentlemen, I give you…"

"Excuse me, Piggsy, very sorry to interrupt…"

"Oh, erm, what is it, Thomas?"

Sir Douglas was not impressed.

"Bloody hell, Thomas! The man hasn't even introduced his yard and you're butting in! What the devil is it?"

"Well, Sir Douglas, I vaguely remember visiting here as a

246

child and seem to remember that there was a pub just over there."

Thomas forlornly pointed to the area where, he believed, a pub had once stood.

Piggsy nodded and moved to put the young man's mind at rest.

"Gone. I had it removed!"

An alarmed Thomas snapped back at him. "You had it removed! How? Why?"

Not seeing any harm in what he'd just said, Piggsy set out to explain.

"I wanted the land for my yard. It was having a quiet day and so I made a few phone calls and got it shut down under health and safety."

"What!?!?"

"Well, erm, how can I put it, when you're commissioned by the Royal Navy, sorry, "Floaty Boat Brigade," to build a vessel, you kind of take what you need and with Health and Safety being the new Thought Police, it really wasn't too hard."

Thomas felt like a busload of deja-vu was coming his way. 'How many times had this situation reared it's head before today?' he thought to himself. He decided he'd ask the question that his mind was desperate to know the answer to.

"Dare I ask how you got the pub shut down?"

Slightly alarmed, Thomas watched as Piggsy took on the role of lead actor in some amateur dramatics presentation. Picking up an imaginary telephone and dialling an imaginary number he spoke.

"Hello! Is that Health and Safety? Aggh yes, Brian Pigg here. That pub on the quay at Mudeford…yes, that one, well I've just caught the plague from it. Can you shut it down please? You can, thank you. Oh and, I'm sure there is some medieval right that says if I've caught the plague from a building then I get that land, so I'd like the land please! Great….paperwork in the post…marvellous, you're very helpful…thank you and goodbye!"

Thomas was outraged.

"You shut a perfectly good, in fact, bloody nice, pub down because you wanted the land!"

"Yep!"

"Just by saying that it had an outbreak of the plague?"

"Yep!"

"Did they not come and check it out?"

"Nope! Too busy. They also said that they were understaffed and that it would impose on their staff's human rights if they asked them to do anything. So nope!"

"That's bloody outrageous! And the restaurant?"

"Gone….plague!"

"And…and….the lifeboat….surely not the lifeboat?"

"Yep!…all gone…plague…must've swept through here with a real vengeance!"

Thomas was getting hot under the collar, whilst Sir Douglas and Sir Horace were humoured by Piggsy's genuine belief that he'd done a good thing for the cause. It was nice, they thought, to watch someone else have a little melt down for once.

"Do you not understand how important a lifeboat is, Piggsy?"

"Oh, of course I do, but if it's got the plague then it's no use to anyone!"

"But that's just it, man, it didn't have the plague!"

"Oh, I'm afraid it did, Thomas. Really, really bad, in fact, so it had to go!"

"But, it was a lifeboat!"

Piggsy felt that, although it was against his wishes, he'd have to spell it out for the distressed young man in front of him.

"Look, they like collecting money, right? We all know that they have far, far too much money, right? Then it makes sense that they can now start collecting for a new lifeboat station at the other end of the quay. So, realistically, my actions have actually helped them make money. Terrible thing, the plague!"

With that, Brian Pigg, boat builder extraordinaire, gestured to his guests to follow him through the gates and into the yard. With the three men in tow, Brian began to explain what was happening in each area.

"So, basically, gentlemen, here we have the yard which, as you can see, is a hive of activity."

As the three men walked behind Piggsy, they looked around, surveying the scene. Everywhere they looked there were men scurrying around with items of equipment, tools or wood. In the central area of the yard stood the newly acquired Mary Rose. Brian continued to explain.

"There's the old girl sited in the middle of the yard. Sectioned all around her are different stages of either build or fittings and materials. The men obviously have an idea of what you guys want and so they're hard at it. The only way I've been able to get them to work on this project is by telling them the craft is for a charity event on the Thames. Otherwise they'd deem the whole thing un-sailable and leave!"

Walking at a steady pace, the four men continued around the yard. To the observer, there was much gesticulating and pointing to be seen. Piggsy continued to clarify various observations.

•

"As you can see, over there, there is a huge pile of fridge and freezer doors. These will form the outer protective skin of the hull, as requested. Over there, you'll see a quantity of type one VW beetles. These will be stripped down to a shell, painted then placed in the relevant positions on her deck. They will then be mated with a telegraph pole from that pile over there and these will then form the ships main guns."

Sir Horace was impressed and couldn't resist another main greeting. He thought that he could couple that with a leading question but it didn't come out quite right.

"Aaaagh Pigggsssyy…that's brilliant work!"

The other men looked at him in a slightly alarmed way. In order to divert their stares, Sir Horace quickly asked another question whilst guiding their attention away from himself with an outstretched arm and finger.

"Ooh…what's going on over there?"

The three other men turned and followed his arm as Piggsy picked up the explanation.

"That, Sir Douglas, is the absolute finest group of craftsmen I have ever known. They are actually making miniature gym equipment. Not only out of wood but also metal and corn flakes packets!"

As he spoke, an air of intrigue came over his face.

"At this point, Sir Douglas, I have to ask. I may be out of

place on this one, and I apologise if I am, but what, exactly, are these miniature pieces for?"

Sir Douglas felt it almost natural to update his old friend.

"Of course you may ask, Brian, my old friend. They are for pigeons!"

"Pigeons?"

"Why yes, of course! We'll have racing pigeons on board. They like to keep fit on long journey's and so this gym equipment will suit them just fine!"

A shrug of the shoulders, coupled with a brief facial expression, was quickly followed by the par-for-the-course rapid change of subject.

"Over there, we have a massive pile of fridge magnets which we will use for the name of the vessel and also some sums and slogans."

Inwardly wincing at what he had just said, he was surprised to find that he had not been picked up by one of his guests for the "sums and slogans" bit. Mentally he noted that he must add some sums and slogans to the finished article. Regaining their attention from the pile of fridge magnets, thirty feet away, he continued with the tour, gesturing to the three visitors that they should walk with him.

"So, Piggsy, are you intending to launch the Ardilles from here?"

"Not really, Sir Horace, the swell off of the quay could prove too great for her. We're intending to move her up the coast a wee bit but, in the event that she looks too fragile to move via road we'll dump her in over there, where the plague ridden lifeboat used to launch."

With the plague still being a touchy subject, Piggsy received a scowl from a still seething Thomas. Sir Horace noted that it had been his full intention to launch from London and that this fact had obviously not been passed on to the boat builder stood before them.

Moving on, the four men stopped at the yard office for a quick cup of tea and a review of the plans, whilst the kettle boiled. Brian felt the whistle stop tour was going very well and was prompt with every answer or snippet of information required. When the kettle had boiled and the cups were filled, the four men stood outside, just in front of the doorway, not only to improve their view of the boat yard, but also to take in the bright sunshine, currently bathing the whole yard in a welcome warmth. Warmth, which seemed to make the whole situation just that slight bit more palatable.

Brian knew his workforce was good, but inwardly glowed at how professional they looked to his visitors. A hearty conversation was taking place, namely between the owner of the yard, Sir Horace and Sir Douglas. To the casual observer, there was much pointing being done. In fact, Thomas, who had taken one or two steps back from this current conversation, had also observed the slightly exaggerated and excessive gesticulating, currently playing out in front of him.

Like so many times previously, a simple thing had seemingly been turned into a competition as a point from one of the three was answered by a more extreme and dramatic point from the next which, surprise, surprise, was answered by the third of the trio pointing in a more dramatic fashion than the previous two. On watching this, Thomas wondered if any of the three really knew what they were pointing at.

Teas drunk and cups returned to the yard office, the tour continued on around the site. No matter what part of the yard they stopped in, the production was still flat out. Another hour or two passed before Sir Horace, Sir Douglas and Thomas had seen enough of this "splendid facility," as Sir Horace had put it, and bid farewell to Piggsy before congratulating him on his work and climbing into the car that would make the return trip to London.

On leaving Mudeford Quay, Sir Horace declared to his fellow passengers that he was "most pleased with the state of play" and that "I might cancel the London launch and stick her in down here!" An alarmed Sir Douglas then proceeded to advise Sir Horace that the launch was already booked and that the Queen wouldn't take too kindly to things being re-arranged.

"I believe, Sir, that her Madge has been writing her very own speech which, her aides advise, are full of Royal gags, or one, at least!"

Sir Horace wasn't about to be put off by the Queen and quickly came up with a plan.

"Ok, here's what we do. We launch in London, as agreed, but not with The Ardilles. We launch HER down here."

A confused Sir Douglas immediately needed clarification.

"Can I ask, Sir Horace, what exactly you aim to launch in London?"

"Douglas, Douglas! Chill, chill! What we launch in London is one very, very large Purple cloak. Underneath, which will be a boat of some sort."

"A boat of some sort?"

"Yes, we'll acquire, just for the day, a boat of similar size. Stick it on the ramp and under the cloak. Her Madge can then launch the boat and she'll be happy but it won't be our boat, because we'll dump that in down here. We just have to find a boat – that's all! Madge will have a boat to launch, although all she'll see is a large purple cloak floating off into the distance, so she'll be happy."

Thomas, who had been sitting with his head in his hands up until this point, thought he'd be sarcastic and suddenly straightened in order to suggest H.M.S Belfast. He was alarmed to find Sir Horace liked the idea.

"Bloody brilliant, Thomas. Bloody brilliant! Douglas, get on the case, we need H.M.S Belfast so we can launch her…. again!"

Thomas sat in despair. His long awaited trip to the seaside hadn't gone very well, as far as he was concerned. Still, he thought, there was still Sir Horace's magical mystery tour, pencilled in for tomorrow, to look forward to.

Chapter Fourteen – Pickering

In the back of a black, Government Issue, limousine, currently making it's way North towards Pickering, sat Sir Horace, Sir Douglas and Thomas, glassy eyed and full of the joys of spring. The reason for this slightly unusual abundance of energy and cheer was due to where they were going and whom they were meeting, once there. Destination, Pickering show ground, North of York and one of the key show sites for 'fancy' birds and poultry. Here, under the McJeffers Act, a pigeon facility had been created and installed which would house, train and monitor the overall health of the pigeons that would serve on board the Ardilles.

On wrestling free of the processional hell, otherwise referred to as "driving through London," the conversation and mood in the back of the limousine had picked up almost simultaneously with the increase in speed of the vehicle. With the end of the stop-start part of the journey and, so too, the mass pondering and 'Pacino-esque' facial gestures, the conversation inside had erupted. Seemingly, as soon as the scenery outside the window became a blur, the thoughts that had been swirling around in the minds of the three men, came to the fore.

Just as the great man, Robin McJeffers, had done

before them, an endless stream of questions seemed to gather momentum inside their heads. Contained by an unwillingness to share, it was simply speed that unlocked the door to the vault. It was Sir Horace who broke the silence.

"Right, Gentlemen!"

On hearing his voice, Sir Douglas and Thomas both sat up with an eagerness that confirmed to Sir Douglas that they were switched on and ready to converse. He continued.

"As you are both aware, we are currently heading northwards on the M1. Our destination is a place, slightly North of York, called "Pickering." Now, does that name ring any bells with either of you?"

Both Sir Douglas and Thomas looked stumped. More 'Pacino-esque' facial shrugs and a few gazes at each other confirmed to Sir Horace that "Pickering" wasn't a place too well known to his two colleagues.

"Not on the radar, eh? Okay. You obviously know, due to our recent briefing, that we are going to meet a man called ""Slit eyed" Vic." Real name, "Victor Ketchup." I think you'd agree, a very unfortunate name but, and here's the "but," Vic is the best at what he does, unless there's someone in a loft somewhere in Barnsley that we don't know about yet, he's the best.

What he does, is train, motivate and generally

258

rehabilitate pigeons. His focus and steely glare is well known throughout the world of "fancy" birds. Now, in his normal working day, Vic wouldn't generally come across pigeons that have come into contact with a stun sub-machine gun and so, this extra attention to detail, has progressed his stare to more of a squint. Hence the name "Slit Eyed!" Any questions so far?"

Sir Horace rapidly realised that the subject of pigeons was a popular one, as facing him sat his two colleagues, both with glassy eyed grins on their respective faces. With no other emotions to work on, Sir Horace felt it was best he continue his address. He had a feeling that every word he spoke was being absorbed in double quick time.

"Now, you see, Pickering is one of the most important venues on the "Fancy" bird and Poultry circuit. I don't think we're quite talking Mecca, but it's quite a key place. Obviously, the Act has placed some rather interesting circumstances in our path and, clearly, one of those is pigeons. So, if we are to use pigeons on our new ship, then we are going to need someone who can train them, motivate them and, in the case of some of our Trafalgar Pigeons, rehabilitate them. Gentlemen, Pickering is where our pigeon facility has been built and where "Slit eye" works his magic."

The pure joy in the back of the limousine, at that

precise moment, made Sir Horace do a double take, just to make sure he was being accompanied on the journey north by adults and not children. On finishing his initial address to Sir Douglas and young Thomas, he found that their enthusiasm for what lie ahead went into overdrive. It appeared, from what he could tell, as though they simply couldn't wait to get to where they were going.

Before he could say anymore there was a steady hum, increasing in volume, and it was coming from his two colleagues. What started as a quiet whisper from one to the other had gradually built into a steady and rather irritating noise. Sir Horace sat watching the other two in quiet astonishment for a short while, before feeling he'd best nip the noise in the bud and bring them back to the job in hand. "Gentlemen, please!"

Mumbled apologies came from the men sat facing him on the back seat in a swift and accepting manner. "Ok, thank you. Obviously, the pigeons are a subject that you are both keen to get to grips with, which is good to see but, I would urge you both to focus your efforts and control your impulses. Now, we'll be stopping for toilet breaks and refreshments in a short while, but I feel we need to get your enthusiasm down on paper. Now, I have here some notepads and pens, that I'd like you both to use, so you can get whatever is in your respective heads, written down."

"What I'm obviously hoping for is valid and excellent questions and/or suggestions as to how we can help Vic or, indeed, how he can help us. I'm not really looking for drawings of pigeons made up as Spitfires or Lancasters with machine guns in their claws! I don't need any of that, nor do I want pictures of your house with mummy and daddy out the front and a few pigeons on the roof. Use this time wisely, Gentlemen!"

On finishing his address, Sir Horace reached to his side and picked up a black leather briefcase. On opening the buckle and flicking the oversized flap over and behind it, he reached in and promptly pulled out three notepads and three pens. After handing two sets of these across the cabin to Thomas and Sir Douglas, he placed the third set down on the seat beside him and, with a swift upwards circular motion that swung the oversized cover back over the opening and down onto the front of the case again, he snapped the buckle shut and returned the briefcase to from where it had come.

Sir Horace inwardly smiled. He loved this briefcase, but didn't get to use it very often. There were thousands of briefcase designs out there and he'd not been interested in any of them, until he'd seen a German officer use one in the film, The Great Escape. With fantastic German efficiency,

261

he'd watched as the officer had marched into a room, swung the case open, did what he needed to do, said what he'd needed to say and then swung the case closed with a magnificent 'snap,' before returning to his staff car, waiting outside.

Sir Horace had instantly given up on the rest of the film and had just watched that scene over and over again for the next hour. After that, he'd started searching for a replica case. He needed to have that impact. Weeks of searching then, after his new purchase had arrived, weeks of practice before, finally, he could do what the German officer had done. He could 'flick' open his case and, more importantly, 'flick' it shut. All with the efficiency of a Hollywood actor portraying a German officer on a set near Munich. He realised that his mind had wandered for long enough and it was time to finish his address.

"Okay, a note pad and a pen each, three rather excited and inquisitive minds. Between us we should be able to come up with something. Gentlemen, let's get cracking! Hopefully, we'll have some ideas to compare or share with each other by the time we stop in about half an hour."

As the black limousine continued northwards, it's three occupants sat, in near silence, forcibly trying to remove anything and everything, that had been swirling around in their heads, and lay it down in some sort of semblance for both the impending stop and also Victor Ketchup, who awaited their arrival a few miles up the road. It was as if the back of the limo had been transformed into an exam centre.

Three grown men sat, pens in hands, mumbling to themselves, licking their lips, gesticulating, contorting their faces into even more 'Pacino-esque' positions, than probably even Pacino himself would know what to do with, enthusiastically writing or sketching then, just as enthusiastically, scribbling it out. Half an hour or so of this passed before Sir Horace looked up from his pad and glanced out of the window. He could see that his driver was pulling off onto the slip road for the impending services. A quick pop from the intercom and a politely efficient "We're here, Sir!" came through. An equally quick "Thank you, my good man" was dispatched from Sir Horace and with that, he shut his pad and closed off his pen. The other two men followed suit.

The vehicle slowed and negotiated its way through the car park, before pulling up in a suitable place. At once, the doors to the rear section opened on both sides and out stepped Sir Horace from behind the driver on one side and Sir Douglas and Thomas on the other. All three men stretched and yawned and finally got themselves in order. The driver window began to lower to reveal the face of the man who had brought them to this point. Sir Horace rapidly addressed the emerging face.

"About forty five minutes, Bob and we'll be back."
A muffled but aggrieved sounding voice came back at him.
"Yes, Sir. And it's Robert!"
"About forty five minutes, Bobby and we'll be back."
"Yes, Sir. And it's Robert!"
"About forty five minutes, Bobster and we'll be back."
"Yes, Sir. And it's Robert!"
"About forty five minutes, Bobaliscious and we'll be back."

Before this charade was allowed to continue, Sir Douglas opened the front passenger door and quickly addressed the increasingly angrier driver, whilst Thomas jogged around the back of the car to guide Sir Horace away.
"Robert, I think you get the idea that we'll be back in about forty five minutes."
"Yes, Sir. Thank you"
"And, please accept my apologies for Gene Kelly over there. He has many faces and the one he's somehow got out of the car with appears to be the "make a thousand names out of one" and, for that, I apologise."
"Apology accepted, Sir. Enjoy your break."
"Thank you, Robert. You too. Please ensure you feed and water yourself as well."

An accepting and courteous nod from both men brought the incident to a close. Sir Douglas hurried off after Thomas and Sir Horace whilst Robert got out of the car and prepared himself for a nice and calming cup of tea. Once he'd caught up with his two colleagues he could hear Sir Horace trying to explain his actions recently passed.

"I was merely trying to make things a bit more familiar between us, Thomas."

"I know you was, Sir, but some people like their names in full and do not take kindly to them being shortened or made into some kind of American soap opera."

"American soap opera?"

"Yes, Sir Horace. His name is Robert. Not Bob, Bobster, Bobby or Bobaliscious, Sir!"

"Oh, ok. Point taken. I was merely trying to be a bit friendly. You know, heart warming. Like Gene Kelly, for instance."

Sir Douglas, happy that he'd just won 'guess the persona,' suggested a suitable eatery to meet after the obligatory toilet break and it was at a table in the eatery that the three men assembled a few minutes later. A sort of drab and dreary open plan coffee shop, come burger joint, come pizza joint, come newsagents come amusement arcade, come toilet affair; it wasn't a patch on the 'Cutty Club' thought Sir Horace, but acknowledged that it would be the devils own job to pull the Cutty Sark around everywhere they went. Or would it? He decided that that would be a question he would address, once back in Greenwich.

Thomas was the last to arrive, but did so with three cups of white coffee. In the process of trying to have a conversation with Sir Douglas and Thomas, Sir Horace realised that, rather unknowingly, he'd created a kind of 'mind games poker.' No matter how he tried or how he approached the subject, neither Sir Douglas nor Thomas appeared to be too keen on sharing with the other two just what they had put down on their pads. After two or three attempts at approaching the subject from different angles, which included "whatcha thinking?" to a "what's on yer pad, me lad?" (The latter being a firm favourite of Sir Horace's), the decision was taken not to delve too deeply into their respective ideas until after the trip.

"So are we all in agreement then?"

An accepting, but hollow, "yes" came back from Sir Douglas and Thomas.

"Good, I must say that I am slightly mystified by your reluctance to divulge your thoughts, but accept that there is a time and a place and that maybe over a coffee in this god awful eatery isn't that place. Ok, who wants to play "I spy?""

Once they'd shot Sir Horace down in flames they

mutually, and rather painfully, struck up a conversation on nigh on anything that didn't involve I spy, pigeons or anyone called "Robert." Thankfully, the forty-five minutes then raced by and the three men ghosted their way outside and across the car park to where a fully refreshed Robert stood, ready to guide them into the limousine and then, once all doors were shut, enter himself. Back up to speed and out onto the motorway, the three men hunkered down into their respective note pads for the final leg of the journey. The time seemed to fly by, as all three rarely seemed to come up for air. Great and wondrous ideas flowed freely from all three as their notepads began to fill.

To begin with, an idea had been shortly followed by it being scribbled out but, as the journey progressed, the ideas that reached the note pads, on the whole, stayed on the notepads. It was almost a relaxing of their own editing powers and, with this relaxation, came more and more ideas and thoughts. So, by the time Thomas glanced up and out of the window to see a rather well kept venue come into site, there was a whole host of possibilities and questions to explore. Soon all three men had put their pens down on the seat beside them and closed their note pads. The elegance and impressively manicured lawns, tree lined drives and pathways had grabbed their collective attention. Sir Douglas felt the urge.

"Bloody hell!"

"By that, are you meaning, "My, what a set of impressive stripes the grounds man has cut into that grass, Douglas?"

"Erm, no, Sir. What I actually meant was, bloody hell, I was expecting one gigantic mound of bird poo!"

Thomas sat stunned by this latest conversation. He accepted that it was in its infancy, but felt that it was doomed, just like most of them between the two men accompanying him in the back of the limo. Still, he suddenly felt the urge to interject.

"Can I just point out that, at a play park, you don't expect to see a mound of children so why would you expect to see a mound of bird poo, Sir Douglas?"

"Because, young Thomas, birds crap everywhere whereas children don't. Generally, you'd expect them to have nappies on."

Those last two words hit all three men like a eureka moment. All at once, precisely at the same time, all three grabbed their respective note pads and pens and, on opening to a fresh page, said out loud and in unison "pigeon nappies." Notes made, smiles smiled and respective stationery closed and returned to from where they came, all three men visually joined forces and, with an accepting nod come smile, drew a line under the cloak and dagger note taking.

As the car came to a stop they could see a rather odd looking man in a white lab coat approaching the car along a grey stoned pathway. Not one to pass up on the opportunity, Thomas felt that a quick question to Sir Horace was in order.

"Can I assume, Sir Horace, that that is our man, Vic?"

"Why yes, you can, Thomas."

"He looks like "Q" out of those bond films. Can we call him "Q" please, Sir Horace?"

"I really don't think that Vic will appreciate being called "Q" though."

"But, he looks like him and so, I'm rather hopeful, his work is along the same lines as "Q.""

"Well, we'll have to wait and see on that one but, for now, lets just address him by his name."

"What about "Slitster"?"

"What?"

"Y'know, like what you tried at the services back down the road. "Robert" became "Bobster.""

"Entirely different, young Thomas."

"Not really, Sir. "Bobster," "Slitster Eyester Vicster"…very similar, although it is beginning to sound a bit Polish, so how about we just call him "Pole?""

"No, Thomas! How about we just call him Vic? Which,

funnily enough, is his name!"

Confused by the hint of a contradiction, Thomas gave up and gave in, mentally hoping that the odd looking man in a white coat, now only a few feet from his car door, really would be their own version of Q. If that were to be the case, Thomas decided, this guy would readily devour the contents of his pad. It was the door nearest to Thomas that was opened first. Feeling very smug and confident, he got out and, on standing up straight, introduced himself to the odd looking man in the white coat, who was nervously greeting him. Six foot tall and painfully thin, he resembled a bag of bones in a white coat. Grey hair, grey skin, the only warm thing about his appearance was his smile. Then there was the squint! "Good morning! You, I am reliably informed, are Mr Victor Ketchup. I am Thomas Jackson, pleased to meet you!"

A confident hand was met by a rather awkward and nervous hand from the odd looking man in the white coat that, against his better judgement, replied in kind. "Good morning to you, erm, Mr Jackson. I am indeed Victor Ketchup but please, call me Vic or "slit eye.""

Whilst the two hands grasped each other and shook cordially, Sir Horace and Sir Douglas were both exiting the vehicle, one behind Thomas and Sir Horace, from the far side, climbing out behind the driver. After stretching and straightening ties and suit jackets, both men moved and positioned themselves next to the, still hand shaking, Thomas and Victor.

On seeing Sir Horace, a wry smile spread across the face of the odd looking man in the white coat, as he moved sideways, away from Thomas, and took up a position directly in front of him. A more confident handshake quickly followed the warm greeting of two old friends.

"Victor, my good man. How the devil are you? How are the wife and family?"

"Sir Horace, bloody good to see you, Sir. All good thank you. How are you?"

The warmest of smiles on both men's faces told Thomas that this was a friendship of some standing and he made a mental note to dig a little deeper to find out more about it, when the time came. In the meantime, Sir Horace, complete with arm around the shoulder of Victor, moved quickly to introduce Sir Douglas.

"Victor, I'd like to introduce you to another good man, Sir Douglas Squires. This is the man who will command the H.M.S Ardilles."

Another warm handshake between the two men was quickly followed by a puzzled look and a quick fire question from Sir Douglas.

"Nice to meet you, Victor. Begging your pardon, Sir Horace, but should information regarding the Ardilles be out in the field yet? I thought it was classified?"

Relieved to see that his man was switched on, Sir Horace moved to put the mind of his concerned colleague at rest. "Oh, it's ok, Douglas. Information is on a "need to know" basis and Vic needed to know, as he has had to do work with the birds regarding wood finishes and habitual environments."

"Wood finishes and habitual environments, Sir?"

"Yes, Douglas! Look, this is one for later but for now, I'll explain briefly. You get the honour of deciding what colour to paint the ship. On the flip side, Vic gets the job of testing that paint on the birds. You simply can't paint pigeon's quarters in whatever you like! Supposing they take a peck at the varnish or paint, suffer a reaction and fall off of their perch or, in the case of a racer and as we shall see in a bit, a waddling machine? We simply can't have racing pigeons on active duty with head bandages because they fell off their perch. It's a very scientific, you know! Now, shall we proceed?"

With that, Sir Douglas gestured for Victor to lead the way with another Gene Kelly-esque arm movement. As all four men started to walk along a very well maintained and grey paved path, Thomas felt he needed to query something. "Sir Horace, did you just say the words "waddling machine?""

Without stopping to answer or even look behind him, Sir Horace, who was walking briskly alongside Victor out in front, turned his head ever so slightly to the side and despatched a quick fire "yes, Thomas, I did!" to the young man, walking alongside Sir Douglas, behind him.

As they walked swiftly along the path, Thomas felt as though he were a child again, almost breaking into a run, just to keep up. In no time at all, the trees that had lined the path from the time they had stepped foot out of the car, gave way to a very impressive, but very strange building. A kind of massive open sided hanger come shed stood before them. A cross between an agricultural colossus and something out of Thunderbirds, whatever it was, it was huge. The closer they got to it, the mightier the structure looked. As the four men continued walking towards, what appeared to be, a front door, a slightly agitated Thomas felt he needed clarification. "Vic, can I just clarify something."

Again, just as Sir Horace had done only minutes before, Victor answered but without either stopping or turning around.

"Of course you can!" came the soothing and almost warm

tones of a man whose confidence had obviously returned now that the meet and greets were over.

"The size of that building indicates that something rather large is inside. You're not training giant pigeons are you? What I mean is, what's the average pigeon coup dimensions? Six or ten feet by that again? What's in front of us is considerably larger than that."

Sir Horace moved to quell the impending storm. "Now, now, Thomas. Just as there is no such thing as a tooth fairy, likewise, there's no such thing as a giant pigeon. Although, come to think of it...Vic, make a note of that one, will you?"

"I know it sounds silly, Sir Horace, but I just wondered, given the size of this building, if we were developing giant pigeons in order to pooh on our enemies with faeces the size of rabbits!"

The men had, by now, reached the main doors, which were in fact, the entrance to a standard reception area. Sir Horace moved to put the conversation to bed, for now at least.

"Now, Thomas. For now, can I suggest that you rest that exuberant young mind of yours? I'm sure what lay behind those doors over there will satisfy even the healthiest of appetites."

Victor had led the party into the reception and, after a few quick, but quiet words in the ear of the receptionist, gestured for them to follow him through the nearest and very non-descript looking door to her right.

Expecting some high tech room full of gadgets, Sir Douglas was somewhat dejected to find a long, white painted room, seemingly stacked with pristine white lab coats on shiny silver hooks. Now definitely in his comfort zone, a confident 'slit eye' addressed his guests.

"Gentlemen, as you can see, we are surrounded by lab coats. Please choose one and place any jackets or jumpers that you wish to remove, on the appropriate pegs. Once suitably attired, we can continue our tour. Thank you."

The three visitors duly did, as asked, and removed jackets and surplus clothing before adorning their own immaculate lab coat. With an acknowledging nod to each other, they all turned to 'slit eye' who responded with another "Thank you!"

Just as Willy Wonka had done at the chocolate factory, from seemingly absolutely nowhere, 'slit eye' opened another door. Sir Horace was struck dumb by this 'no door – door' scenario, but could only muster a brief "Well bugger me! Where did that door come from???" Victor, happy that his guests were impressed, without even getting to the pigeons, smiled and gestured for them to follow him on through and beyond. Once through this amazing appearing door, the three guests came face to face with their first 'lab' type room. "This," Thomas thought to himself, "is about to get interesting!"

As the three men walked behind Victor, their respective eyes were everywhere, glancing this way and that. It was if there wasn't enough time and what time there was had to be rationed. A split second here, a split second there. There was simply too much in the room for them to see everything and spend time on everything. There were simply too many men and women in white coats and, more importantly, too many pigeons in this one room. Victor, on seeing the glazed expressions on the faces of his guests, felt he'd best explain what they were clearly struggling to take in.

"Gentlemen, here we have the first room in what you might like to think of as a filtration process. This is the very first stage of the rehabilitation/training program and focuses on the arrival of the birds, here at Pickering. As and when they arrive, they pass through this room and are given a full health check and condition inspection. Regardless of variety, both Racing and Trafalgar share this same room."

Sir Douglas felt the urge to question the lack of segregation and spoke up before really giving himself a chance to think it through.

"Victor, do you think it is socially acceptable for these two vastly different classes to mix and be in the same environment. After all, one is quite high up the class ladder and one is not. I'm really not sure that it is, erm, "cricket" for these to mix like this!"

Before Sir Horace and Thomas could evaluate what their colleague had said, 'Slit Eye' had come back with a corker that made Sir Douglas really want to think twice and maybe three times before saying anything more.

"They're birds, Sir Douglas! They both eat, both shit and both fly! The only difference is that one type is a bit quicker in the air and the other type can roll a fag by the time they leave here!"

Feeling rather like a naughty school boy, who'd just been corrected by his teacher, Sir Douglas was only able to reply with a mere "ok then!" before Victor continued his explanation.

"The birds arrive at Pickering and are booked or registered in this room. They are then also checked and assessed in this room. Once checked and tagged, they are fed and watered and then and only then, Sir Douglas, are they segregated and passed from this room to the next phase of the program. Obviously, from here on in, the program changes depending on what type of bird you are and what your condition is. If you're a racing pigeon and you're seen in this room as healthy, then you go through to the fitness centre, which we will visit shortly." Vic couldn't help, but note the enthusiasm, oozing out of every pore and orifice of his guests, and felt he must continue whilst the passion was still there.

"If you are a Trafalgar type and have two of everything that you should have two of, then you pass through to a certain stage. If, however, you are a Trafalgar type and you have bits missing, legs, eyes etc etc, then you will go a different route to the previously mentioned "complete" Trafalgar. Quite obviously, if you've had a run in with a stun sub-machine gun then you're going to need more than just a fag before starting active service. And so it goes on etc etc."

Suddenly, for Sir Horace, Sir Douglas and Thomas, the whole project had become real. Disregarding the various other trips and the training of the accountants, standing in an immaculate lab-type room, surrounded by men and women in pristine white lab coats of which each and everyone of them were giving their utmost attention to a whole load of pigeons of various colours, conditions and sizes brought the whole situation home in an instant.

For here was a room, where pretty much everything

was white in colour, except the birds or, as they looked to Sir Horace, the patients. Rows and rows of examination benches were filled with rows and rows of staff in white coats and all of these were, in turn, examining rows and rows of pigeons. No segregation or discrimination as of yet, as each bird was assessed then moved on down the production line. All of the while these thoughts and observations had paraded themselves through the minds of the three, Victor Ketchup had stood their watching them. Knowing that the truth and reality of the whole project had hit home, he felt it was time to move along.

"Gentlemen, I think we can safely tick the box, as far as seeing this room goes. Please follow me to our next port of call."

An agreeing nod from all concerned and off they walked, following Victor through a door, down a corridor and into another ridiculously white and spotlessly clean room.

"Now here we are in the fitness management suite for the Racing pigeons. As you will note as you look around, there are a lot of different types of mini fitness related apparatuses. The objective in this room is to train and condition the birds in the use of this specialised and rather bespoke equipment. Obviously, being of the racing variety, they are used to being trained and used to being fit. We are taking them out of their rather comfortable comfort zone and sticking them in the middle of a sea somewhere, down below in cramped and confined quarters. This habitual change takes time to implement and this is what is happening around you as I speak.

It was at this point, as the three men looked around the room, that Sir Douglas spotted something odd that needed addressing. For there, on a perch, on a mounted plinth, in the middle of the room, sat a very large and slightly unkempt looking pigeon. No white-coated personnel in attendance or, in actual fact, anywhere near it. It seemed to be comfortable in it's surroundings, not fazed by the commotion all around and was simply minding it's own business. If a pigeon could wear a smoking jacket and slippers, it would've been this one. Sir Douglas caught the eye of Thomas and diverted his eyes towards it. A less than subtle reaction followed.

"What the hell is that?"

"Thomas, I was rather hoping that you would be slightly more subtle in your astonishment!"

That reaction brought the focus of 'Slit Eye' and Sir Horace down on them. It was 'Slit Eye' who casually brought an air of calm explanation to the proceedings.

"I see, Gentlemen, that you have met Richard."

"Whom, may I ask, is Richard?"

"Sir Douglas, you may ask anything you like and, in answer to your question, that pigeon right there is Richard!"

Thomas felt confused and ever so slightly angry at the fact that he did so annoyingly not have a clue about what was going on. He moved for clarification in a pressing manner.

"Right, Vic. Can you please explain to the three of us why, in a room where all the pigeons are certified healthy and racy but, as yet, don't have names and, as yet, only have numbers, why in the middle of the very same room, on a perch which might as well be an armchair, sits a slightly less healthy looking pigeon by the name of "Richard?""

Very calm, cool and relaxed, Victor Ketchup smiled and answered his ever so slightly annoyed guests in a very calm, cool and relaxed manner.

"Of course I can, Thomas. That, there, is Richard Burton."

"Richard Burton? Why do you have a pigeon called Richard Burton? Of all the people that you could have named him after, why Richard Burton?"

Before Vic could answer, Sir Douglas mustered a feeble "Where's Liz?" and giggled to himself in a somewhat teenage girl-esque manner. A sturdy stare from Sir Horace ended his fun and all ears were once again on Victor, waiting for the answer to Thomas' question.

"My dear Thomas! That isn't a pigeon called "Richard Burton." That IS Richard Burton!"

A kind of stunned silence greeted Vic at that point. In his mind, he was expecting an accepting nod and an understanding that the once great actor had now taken the form of a pigeon, on a perch that resembled an armchair, in a pigeon training facility in Pickering. What he seemed to be confronted with was an air of disillusionment and astonishment. To back this up, it was Sir Horace who felt it right and proper to question his long-standing friend and colleague.

"Now, Vic. That there is a pigeon, as I am sure you are aware. I am also sure that you are aware that Richard Burton was, and I'll stress that bit, was, a human. There are two elements of my last sentence that I would like to focus your attention on. Firstly, the bit where I mentioned the word "was," which, like in many cases of its use, implies a past tense. The other little bit of my statement, which I'd like you to focus on, was my use of the word "human." Now, if you put the two together, implying that the subject, in this case, Richard Burton, was a human, as in no more, as in passed away, as in dead."

Victor had stood soaking up this address, but now took his turn to respond, in his own aggravatingly calm manner.

"I understand what you are saying, of course I do. But, please let me explain. This pigeon wasn't here. It wasn't physically around, at all! Richard Burton dies and it appears. How, I ask you, do you explain that?"

Sir Horace grew agitated, almost annoyed. There were two, seemingly glaring issues, that he needed to bring to the attention of the man, defending the pigeon, stood before him.

"Victor, my friend. I hate to say this to you, but there are two facts which, when addressed, will demonstrate that this pigeon cannot be Richard Burton."

Victor felt obliged to remonstrate with his colleague.

"Sir Horace! In all of our years of friendship..."

"Victor! Richard Burton died in 1984. A pigeon formed Richard Burton would also have died by now! It simply isn't possible for that Richard Burton to have become this Richard Burton. I think that this Richard Burton is simply a pigeon imposter!"

Again, the response was delivered with a cool, but very calculated aim.

"Now, Sir Horace, that is where you are wrong! Records suggest that the oldest authentically recorded age of a pigeon is that of Kaiser, captured in a basket of pigeons during the

Meuse-Argonne offensive in 1918. Kaiser, gentlemen, was reported to have died at the age of thirty-two years eight months. That makes it entirely possible and factually correct for that pigeon to be Richard Burton!"

As if to prove that there was an element of truth about what Victor had been saying, Richard Burton, the pigeon, had a brain haemorrhage, just as his namesake had done, fell off of it's armchair-esque perch, and died before their very eyes. Immediate reactions varied from Sir Douglas' "Well, bugger me!" to the absolute heartfelt public display of sorrow and pain from Victor. This was demonstrated with a banshee like cry of "Nnnnnoooooooooooooooo! Richard!!!!!!!!"

Feeling that they were going to have to scrape this normally mild mannered man off of the floor, Thomas, Sir Douglas and Sir Horace quickly looked at each other to decide what to do. Before any of them could act, an assistant, who had stood silently in the corner of the room and dressed, as were all the other assistants dotted around the complex, in an immaculately pressed white coat, suddenly sprang to life and rushed forward to bring his clenched fist crashing down on a red plunger type button. He then proceeded to open the door and run, screaming hysterically, for the exit. Instantly sirens sounded and yellow lights with crudely stuck on "x's" in black electrical tape started to flash. The noise was deafening.

Straining to hear himself speak, Sir Horace started to address Victor who, by now, had composed himself and seemed almost immune to the seemingly million-decibel howl all around them. As he started to speak, he noticed a change in Victor. The sorrowful collapse, witnessed by all only moments before, had been replaced by a stronger, steely-eyed version, rising from the flames of sorrow.

"Victor! I'm truly sorry about Richard, I really am but…"

"Get out! Everyone out! The tour is over, the visit is finished and Richard is dead!"

"What???"

"Out! Sir Horace, out! Everyone out! The complex is shut down as from now and a five-day mourning period will commence shortly. Please, Sir Horace, leave the complex and assemble in the main car park. I'm awfully sorry, but the visit is terminated. I have to deal with Richard."

And with that announcement came the waving of the arms and the shepherding of the three visitors out of the complex. All the while the sirens and flashing lights continued. Sir Horace began to remonstrate whilst being herded out of the building, but it was all to no avail. Victor had made up his mind and, to him, the only way to deal with the sudden collapse and death of Richard Burton, the pigeon, was to close the complex and mourn for five days.

In the car park, the scene was one of tragedy and despair. Men in immaculate white lab coats stumbled about all over the place. All were in various stages of personal collapse. Out of the chaos of sirens and lights came Sir Horace, Sir Douglas and Thomas, striding purposefully through this saddened crowd and hastily looking for their limo. On finding it already prepared and with Robert standing by an open rear door, first Sir Horace and then Thomas climbed in before Sir Douglas checked himself, turned to look at the tragic scenes behind him and simply said "That's a bit bloody weird for my liking," before climbing in and requesting that Robert return them to London, without "sparing the horses."

"Like everything on this project," he thought to himself, "everything was a complete shambles, but maybe it was supposed to be that way?"

After a very relaxing weekend of doing nothing and nothing respectively, Sir Douglas and Thomas entered the Museum for their nine o'clock briefing with Sir Horace. Both men were in fine fettle, as they passed the familiar paintings and exhibits along the corridor to the Main Hall. However, upon entering the hall, they were not quite met by the calm they were expecting.

Workmen of various shapes, sizes and attire filled the room. This was alarming, but the lack of the blue whale was even more so. For once, both men did not reach for their dusters, as they closed in on the area where the disjointed lower jaw had once hung. Instead, they stopped and took in what was happening around them both.

Workers, all with their respective trades' fashion accessories hung from their bodies, tried to act busy in between breaking wind and talking more cockney slang than the next guy. If one had a bright yellow 14v drill hung from his hip like a Magnum 44, the next guy appeared to have a blue one that had a shiny 18v sticker on it. All around them, men struggled to move under the weight of the attachments hung from the tool belts, draped around their waists.

Thomas looked at his watch. 08.55, time to get below.

He saw a large cardboard box over on the far side of the room at the same moment that Sir Douglas did. Sir Douglas reached deep within himself, searching for that high, panic-stricken voice that signifies alarm, and began a sentence before being cut short by Thomas.

"That's bloody…"

"Yes, I know, now come on or we'll have some explaining to do!"

After descending the stairs and negotiating a brief series of corridors and turns, they arrived at the intended room. As they opened the door, the figure of a rather concerned looking Sir Horace came into view. Without so much as a "Hello," Sir Douglas tried to lodge a complaint regarding the scene above them in the Main Hall, but was cut short again, this time by Sir Horace.

"Sir, I feel I must complain at the highest and strongest…"

"Ssssh Douglas, I have something to read you both."

Sir Douglas stopped his tirade and took a seat, Government Issue. Silently, Thomas did the same. As their minor adjustments to the seating arrangements died down, Sir Horace looked at his colleagues and began his address to them, his face pale and drawn.

"Gentlemen, good morning. You are as aware as I am of the letter received recently, regarding the changing of the times and also our gate monitor, the blue whale. I'm guessing that you were both, like me, not really expecting anything to come of this and that we would see out our days on the project, sliding underneath the distorted lower jaw of our old friend, Balaenoptera Musculus. However, as you can both see, it would appear that the threat to replace our old friend has now been carried out and Lord only knows what will happen next."

Again, in a pose and tone of voice similar to Neville Chamberlain, some years before, he held up a letter and continued.

"And so, Gentlemen, I have received another letter. Well, actually, a bit of a letter, that I would like to read to you. Afterwards, I will ask Thomas to fetch some glue, so that we can complete the order! Anyway, I shall proceed."

"To Sir Horace Hargraves and all of the team working on "Project New Boat."

Further to my previous letter, I have now added a few lines (see below). Please, feel free, to cut and glue these onto the bottom of the previous letter, in order to see the complete picture.

You will note that, as previously mentioned, the installation of a replacement and far friendlier gate monitor has commenced. As for the Blue Whale, that is currently residing at the Tower Of London, behind bars.

Even though it is a hundred odd foot example of what fibreglass can achieve, the Queen is so disgusted with it that she wants to teach it a lesson. It has been sentenced to six months there, with no time off for good behaviour.

Many people have attempted to get the point across, regarding the inanimate characteristics of the thing, but the Queen will not have it any other way. She simply will not accept that it isn't real. As far as she is concerned, it represents its species and so must serve the custodial sentence on their behalf.

Carry on!

Yours truly,

Robin McJeffers – of the "Sir" variety"

Sir Horace lowered the letter, or part thereof, and gestured, with two out stretched hands, for any questions. He'd felt that this would be best delivered with another 'Pacino-esque' facial gesture. Unfortunately, for him, his two colleagues were a little bit too far withdrawn for that and, almost, a little too far into their own thoughts for any questions. A glazed expression sat on both of their faces, as they inwardly struggled to comprehend what had just been read out.

Knowing exactly what was needed in order to bring these two back to the present, Sir Horace continued. "Cutty Club, anyone?"

Before either of them had a chance to think through exactly what had just happened, Sir Horace had walked towards the door and, without stopping to wait for them, switched off the lights and continued towards the stairs, that led up to the Main Hall.

That certainly seemed to do the trick as, both Thomas and Sir Douglas were startled back to the present and, after a quick shake of the head and rub of the eyes, were out of their respective chairs, Government Issue and out of the room, high tailing it after Sir Horace.

Once up and out in the Main Hall, the emptiness that the lack of blue whale brought to the room was mind-boggling. All three stood looking around at the chaos that surrounded them, before quickly scurrying off towards reception and, Thomas thought, an even earlier appointment at The Cutty Club than even they had managed before.

Chapter Sixteen – And then there was Nemo

It was now Thursday and the hangovers were finally gone. Two full days of recovery were complete and the searing pain, dehydration and general sickness had all but disappeared. Back in the land of the living and able to stand up straight, without being overcome by the symptoms of vertigo, Sir Douglas and Thomas stood in the Main Hall at the museum, staring.

The focal point of their combined stare was fairly obvious, as pretty much everyone in the Main Hall at that point were also staring at the very same thing. That 'thing' appeared to be a rather makeshift Punch and Judy booth, complete with hastily painted 'Punch and Judy' slogans.

As if this wasn't odd enough, it seemed to be positioned over the previously concealed entrance in the floor to their Headquarters below. And to top off this somewhat unfortunate scene, there was a full-scale, fifteen centimetre, fiberglass clown fish, suspended from the ceiling and swinging around uncontrollably every time it caught a gust of turbulence from a passer by or the breeze from an open window.

Thomas looked at Sir Douglas. Sir Douglas looked at Thomas, who then promptly gestured for him to enter through the back of the Punch and Judy stand first. An accepting nod from Sir Douglas and he was through the curtain and down the darkened stairway, swiftly followed by Thomas. The, almost customary distant lights, that were on to illuminate far off corridors and rooms, but somehow still managed to light their way, shone out as normal.

It was this light that, like so many other times, guided them around corners and along the corridors, until they entered the same old room and where they were met by the same old image of Sir Horace, standing and anticipating their arrival.

Sir Douglas felt he'd best question the scene upstairs, but was cut off, as seemingly always, in his tracks by his superior.

"Erm, Sir. About..."

"Save it, Douglas, already on to it."

"But..."

"I know."

"Erm.."

"Yes, I know!"

Thomas could see where this charade was heading and so stepped in to save the pair of them from seemingly becoming some sort of contestants in a nineteen eighties game show. As he took control, he had a quick glance at Sir

Douglas, which confirmed to him that he could actually be Lionel Blair. That would have to mean that Sir Horace would need to be Una Stubbs. Slightly weird to think about but, anyway, back to the task at hand. He addressed them in a raised voice.

"Gentlemen!"

To his own amazement, the staggered and pointless conversation between Sir Horace and Sir Douglas stopped, as both men simultaneously turned to look at him. Feeling somewhat more powerful than he'd felt in a long time, he realised that this feeling wasn't going to last and so there would be no point playing on it. With a normal voice he asked, "Can we just get on with what we need to, in order to fix the problem, please?"

Instantly, Sir Horace regained control and addressed his men.

"Yes! Erm, right. Well done, young Thomas, my lad. And thank you! Right, gents, please take a pew. The kettle is on and I need to read you something.

Almost in unison, both Sir Douglas and Thomas answered in dismay.

"Please, not another letter from the office of McJeffers!"

They knew the answer almost immediately, as they saw Sir Horace prepare to read from a piece of paper he now held firmly.

"Now, now, Gentlemen! As you can see, on your way in this morning, there has been a little mix up that has hastily and, I say hastily in the loosest sense possible, been corrected. I will now read to you a letter, the latest letter, to come out of the McJeffers office."

Sir Horace seemed to stand to attention before reading it. The two others took it upon themselves to stand and hold a clenched fist salute across their respective chests. Sir Douglas, unsure of why he was doing this, looked at Thomas. With an agreeing nodding gesture he simply said "El Presidente!" Sir Douglas liked this sudden mockery and smiled back, continuing to hold the same pose. Sir Horace, rather than be shocked and rebuke his men, smiled at the gesture and left them to their own devices. He continued.

"Gentlemen. You are as aware, of the calamitous error of judgment, as I am. Instead of walking in this morning to find a monstrous Nemo model guarding the entrance to our head quarters, we have all encountered a fifteen centimetre model, swinging in the breeze, and, to top it off, and to make it really a showpiece of incompetence and, in no way designed to hide the error at all, a hideously poorly constructed Punch and Judy booth, seemingly dragged over our entrance. Now, I'm sure that in his last address to us, Sir Robin McJeffers never meant for our beloved blue whale to be replaced by a matchbox model but, seemingly, that is what has happened. The tradesmen, who installed the replacement model, have reported the error to the office of Sir Robin McJeffers and here is the reply."

He took a final look at his two colleagues before continuing to read the sheer absurdity that he knew was laid in ink on the very paper he held. He began.

"To Sir Horace and the team at "Project New Boat."

It has come to my attention that the Nemo model, brought in to specifically take over gate duties at your illustrious HQ, has been made to life like proportions. Whilst, I am told, the actual model is very detailed and professionally done, I understand that it falls some way short of being able to perform it's main task, that of concealment. This, I can understand.

I have had the finest mathematicians in the land look at the facts and figures and all have failed to come up with any formulae, which would allow a fifteen-centimetre model fish to cover a five-foot by five-foot hole. I am reliably told that the model would need hilariously over sized fins in order to get anywhere near the coverage and, based on the fact that this could be humorous, I have instructed the staff at the Sea Life Centre, Weymouth, to start a cross breed program with immediate effect.

Hopefully, within a couple of years, you could have a life-size model of a giant clown turtle hanging over the HQ entrance. It would still have a small body, but its massively oversized fins would really conceal the entrance well. I will keep you updated with regards to the Giant Clown Turtle breeding program.

For now, though, all I can do is apologise for the slight error in calculations and will endeavour to get a larger than actual scale Nemo model made and installed quicker than you can say "Hello, is that Weymouth Sea Life Centre? What are the chances of breeding a giant turtle with a clown fish?"

What of the blue whale, I hear you cry? Well, it would appear that your friend, the blue whale, isn't eating his plankton, like a good whale should, and appears to have gone on hunger strike. We are trying to get an I.V line into his fin but are finding his surface skin to be tougher than we expected. I will update you on this in due course as well.

Finally, and until the replacement model arrives, please feel free to watch the Punch and Judy show as many times as you wish. It really is terrific!

Yours truly,

Robin Mcjeffers – of the Sir variety!

Silence prevailed. Sir Horace looked up from the piece of paper that he had just read aloud from. He looked at Sir Douglas and then at Thomas. Both of these men stood statue still and ever so slightly stunned. Sir Douglas felt it was a good time to question Sir Horace.

"So, Sir!"

"Yes."

"What you are…"

"Yes, Douglas."

"No, but what I was…"

"No, Douglas…"

"But, Sir!"

"Yes, Douglas?"

"About the…"

"No, Douglas!"

"But, Sir!"

Thomas, once again, assumed control and, with a heavy heart, he shouted "Guess I'll make the coffee then!"

With the mention of the word 'coffee,' probably more than the loud voice, both Sir Horace and Sir Douglas brought their pointless and meaningless conversation to a close. As before, Sir Horace regained control. Whilst Thomas drifted into the kitchen to make three cups of coffee, Sir Horace motioned for Sir Douglas to help him set up, what appeared to be, another 'overhead projector thing.' On seeing this piece of office equipment, Sir Douglas's mind drifted momentarily back to the first day on the project. He recalled how his boss had struggled that day and decided that today would not be a repeat of then. With calmness and conviction, he assisted Sir Horace with cables and a mains leads. This time, Sir Horace upped the level of sophistication by introducing a laptop.

Sir Horace was pleased to note the surprise on Sir Douglas' face and acknowledged it with a smugness that he had rarely had a chance to use of late.

"Laptop! Like it, eh?"

"Why, erm , yes, Sir Horace!"

"Thought it about time we got more sophisticated."

At that moment, Thomas entered the room with the coffee. As he sat down, he placed them on three place mats before declaring, "It's just a laptop!"

Mortified, Sir Horace rose to the challenge.

"It may be only a laptop to you, Thomas, and your young generation of computer games this and streaming that but, to Douglas and myself, who's only real knowledge of a stream is either what you paddle in or what your nose does, it is somewhat more than just a laptop. This is the next level for our project and, indeed our team!"

Feeling ever so slightly smug, Sir Horace lowered himself into the nearest chair and reached for a cup of coffee. Thomas, feeling that he could win this, continued.

"What are we to use this wondrous piece of technology for, Sir Horace? Are we going to re-design the Ardilles using Cad sophistication? Are we going to arm her with something slightly more dangerous than a VW beetle and telegraph pole and maybe even program the weapon systems from here? Please, to put my young and inquisitive mind at ease, please tell me why we have this laptop?"

It was now Thomas who felt smug and leant forward to sip from his coffee.

The scene began to play out like some game of poker from a western movie. Beads of sweat running down cheeks, steely glances across the table at each other, each man trying to out guess the other. Sir Horace who, by the fact that he knew why he had the laptop, and was therefore about to win the hand, broke the Silence.

"Thomas, we have the laptop, not so we can re-design our ship, nor so we can arm her with better weaponry or, indeed, program those systems but so that we can watch this!"

And on his very own cue, he pressed a couple of buttons on the laptop and there, projected onto the wall in front of them, began a film presentation.

Immediately, Thomas was alarmed to see that the quality of production was severely lacking. What he was hoping to see was a polished presentation, detailing some important updates on the project or some vital information that the three of them needed to know about. What he, Sir Douglas and Sir Horace were now watching had just creaked and crackled onto the wall, announced by some warped sounding trumpets and a very posh 1930's style announcer who promptly declared, "This is Pigeon Pathe News!"

At that point a huge and rather poorly animated pigeon waddled across the screen, before disappearing off the other side. Preparing himself for the worst, Thomas quickly rose from his chair, ran to the light switch, switched off the lights and returned to his chair and, more importantly, his cup of coffee. He knew that things were about to get interesting. Meanwhile, the film continued in an awkward and disjointed manner. The posh 1930's announcer continued to talk over the images there before them.

"Here, at Pickering, we have the most top birds ready to serve their King and country...Queen and country. No! Saucy fellow...not those kind of birds! You really are a cheeky chappy! I mean Pigeons and clever ones at that!" Thomas sat back and smiled. This was looking like a class way to spend a morning. The film rumbled on and showed various types of pigeons on various tables or worktops, all being checked over and booked in. From racing pigeons being washed to Trafalgar pigeons being fitted with stumps, the film showed it all. The posh sounding 1930's announcer continued, unabated.

"Here, at Pickering, we have established an establishment of enormous importance to the project. For here, at Pickering, is where untrained pigeons become servants to the King...Queen! Here's a scruffy chap, what with beard and all. But, wait! What's that missing? Why, it's a leg! The little blighter's only gone and had it shot off! And, by a stun sub-machine gun, I wouldn't half betting with someone. Never mind though, as here, at Pickering, we have the ability to rebuild and re-leg little blighters like this unfortunate fellow.

The film skipped and jumped in a rather disjointed fashion, to the next stage of what the posh 1930's announcer was commentating on.

"Here you see a rather skilled chap carefully fitting a stump to our feathered friend. A few tentative steps, a little stumble, then the one legged wonder is placed on his perch with a cigarette for his troubles. Well done skilled person and well done scruffy pigeon!"

Lots of triumphant, if slightly warped, celebratory music followed and the film cut to the next shot, which was even more alarming. There, before them, was a seemingly hastily arranged and very poorly acted scene of contentment. The rather skilled chap, who they'd just watched fitting a stump, now sat in a large padded armchair with a cup of tea on the arm.

Massive smiles and fake nods of approval were flowing from this gentlemen and all aimed at his patient, the pigeon, who stood on the arm of another armchair, looking ever so slightly perplexed by it all. The pigeon was naturally smoking a cigarette, but had had a cup of tea placed next to him for the purposes of the film.

The posh 1930's gentleman continued.

"We're all friends here at Pickering and what better way to enjoy a cup of cha than with your stump fitter buddy or pigeon with a stump! Here we see the skilled chap enjoying a cup of tea with his latest pal, the pigeon who he just fitted a stump for. See how they laugh and enjoy each other's

company. Two real pals forever! Hurrah for the skilled chap,
the pigeon with the stump and hurrah for Pickering!"

Even though it was digital and being played from a
memory stick, it appeared that quite a lot of effort had been
put into making the film end as though the reel of an old
projector had just run out. The image on the screen crackled
and the repeated image of the end of a reel flapping all over
the place continued to play out. Sir Horace reached forwards
and pressed a few buttons to stop the film and close down the
laptop, whilst Thomas switched the lights back on and
returned to his seat. Sir Horace broke the silence.

"Well, gentlemen. What do you think of that?"

Thomas spoke first.

"Was that for real?

"Why, yes, Thomas. That was designed to fill in the gaps, so
to speak. To tell us about the bits we didn't get to see last
week, because Richard died."

Thomas, with frustration seemingly bursting from
within, decided that bluntness was the best weapon.

"But, Sir Horace, that place at Pickering was massive. It was
huge. We saw three maybe four rooms in the entire place. All
of those rooms were either reception or clerical or basic
rooms where the pigeons were checked in. This dreadful

film, that we have just watched, has still not filled in the gaps. I mean visually, at least."

"Oh come, come, Thomas! Of course it has."

Angered and somewhat frustrated by the ignorance of his boss, Thomas snapped back.

"Oh really? Have you actually seen a Racing pigeon on a running machine? Or even on a waddling machine? Have you actually seen a Trafalgar pigeon roll a cigarette? Or even smoke one, although scrap that, there was a smoking pigeon in that film. I'll give you that one. But, you get my point!"

A very smug and assured Sir Horace calmly responded to the young man's protests.

"Thomas, points taken on board now, please, be a good gringo and turn the lights out. In fact, make some more coffee then turn the lights out. I have something else for you two to watch."

Sir Douglas, always one for surprises, felt he needed to try and guess what it was.

"Is it The Cruel Sea, Sir Horace?"

"No, Douglas, it isn't."

On re-joining his colleagues at the table with three fresh cups of coffee, Thomas nodded to Sir Horace a nod that said, "please proceed." Sir Horace leaned forward and pressed play. Once again, a creaky and poorly made video presentation appeared on the wall in front of them. Almost instantly another poorly animated pigeon appeared and their old friend, the posh 1930's announcer began his address.

"This is Pigeon Pathe news….again!…England…home of the English people…and some other chaps too…also the Spitfire, Hurricane and Lancaster and burial place of Richard Burton, the pigeon. Also, here in England, but more specifically up in the Northern bit, is Pickering, mecca to all of those chaps who like their birds to have feathers. The type of bird that is as happy having a poo as flying…"

Sir Douglas leaned over to Thomas and whispered in his ear, "Not the most poetic openings on film!"

In a rather awkward fashion, the film suddenly jumped to another scene, accompanied by some 1930's style music. The posh 1930's announcer continued.

"Here, at Pickering, we have two types of birds. No, not those birds you cheeky chappy! Of the feathered variety! One type are thoroughbred racers, destined to earn fame and glory for their kind, country, and King…Queen! The other type, are destined to train religiously until they can roll a cigarette whilst in mid-air!"

In a seemingly obvious rush to display the images required and end the film, the posh 1930's announcer suddenly upped his game, and his speed of voice, and rapidly described the next few seconds in machine gun style.

"Here we have a racer, checked, booked in and now on a waddling machine. See how fit he is becoming! Here we have a Trafalgar pigeon, complete with dirt, eye patch, leg stump and beard. See how he rolls a cigarette to perfection then lights it with a specially developed pigeon lighter. Hurrah for Pickering! The End!"

This time, there was no simulated end of the reel of film thing for the three men to stare at. The film simply stopped, with absolutely no warning of the impending and abrupt end to come. Thomas, as shocked as the other two men, rose from his chair, turned the lights back on and returned to his seat. Silence ruled. All three men too shocked to talk. Sir Douglas could only muster an "Erm!"

On hearing that, Sir Horace rose to the challenge and declared "mmmm..." Thomas, not wishing to be outdone, followed soon after with a short, sharp "wow!" In order to win this war of sounds, Sir Horace felt a quick, succinct, address to round off what they'd all just sat through would be beneficial.

"Gentlemen, you have now seen pigeons on running machines and other pigeons rolling cigarettes. Lord only knows what the hell that was that we have just watched but,

I'm guessing, they feel that they can tick all the boxes regarding showing us what is going on there. I now have a massive headache and am going home. Please submit your reports over the next few days on what is happening with fitting out, launch and trials please. I will contact you over the next few days to discuss what happens next."

As he finished his address, Sir Horace left the room, rubbing his head. It was left to Sir Douglas and Thomas to clear up, wash up and pack away the laptop. All done in near silence, the both of them knew that there were still a large amount of blanks that required filling. Only time would tell if they would get filled in or if the Ardilles would set sail with a whole bucket load of uncertainty around her.

With everything packed up, washed up and put away, it was time for home. Thomas knew that the build was nearing completion now and the launch would sap every ounce of strength from him in the coming weeks. It was time for home, and rest, and to ponder what lay ahead.

Chapter Seventeen – Deals

Monday morning had come around again and Sir Horace stood in the Operations Room, making three cups of coffee. Having filled the respective cups to an acceptable level, he replaced the kettle, Government Issue, back onto the worktop and checked his watch. Whilst he wouldn't wish to admit it, the whole Ardilles and Floaty Boat Brigade thing had made him an obsessive timekeeper. Always to be seen checking his watch, sometimes seemingly for no other reason than to ensure it was actually on his wrist, Sir Horace was a stickler for courtesy and people being where they should be and when they had agreed to be there.

Another glance of the watch and the conversation from the previous week came back into his mind. *"Gentlemen. First class efforts all round! Shall we say ten o'clock Monday for an update session?"* The two men, whom he had been addressing and whom, in turn, nodded an acknowledgement, were Sir Douglas and Thomas. After a sort of secret pact exchange of nods, that almost got out of hand and become winks, all three men had departed from the scene, their own separate ways. All three looking forward to a well earned weekend of relaxation.

So there he stood, recalling the conversation from the

previous week and checking his watch…again. As the minutes, to the designated meeting time, gave way to seconds, he felt a slight twitch run down his spine due, he was aware, to the thought of his men being late. Just as he checked his watch against the clock on the wall and saw the hands strike ten o'clock, he was pleased, and somewhat relieved, to see the door to the room open to reveal both Sir Douglas and Thomas entering. An ecstatic Sir Horace greeted the men with a Gene Kelly-esque shuffle-come-tuneful-greeting.

Sliding across the floor, in a manner he hadn't used for a while, he hit his finale pose, back stooped, arms outstretched, one pointing diagonally down, the other diagonally up. As he held this posture, he thought to himself that he'd absolutely nailed the Gene Kelly thing. For some reason he could only think of the great man's dance with Jerry the Mouse but, he was sure, he must've struck this pose at the end of that routine. With razor sharp timing, just as he snapped his arms out straight and in their respective directions, he let out a "Gentlemen, good morning!" He was inwardly very pleased with himself.

This feeling was quickly replaced by confusion as Sir Douglas and Thomas both came rushing to his side and helped him sit down in a chair, rapidly gathered by Thomas.

"What the bloody hell are you doing? Let go of me!"

Sir Douglas felt an explanation was called for.

"Sorry about that, Sir. We both thought you'd slipped a disc or something! Thought we'd best sit you down."

"Slipped a disc! Jesus man! I was merely saying good morning. All be it in a rather over enthusiastic way, I grant you! Having said that, I understand where the confusion arose from, so let's just draw a line under the morning greetings and continue. Thomas, get the coffee from the side in the kitchen will you? There's a good fellow!"

Thomas acknowledged Sir Douglas and turned towards the kitchen. On returning with a small tray, on which the three cups of coffee sat, he placed the tray on the table in front of Sir Douglas and Sir Horace, before joining them at the large conference table. He then proceeded to slide one across to each man, sat across from him. An acknowledging glance from Sir Horace and Sir Douglas brought a rather bizarre five minutes to an end as Sir Horace spoke up.

"Gentlemen, we are approaching the last few days before the H.M.S Ardilles takes to the water for the first time. The launch itself will be a monumental day for us all. We are, I believe, at the dot the i's and cross the t's stage. With this in mind, I thought it would be a good idea if you could both update me on exactly where we're at." Sir Douglas

311

spoke first.

"Well Sir, from my point of view, the accountants are all trained and are awaiting final orders, as are the bookkeepers. The H.M.S Ardilles is coming along very nicely now. The decks are complete, as is the outer skin, along with fridge magnet name. On that subject, we had severe problems obtaining giant magnetic letters. The biggest we could get seemed to be from Mothercare, so we bought those. We figured the first big wave will wash them away anyway, so even if they only stay on long enough for the launch then, in a way, it's mission accomplished and box ticked."

Sir Horace felt that he should strike a thoughtful pose and almost over did things as he just stopped himself stroking an imaginary goatee beard in time. This near miss was quickly followed with an "I see. Please, Douglas, continue." Sir Douglas, watching his boss narrowly succumb to an "air beard" stroke, continued.

"The finish of the wood is, what we believe to be "Battleship Grey" but, due to the wooden structure of the vessel, had to be a garden wood stain of similar shading. The colour I chose was actually called, "Asteroid," by a company called, "Sadolin." We received a very good bulk-buy deal from them by telling them we were building a life-size mock up of the H.M.S Hood for a new version of The Royal Tournament."

"Douglas, that really is very excellent work, my friend. If you have any left, I'd love to paint my shed in the same colour as the Ardilles!"

"Thank you, Sir! They were only too happy to supply us and, yes, there is some left. It has cost us a fair bit of our budget, but that was an expense I felt was justified."

Before Sir Horace could reply, Thomas interjected. "I can reclaim that cost....and probably that cost again...and, actually, maybe that cost even three or four fold!"

Both his colleagues, currently sat across the table from him, looked alarmed and both tried to show this with their very best 'alarmed' expressions. Sir Horace had felt that his was good and probably worthy of an Oscar but, on glancing across at Sir Douglas, realised in an instant that it was not a match for his favourite underling and the reality struck that he probably looked as though he was breaking wind in comparison.

For Sir Douglas had pulled out a real gem of an 'alarmed' expression and even appeared to be holding it too. Deep, angled eyebrows, coupled with a fantastic facial expression, it left Sir Horace inwardly mightily impressed and Thomas ever so slightly worried.

Silence and hesitation filled the air. Minutes seemed to pass although, in reality it was a few seconds, before Sir Douglas snapped out of his potentially award winning expression and responded to Thomas's declaration.

"I say, Thomas! That's a mighty big statement that you've just made there! May I ask just how you believe you can recoup this money?"

Thomas happily obliged, for these last few weeks had seen him set out on and achieve his finest work, since joining this ridiculous project.

"Two words, Gentlemen, two words. Corporate sponsorship."

Sir Douglas looked at Sir Horace who, in turn, looked at Thomas. Aware that there was a distinct possibility of yet another farcical situation taking hold, he decided to act quickly by way of a reply.

"Corporate Sponsorship? Thomas, I'm intrigued. Please explain what you mean."

Thomas gladly obliged.

"Well, Sir Douglas. A couple of weeks ago, I took it upon myself to see if there was any way in which we could cut down on our outlay and yet, maybe, add a little extra to the project. I knew, obviously, that there wasn't much in the coffers and that what there was, was being diminished at a fair rate of, erm, knots, if you pardon the pun. So, I started looking at what we had and what the world around us had and kind of married some of it up. By the world around us, I mean companies and products."

Feeling ever so slightly enthused by what Thomas was saying, Sir Horace moved to find out more.
"Go on, Thomas, I'm liking the sound of this. Please, proceed and tell Sir Douglas and myself what little delights you envisage!"
"Okay, there are a few deals in the offing and I'll outline them, briefly, to you both now:
Firstly, Pigeons. You're aware that there are two types in use. One type, ridiculously healthy, and the other ridiculously unhealthy. For the racing variety, we have already factored in mini gym equipment and air conditioning into their quarters and for the "Trafalgar" pigeons, we are installing several seed bars and smoking perches but, here's the thing. Why not get companies involved for these two areas? What I have lined up, barring the final say so from your good self, Sir Horace, is white sports vests for the racing pigeons…"

Sir Horace felt that he needed to jump in and question the young man, sat before him.
"White vests, Thomas? White vests? How the hell does kitting out our entire entourage of racing pigeons with white

315

vests bring in any money? Unless I'm sorely mistaken, wearing a white vest doesn't attract any income at all!"

Sir Horace felt very satisfied and professional with his quick and succinct assassination of the young man's ideas. This feeling didn't last very long as Thomas quickly finished what he was trying to say.

"It does if it has the "tick" logo of the sports giant "Nike" on it!"

"Nike?"

Thomas continued.

"Sir Horace. I have a rather substantial deal lined up with that company, whereby they will pay us a considerable amount of money if our racing pigeons where a white Nike vest with their slightly amended slogan on them."

A little uneasy with this developing thread, Sir Horace sought clarification.

"Thomas, dare I ask what the slogan is normally to be seen saying and what you or them, or whoever, is proposing?"

"Yes, Sir Horace, of course you can ask. Normally, in our every day human orientated world, the Nike slogan can/could/would/is seen to be "Just do it." Their creative team and myself have come up with, and this was after many hours of deliberation, "Just poo it!""

Sir Horace, now enthralled by the topic of

conversation, pushed for further clarification, as the excitement he now felt inside was clouding his ability to create the image in his mind. At present, the only thing he could conjure up was a bird, similar in appearance to that of a Dodo, wearing a football shirt. Alarmed, and somewhat agitated by his failure to muster a pigeon in his head, he pushed on regardless.

"Go on, Thomas, go on!"

Thomas, realizing that he was not only on a roll, but also most definitely in favour, pushed on, as invited. "Well, with that deal lined up, I felt I needed to look at something for the Trafalgar birds. A combination of a clothing giant and a somewhat antiquated slogan from the mid 80's combined to produce a rather classically styled, yet very apt item of apparel for our less than healthy crew members."

"So, to go with white vests, Nike and "Just Poo It!" we have…."

Sir Horace was edging, ever closer, to the edge of his seat.

"Well, I'd like you to picture the comparison, if you will. In the red corner, so to speak, we have a luxury themed, air conditioned, gym of excellence, populated by the finest athletic specimens of the pigeon populace, all wearing figure hugging, but breathable, white flying vests, emblazoned with a big black Nike tick logo and the slogan "Just poo it!" All the accompanying pillows and gym equipment will all carry the Nike signage."

Whereas, in the blue corner, so to speak, will be our less than perfect, ever so slightly unfit "Trafalgar" pigeons, complete with beards, eye patches, stumps and fags. These beauties will be kitted out in one-piece, Burberry patterned tank tops, and complete with the old British Rail slogan, "We're getting there." There are options for other corporate logos to be added to stumps and eye patches etc, but these are just ideas at the moment."

Sir Horace was, by now, thrilled with what he was hearing and pressed for more.

"Go, on, Thomas, please go on! This is just fabulous!"

"Why, thank you, Sir Horace! Ok, other possible deals, that are all lined up, bar the shouting or, in your case, the signing, are things such as the old Canon classic "Image is everything" or the Burger King favourite "We do it our way," and even the use of the British Army slogan, "Join the professionals," has been successfully negotiated and it's use agreed."

"These three slogans are ready to be emblazoned on all stumps and eye patches on board if, as just mentioned, you like the idea. Now, I know you're going to mention it, so

I'll just continue. Cigarettes. I'm thinking that you're thinking that we need a slogan on every cigarette on board and, I'd agree, yes we do. However, none of the aforementioned cigarette companies wanted in on any deals and so I lined up Cadburys instead."

A joint "Cadburys?" came back at Thomas. "Well, yes. The best I could muster was "Are you a fruit and nut case?" To be printed on every cigarette and smoking perch and ashtray. Total sum for all of these companies sponsoring the birds will be close to half a million." Sir Horace was having a good day. "Bloody hell, Thomas! That's bloody fantastic work!"

"Thank you, again, erm, Sir Horace, but I've not finished. That's just the birds. If you add the Andrex slogan "Soft, strong and very long" as well as the other Cadburys slogan "and all because the lady loves milk tray," to the oars then that is more income and, and this is my absolute favourite, Mumm Champagne."

There was a classic TV ad in the 70's or 80's, where a lady was launching a liner of some description. As it slid down the slipway she exclaimed, "Good heavens, this is Mumm Cordon Rouge champagne, that's far too good to waste on launching a ship!" The next thing you saw was the liner at sea with those very words painted repeatedly all around the ship. As a tribute to that very advertisement, myself and Mumm have been talking and have agreed a deal for it to be on our ship in fridge magnets, subject to signatures, of course!"

Sir Horace was now becoming a touch too enthusiastic and it was left to Sir Douglas to take control of the situation.

"Good work, although I am a little sceptical, shall we say? Whilst the money would be nice, I'm not sure about turning the most important vessel of our time into a bobbing advertising hoarding!"

Thomas, not wishing to be cut short, addressed Sir Douglas' concerns immediately.

"I understand your concerns, Sir Douglas, but please bear in mind that we're not talking about your average, technically gifted, floating killing machine here. We are, in fact, talking about the opposite. A craft so unstable, so technically retarded, so devoid of anything remotely advanced or, indeed seaworthy that we're aiming to bluff the entire planet into thinking we have something they don't. Why not add to their confusion by doing exactly what you wouldn't normally do with a warship, emblazon it in brightly coloured advertising slogans. All against the battleship grey or "Asteroid" grey? Why not add the word "confusion" to the words "deception" and "death trap?""

Almost in unison, both Sir Douglas and Sir Horace shrugged their shoulders and pulled a brief, but accepting Pacino-esque facial expression and it was Sir Horace who gestured for Thomas to continue once more with a rolling queen-esque wave of his hand.

"So, approximate total for everything mentioned so far is approaching seven fifty thousand but, there's more. You see, I was thinking. What happens if boredom sets in? I mean, with the accountants. What happens if, due to the wait for them to get their orders, they get bored? Can either of you suggest anything?"

Both Sir Douglas and Sir Horace sat staring at Thomas with blank faces, as though they were school children, confused in a lesson.
"Okay, here's what I've thought up, and run with for the last two weeks. Bingo!"
A joint, and rather sarcastic "Bingo?" came back at him and it was Sir Horace who felt that a sarcastic put down was in order.

"Bingo! Thomas. Bingo? Can I just clarify, at this point, that we are talking about the same specimen? The accountant. The noble, honest, patriotic backbone of British society? The esteemed and respectable Gentleman, who will row and power the most important vessel ever put to sea and who will do that with the utmost endeavour? Are we? I ask you? The humble, religious, respectable accountant? Are we talking of the same man?"

Sir Horace felt good. Of course, he wouldn't normally move to put anyone down, but he couldn't resist it on this occasion. Thomas, however, had his reply loaded and waiting in the chamber.

"Sir Horace, let me explain. But first, let me satisfy your quizzical mind. Yes, I am talking about the very same man as you and yes, I am talking about our beloved accountants and yes, I'm afraid that they have been close to boredom. Please take note that I said "close to" and not "were bored" or something similar."

"You see, as you are both aware, the accountant is a noble steed. Honest, reliable, God fearing and, above all else, hard working. Having spent quite some time around them in recent weeks, I felt that they were missing something. Something just wasn't quite there. Just a part of their day wasn't right. Sure, they threw themselves into training and the belief that they held and, indeed do still hold, for this whole project is truly inspiring, but something was missing."

Sir Horace, not satisfied with one shot across Thomas' bow, went for the second.

"Thomas, please spare us the analysis. What, in your professional opinion, are the accountants missing? What could they possibly need? I, and I'm sure Douglas here, really can't wait to find out. I say that because I can't think of anything. Douglas, can you? Can you honestly tell me that something is missing in their lives right now? Can you, Douglas, eh?"

Sir Horace felt a little guilty. He knew that there was absolutely no need for him to act in that way and speak with such sarcasm but, if the truth be told, he was actually frustrated that he couldn't guess the answer. Thomas' response, by way of giving him the answer, hit him, indeed both Sir Douglas and Sir Horace, right between the eyes, with the force of an express train. For, as soon as Thomas said his next word, it was obvious. And now he really felt guilty for speaking with such a tongue!
"Numbers!"

It was as if Sir Douglas and Sir Horace were in the middle of a pub quiz and listening to the answers to a previous round. Both let out a sigh. It was so obvious and yet neither of them had thought of it.
"Bloody hell, Douglas! Numbers! It's obvious, isn't it? Thomas, please elaborate."
Thomas, deciding not to either dwell on or highlight the fact

that Sir Horace had just shot himself in the foot with his sarcasm gun, proceeded with his explanation.

"Gentlemen. Accountants need numbers in their lives, just as they need their God. I have merely combined the two and created "Holy Bingo." Across the road, from the building in which we are currently sat, is a church. A church that, on a Thursday for the past two weeks, has been filled with our accountants playing "Holy Bingo.""

"The format is quite simple. They all file in, take a seat in the pews and accept a laminated card from the vicar. Although, that's precisely what he isn't, a vicar. The man in the robes, who looks like a vicar, is actually the owner of the fancy dress shop over by the station. By offering him the chance to dress up as a religious vicar-type person and put on a deep and very monotone voice, we are killing two birds with one stone. He has the chance to pretend to be a vicar…no questions asked, and we get someone to call the numbers, who looks religious. Anyway, the laminated cards are obviously in place of the service or what have you cards."

Whilst Sir Douglas nodded approvingly, it was Sir Horace who spoke up.
"Thomas. I mean, bloody hell! Simply fantastic! But what do they win?"
"Well, Sir Horace. After a few pretend prayers, to the God of

the balls, obviously led by our fancy dress shop owning "Bingo-Vic," the guys settle down to an afternoon of "full house" games. Each winner is praised by the Lord, and then given a voucher for a free sandwich and a cup of tea from the deli on the station concourse. It all works rather splendidly, even if I do say so myself."

"And this is what they've been missing….numbers?"

"Yes, Sir Horace. Well, actually, it's probably a little combination of numbers, activity, akin to what they would normally do, and something a little thought provoking."

"Just plain stunning. Let's do lunch!"

Enough was enough for Sir Horace. The routine of phoning for his driver and fake dusting, the now newly sited Nemo, before meeting said driver, complete with car, at the reception before entering and speeding off around the corner to the Cutty Sark and, indeed, the "Cutty Club," swiftly followed.

All in all, he pondered, a morning worthy of being a day. More than enough updates and more than enough deals. All he wanted now was to get three pints of lager ordered. He was mighty proud of his men, and he really wanted a game of 'Holy Bingo.' Next up was the launch. A wry smile developed, swiftly followed by a smug and very warm feeling within. These were happy days.

"Launch day!" declared a rather relaxed Sir Horace, as he slumped back into his official, bought in for the occasion, Government Issue, red leather armchair. Surprised by his sudden change of character and almost normal demeanour, Sir Douglas and Thomas thought it best that they find a spot in the other armchairs and do the same.

Walking from the doorway, where they had watched Sir Horace fall into the armchair, around the side of the seemingly oversized piece of furniture, they realised that Sir Horace had also installed a massively oversized TV, on which to watch the launch of the Ardilles. As the two men slumped into their respective armchairs, it was Thomas who sought clarification first.

"Can you explain to me, Sir Horace, why we are not at the launch?"

"Because, we're here."

"I can see that we're here, but why? Why are we here?"

"Because we're not there!"

"But why are we not there?"

"Because we're here!"

"I understand that we're not there, because we're here, but why are we here, slumped in leather armchairs, instead of being there to meet the Queen and launch our vessel, Sir?"

"Now, that's a good question, Thomas, my lad. One that I will endeavour to answer to my utmost best ability but, one that will only become clear, when the vessel hits the water."

"That is the most unhelpful and cryptic answer to a question that I have ever been given, Sir. With obviously all the respect etc etc!"

Sir Douglas became alarmed when there, right in front of his very eyes, Sir Horace took on a kind of Bob Marley meets Mr Bean persona. In an attempt to do a Jamaican accent, he'd overplayed it and the words "Thomas, chill man!" had actually sounded more like a cow in heavy fog, rather than the quintessentially controlled voice of the Reggae star.

It had all gone wrong in an instant and he watched as Thomas stood staring at Sir Horace in disbelief. Sir Horace, slightly overcome by what had just emanated from his mouth, felt a stare back was the best way to deal with it. This poker match of stares was becoming annoying, so Sir Douglas decided, there and then, to step in.

"Thomas, just accept what Sir Horace says and question him after the event. I have no idea either and am perfectly willing to accept that afterwards and not before, is the time to get answers."

A nod from Thomas and the stares were broken.

Having just watched Thomas sit down, Sir Horace made a suggestion.

"How about you wander into the kitchen and pour us three pints of lager, young Thomas, me lad?"

A huff and a puff and a quick "bloody hell!" thrown in for good measure, saw Thomas rise promptly from the chair he'd just sat in and head off towards the kitchen. All the while the TV had been on, but with the sound turned down. As Thomas trudged off towards the kitchen, Sir Horace reached for the remote control and turned the volume up.

The BBC reporter was plum in the middle of setting the scene:

"...and so here, alongside the North bank of Tower Bridge, a slipway has been built and, we are led to believe, the newest ship to enter service with the Royal Navy, or soon to be Floaty Boat Brigade, The H.M.S Osvaldo Ardilles, sits on it, ready for her big moment.

The crowds are growing increasingly larger and all are straining to get a view of, not only the impressively built slipway, but also the giant purple silk sheet that covers the Ardilles. I have to say, and I'm in no way an expert, but I have to say that, for a vessel so large, and I'm only going on the data sheet that I've been given, it doesn't appear to be very large under silk. If anything, I'd say very triangular in appearance."

Sir Horace was impressed and felt that his considered opinion of the reporter wouldn't be out of place.

"He's very sharp, that guy. He'll go far!"

Thomas caught this assessment as he returned from the kitchen, complete with a tray of three pints of lager.

"Why will he go far and why is he so sharp?"

Sir Horace, not wanting to give anything away mumbled a quick "oh, no reason," before reaching for a pint of lager from the tray and proposing a toast.

"I'd like to propose a quick toast to the Ardilles and all who sail in her!"

With that, he raised his glass in the air. Sir Douglas quickly followed suit and appeared to think nothing of it, whereas Thomas was ever so slightly suspicious. Alerted to some kind of shady goings on, he was now monitoring the every move and sound that Sir Horace made. Something, he'd decided, wasn't right. Rather than draw attention to his suspicions, Thomas quickly decided to slump back in the chair and just drink.

Meanwhile, the commentary of the sharp BBC reporter continued on screen. Cameras were panning around and showing the crowds around the launch area slowly starting to swell. A few different distance shots confirmed to Sir Horace that intrigue from the populace had, in turn, spawned interest for there, along the river banks of the Thames, was a constant and steady gathering of people. Each and every one of these, he thought to himself, have turned up there to see, or at least catch a glimpse of, the Ardilles. The voice of the reporter continued to comment on the weather, the crowds, the expectant Nation, and the duties of Her Majesty The Queen, due in the area shortly.

Alongside the slipway was a grand and rather pompous looking section of seating. Completely out of context with the launch, the slipway and The McJeffers Act itself, it was finished in a bright red cloth and fake gold furnishings. Each individual seat had fake gold inlay on it and the whole structure looked very awkward and out of place. As the camera panned across this gigantic lame duck of a structure, Sir Douglas saw it on the T.V and reacted first.

"Bloody Hell! What is that and who put it there?" Before anyone could answer, Thomas added his thoughts. "It looks like something out of a rap video. All fake and pompous!"

Sir Horace felt it would be a good idea to nip this one in the bud, as quickly as possible, and so promptly proclaimed, "I put it there!"

Shock and surprise were followed by a joint "Why?" from Thomas and Sir Douglas.

"Because we needed some seating for her Madge and old McJeffers and his gang."

A secondary and near identical joint "why?" came at him again.

"Because they all have to sit somewhere!"

Thomas took hold of the potentially game show-esque situation and moved to do all he could to stop this particular conversation from going south any further.

"But why? And where did it come from?"

"Oh, that bit is easy, Thomas! We needed seating for her Madge, as previously discussed, and all of our budget had been spent on accountants, Arthur Pounder, pigeons, people to care for the pigeons, fridge doors and their associated magnets etc etc. That entire situation was fine, but we still needed seating. Looking around and speaking to a few people "in the know," I was offered and then able to secure the loan or borrowing of said seating!"

"But where did it come from?"

"Oh, right! Well, erm, some very dodgy and, dare I say, talentless teenager, who sees himself as the next puffing daddy or whatever the guy's called, has just shot his first video in London. The budget was miniscule, but the impression was intended to be large. You know, fake gold, fake diamonds, tigers, big fur coats, private jets and opulent sections of seating, apparently!"

As this conversation continued to gather momentum, Sir Douglas noticed that the BBC reporter had also picked up on the seating and had directed the cameras in for a closer look of the structure. Alarmed at what he was seeing, Sir Douglas let out a panic stricken cry.

"Oh my bloody Lord! Are those…are those toilet seats in that stand?"

Sir Horace moved to explain the situation, but hadn't bargained on another panic stricken cry, before he'd been able to issue his explanation.

"Jesus! Is that gold leaf writing, on toilet seats, in that stand?"

"No, Douglas, it isn't gold leaf writing on toilet seats in that stand!"

"With all due respect, Sir Horace, I know gold leaf writing when I see it and that is…"

"FAKE, gold leaf writing on real toilet seats in that stand, Douglas."

Thomas, not wishing to ask anymore questions on this subject and glad that Sir Douglas had jumped in with such abandon, rose from his chair, with freshly emptied glass in hand, and headed for replenishments in the kitchen. Meanwhile, Sir Douglas pushed for more answers. He realised that he hadn't felt his heart racing so fast since first being introduced to the project.

"So, Sir Horace, can you please explain to me why I am looking at a large temporary seating structure, draped in the most god-awful red drapery and fake gold furnishings which, quite why, I have no idea, has toilet seats with fake gold inlay on them for seats, instead of actual seats?"

"Well, Douglas, as I have already said, I did the project proud by securing a large section of very expensive temporary seating for absolutely no cost to us at all. Unfortunately, what I didn't realize was that it had been used by an up and coming rap artist for his debut release, thus debut video. As is the usual thing with this kind of "artist," the name of the game was to shock. I admit that I didn't really grasp the true meaning of said debut release and simply received the seating with thanks."

On returning from the kitchen with more lager, the new Floaty Boat Brigades' drink, Thomas could not help but hear these words and instantly sought clarification on some of them, as he placed another tray of lagers on the table and sank back down into his chair.

"Woa, woa, woa! Stop right there please and rewind a bit!"

Sir Douglas instantly hated the fact that he was stumped. He was inwardly annoyed that Thomas had picked up on something that he hadn't. It was just like the early days of the project and he didn't like it.

As with the early days, he thought he'd best just go along with the conversation and add a few facial gestures which, would hopefully indicate to Thomas, that he was 'up with play.'

"What, exactly, would you like me to rewind to, Thomas, my boy?"

"Erm, actually, Sir Horace, I'd quite like you to rewind to the bit about "not really grasping the true meaning of the song," or whatever you said!"

A sudden reality took hold of Sir Horace, as he realised that he had been rumbled. Sir Douglas now sat with a rather smug look on his face. Finally up with play, he thought his best 'wonder how you are going to explain this one?' face would do the trick, although he was instantly brought crashing down by Sir Horace who exclaimed "Douglas, have you got wind?"

Before Sir Douglas could answer this most embarrassing of questions, Sir Horace moved to bring some sense of clarity and, more importantly, closure to this conversation. His explanation, however, meant that this objective was never going to be met.

"Ok, Thomas, ok! The name of the song, that I refer to, and the one of which, I admit, I never fully grasped the meaning of is, "messing in da stands.""

"Messing in da stands?"

"Yes, Thomas, "Messing in da stands!" I thought that the song title referred to a teenager's attempt to relay the story of his youth and growing up and experiencing all of its little foibles. Of how this guy, and his friends, took on the angst and pain of teenage years and all of it's problems, all within the setting of a football stadium."

"Did you now?"

"Yes, Thomas, I did! What I know now is that the writer and performer of the song didn't ever have the intention or, as it turns out, the ability to describe such a struggle and the name stroke song literally means or describes taking a dump in a stand. This is why we now have the Queen making her way through London, for the launch of the Ardilles, in order to sit on a toilet seat with fake gold leaf lettering."

Sir Douglas, all the time keeping one eye on the T.V, felt he'd best get the attention of his two colleagues, as the cameras and the reporter had really become interested in the seating by now.

"Erm, gentlemen, can I draw your attention away from discussing said seating in order to look at the T.V who, by some coincidence, are also discussing said seating?"

All three men's focus returned to the T.V coverage and the voice of the BBC reporter, who was cautiously describing the toilet seats and the gold leaf inscriptions on them.

"For some reason, and a reason unbeknown to myself, all of the traditional seating, usually found on these temporary stand type structures, has been removed and replaced with toilets and toilet seats. On each seat is some gold leaf lettering, but I am unsure of its exact meaning. On the lid, once in the down position, are the words "Hiding da mess!"

If you lift up the lid, to reveal the actual seat, you can clearly see the words "creating a mess!" And to complete the set, so to speak, if you lift up the seat, you can see that, again in gold leaf writing around the rim, are the words "smelling da mess!"

Now, as I have reiterated, I am unsure of what all of this means, but one cannot but feel concerned and somewhat alarmed that the Queen is coming to launch a ship and sit on a toilet seat in public. Surely, this cannot be right?"

Sir Douglas looked at his two colleagues with a very alarmed expression that, he was sure, would be identified as alarm and not as wind.

"Sir Horace, care to elaborate any more?"

"Douglas, stop panicking!"

"But, Sir! Her Majesty the Queen is very close to sitting on a toilet seat to launch our ship and, what's still not clear, but plainly obvious is, we're not there to greet her!"

"Douglas, my friend. Her Madge is in on the deal. She is fully aware of what is going on, so don't panic!"

Having just spat his lager all over the coffee table, Thomas felt a very dramatic "WHAT!" would best be the order of the day.

"Gentlemen, Gentlemen! Let me explain. We're not there, because the Ardilles is not there. If the Ardilles is not there, then why would we need to be? Her Majesty and Lord McJeffers are aware of both of these facts and have agreed that, for the sake of the Nation, they will attend and carry out their duties, as though nothing has happened."

Expecting questions and hysteria, Sir Horace had briefly stopped his explanation but, on looking at his two colleagues and finding them open mouthed and somewhat paralysed, he continued once more. All the while, in the back ground, the sharp BBC man continued to set the scene, apparently having had his fill of the seating, he had now moved on to describing the arrival of Her Majesty the Queen and the various dignitaries of the day. The cool, calm and ever so professional voice of the commentator continued to emanate from the T.V beside them.

"*Here is Her Majesty the Queen, resplendent in an ivory coloured dress and matching hat. I'm sure the likes of OK magazine have already managed to turn a simple step out of a car into a ten-page spread. Guided, as she is, to her seat in the rather red and overly opulent seating area by Lord McJeffers himself. The man, whose foresight and genius, has brought us all here today.*"

"Ok. As the sharp BBC man is saying, her Madge is about to take a seat on the loo in public, and that is ok. She will then say a few bits and bobs like she has done countless times before. But, and here's the "but," what she launches won't be the Ardilles. It will, if it goes to plan, be a large triangular shaped purple silk sheet. I would say, in fact I'm pretty sure, it's exactly the same as the one sitting on the slipway right now."

"She will speak and it will slide into the water. The official line will be that it is still a top secret vessel and so everyone will just have to be happy that they've seen a large purple sheet float by. That is the plan. I'm going to ask if there are any questions, although I know there will be. Thomas, you're mouth is slightly less of a dribbling mess than Douglas,' so why don't you go first?"

It was certainly true that Thomas was ever so slightly more in control of his mouth than Sir Douglas and, as he quickly regained his composure, he thought of a few things he wanted to say.

"So, firstly, why? And, erm, secondly, why? Realistically, all of my questions, that I would like to put to you, Sir Horace, involve the word "why?""

"Right, ok then! The Ardilles is potentially, a very unstable vessel. I think, in fact I'm sure, that you will both agree."

Waiting for a nod or an accepting gesture from either or both of his colleagues, which didn't materialise, he continued.

"What we couldn't afford was a public sinking immediately after launch. So, with that in mind, we put the Ardilles in at Christchurch three days ago. The whole of the harbour mysteriously contracted the plague and shut down under quarantine conditions. She has spent three days floating in the water, under test."

Thomas moved to question Sir Horace in an almost sarcastic manner.

"Under test, Sir Horace? Let me guess! A test to see how long it can remain, undetected, as a giant floating mass of purple silk? Or, how long it can withstand the onslaught of the plague, currently enveloping the harbour all around it? Or what, exactly???"

On seeing that frustration was clearly taking hold of the young man, Sir Horace quickly moved to clarify a few things.

"Ok, Thomas. The Ardilles has been floating in Christchurch harbour for three days now, in order to assess two things. Firstly, whether she sinks and secondly, if she doesn't, does she take on any water. The answers to these questions are as follows: No, she hasn't sunk and, remarkably, no, she hasn't taken on any water. This means that, as of 0800 hours tomorrow, she is on full sea trials and you, Gentlemen, can take up your posts in a further three days time, if she remains afloat and dry!"

Stunned by what they had just heard, Thomas and Sir Douglas snapped out of their delirium and instantly went to the opposite end of the spectrum, becoming highly animated with almost verbal diarrhoea. Sir Horace moved to calm the two men down, as their over exuberance had caused the volume level in the room to go sky high.

"Gentlemen, Gentlemen! Please! I understand your excitement but, please, let us have some calm restored to proceedings!"

Without waiting to finish, or even start, his next lager, Thomas walked off towards the kitchen for another. Once peace and tranquillity had been restored and all three men had returned to their respective armchairs, all eyes re-focused on the sharp BBC man's commentary, continuing unabated from the slipway next to Tower Bridge.

"And now…with Her Majesty The Queen and all of the respective dignitaries seated on their toilet seats, the ceremony can begin. Here to start proceedings with a specially written sea shanty entitled "Oh Lord, what have thy done?" is the band of the Royal Marines."

"Very apt!"

"Yes, Douglas, it is. I wrote it!"

Sir Douglas was surprised at how musical his boss was and that he'd never even had an inkling of this being the case. Thomas chose to dig a little deeper.

"Are there any words to this sea shanty, Sir Horace?"

"Erm, well, only a few, but not until later and certainly not in the version the band of the Royal Marines play!"

On T.V, the band played on a little longer before ending in an almighty crescendo of symbols and drum rolls to fade. The commentator, having taken his voice to smooth and deep over easy, continued with his voice over.

"And now, following a blessing by the Archbishop of Canterbury, Her Majesty the Queen will read a poem of the seas before officially naming the vessel."

Sir Horace, Sir Douglas and Thomas found themselves standing in silence, whilst watching each every move made by each and every person on the screen in front of them. Sir Douglas made a mental note not to buy in leather armchairs for any successive launches, as people seemed to prefer standing. Mental note made, his concentration returned to the T.V in front of them. All the while, the chocolaty smooth voice over continued.

"Having given his blessing to this, the newest craft to serve in Her Majesty's Navy or Floaty Boat Brigade, the Archbishop of Canterbury now steps aside and makes way for Her Majesty the Queen to step up to the microphone and address the Nation, indeed the World."

"There's a slight cross wind blowing, which is just doing enough to ruffle the triangular lines of the purple silk sheet covering, we are led to believe, the Ardilles. Her Majesty stands up and walks away from her toilet, to where

the microphone is located. Accompanied, as ever, by Lord McJeffers of Beckenham, who is assisting the Queen with various notes and is even now, holding her handbag. I can see the headlines tomorrow; "Lord Mcjeffers and his maam bag!" Her Majesty composes herself before speaking, as silence falls all around…"

Sir Horace, aware of what was to come, chuckled and couldn't help but spill the beans.

"This is going to be hilarious! Bless her! She's been practicing this all week!"

Unsure of what he was on about, Thomas and Sir Douglas chose to ignore him and watch on, as with seemingly everyone else, in silence.

" The Lord giveth…and the Lord taketh away. I name this ship H.M.S Osvaldo Ardilles."

Turning to question Lord McJeffers, she continued.

"I say, McJeffers. Wasn't Ardilles the fellow that said "give me the ball and I'll do this, and this, and this and goal!" In that football film?"

A rather embarrassed Lord McJeffers could be heard mumbling, "Erm, No, maam and your microphone is still on!" The realisation, that she had been overheard by the entire planet, failed to faze the monarch, who simply shrugged her shoulders and continued on the subject.

"I'm sure it was him you know. The Brazilian chap who beat Bobby Moore at Poker in 1970."

Again, mumblings from Lord McJeffers was met by further proclamations from Queen Elizabeth.

"They escaped from the Germans you know. By going down the plug hole or something very, very similar!"

Whilst he had been in on the situation and had, indeed, rehearsed the launch at Buckingham Palace with Her Majesty, it had actually only been the lines up to and including "this, and this, and this and goal!" Up to and including that bit, McJeffers was comfortable, now, as the Monarch tore into some kind of stand up routine before his very eyes, Lord McJeffers of Beckenham wanted to run and hide under the gigantic purple silk sheet, currently catching the breeze before him.

An accentuated clearing of his throat hadn't even interrupted Her Majesty and so another more violent attempt had stopped her in her tracks and had also tore through the microphone system. Believing it to be the signal that they were waiting for, the staff on hand to pull the levers and dislodge the giant wooden buttresses that were in position to keep the giant purple silk sheet on the slipway promptly pulled levers and swung heavy mallets at giant buttresses.

In only a few seconds, the giant purple-sheeted framework began to slide down the slipway and into the water, much to the delight of the waiting crowds. McJeffers could be clearly seen on TV reeling away in an uncomfortable embarrassment, whereas Her Majesty appeared to walk nonchalantly back to her toilet, lift the lid and seat up to reveal "smelling Da mess!" and walk off down the steps towards her car. McJeffers, having seen this, scurried off after her, in order to assist and open car doors.

Meanwhile, watching from the Floaty Boat Brigade HQ, Sir Horace began to roar with laughter.

"Oh she's a beauty! That was priceless! She absolutely deserves to award herself a medal for that. Absolute GENIUS!!!"

Sir Douglas and young Thomas stood dumbfounded. Not quite sure if their respective brains had actually managed to compute what had just played out on National television, they both found the going quite hard. Thomas spoke first.

"Is that acceptable, Sir Horace?"

"Is what acceptable, young man?"

"Having the Queen perform some kind of stand-up routine live on TV!"

"Oh, of course it is. Her Madge has just done this country an absolute world of good by doing what she has just done!"

Angry in a fashion similar to how he felt about the Mary Rose, Thomas hissed back "And just how to you come to that conclusion, Sir Horace?"

"Well, Thomas, she has just made people think about the film industry and the gaming industry and Bobby Moore and the Germans and the War and toilets and…"

"Ok, OK! Enough! But, we have just watched Her Majesty the Queen make herself look senile in front of the world!"

"Nonsense, young Thomas! The Queen has just performed a routine of pure comedy gold. Absolutely brilliant stuff from her Royal self. She has taken the emphasis off of the boat itself and put it onto the name…and footballers who never even had anything to do with it. I bet if you ran a survey in amongst the crowd there now, you'd find a high percentage of them wanting to find out if Pele played Bobby Moore at poker in 1970!"

"But she's the Queen! She shouldn't be doing that sort of stuff!"

Meanwhile, in the background, the smooth voiced commentator continued with his voice over.

"And as Her Majesty departs, so does the Ardilles, albeit under giant silk and purple cover! We are led to believe that she is still designated "Top Secret" and so will be towed away, complete with giant silk and purple cover, to a

destination down river. As the Ardilles makes it's way along the Thames, swarms of people have stayed on in order to wave and cheer as the giant purple triangular structure is towed past. Huge cheers greet her as she floats on by. I can honestly say that I have never seen this much support and appreciation for a purple triangle. Simply amazing..."

Reaching for the remote control, Sir Horace turned down the volume and, after dropping the controller onto the coffee table, rubbed his hands with glee.

"Gentlemen, I need to go to the Palace, to congratulate her Madge on a scintillating performance. You guys can finish up here and then report to Christchurch in three days time. From there on in you will be on board pretty much all of the time."

"There will be sea trials being conducted without you – in case she sinks at sea, and if she doesn't, then you guys will be on board in three days time to continue said trials. Once these have been completed, you will set sail for the shipping lanes between France and us. Your mission, to sniff out trouble and defeat it!"

With his Churchill-esque speech over, Sir Horace saluted both of his colleagues and then walked off, through the door and into the dark corridors beyond. With both Thomas and Sir Douglas ever so slightly mystified by the

347

entire goings on, both on the TV and in the room, there were only three things to do. Tidy up, turn off and go home.

When all of these were completed, the two men left the HQ and walked off into the afternoon sunshine to wait for their car. With their minds on many other things, they were in no hurry to get anywhere. Once inside the car, both fell asleep, almost instantly. The pressure of another day taking it's toll, for they both knew that it was time to set sail in what McJeffers had created.

Chapter Nineteen – All at sea

With the ridiculous launch now almost a distant memory and a week of sea trials behind them, Thomas stood on the bridge of the Ardilles, pondering his life to date. This pondering had been short lived, as the news had reached him that the Italian vessel, Signore Del Piero, was nearby. Arming himself with a pair of binoculars, he walked outside onto a viewing platform and began to search the cold, unforgiving sea that surrounded the ship.

As he gradually widened his search, he became bored of seeing grey wave after grey wave and found that, within minutes of this tedium, his mind had begun to wander. Nothing, not even a seagull, broke the repetition and monotony of grey wave after miserable grey wave. He felt as if it was now down to him to find this ship, as if now that the message had been passed to him, everyone else had gone to the canteen, leaving him and his wandering mind to wrestle with the sea and horizon for an answer.

The legs beneath him trembled and he was unsure if this was due to vibration or just plain fear. Not fear of the Del Piero, or indeed the finding of, but the fear of the vessel he stood on, for it creaked and groaned with every passing wave. It was moments like this, he thought, just those odd, infrequent split seconds, where he wondered why he'd tied himself to this particular proverbial track. If he thought about it long enough he was sure he'd recollect many other tracks he could've laid down on but, here he was and, anyway, enough of that. He was here, on board, and trembling. Another series of creaks and groans and an anxious peer over the side explained why.

Looking over the starboard side he could see many oars, all seemingly in sync with one another, but all under the influence of grey men in grey suits. More or less as one, these oars would rise out of the water and arc forwards, water escaping from every blade at every given opportunity, before they crashed back down into the sea again to begin another stroke. And with six hundred oars again projecting the Ardilles forward, came another series of creaks and groans. He quizzed himself why such force and violent motion seemed audible only when you stuck your head over the side. Step back and you only heard the creaks and the groans. Step forward and the sea grasped your senses and shook you again.

He went to walk back to his viewing platform, but another thought grabbed him, causing him to stop, turn back towards the edge and, with one pace forward, lean over to see those blades again. There it was, the same rhythmic cycle that he'd just witnessed. Once, twice, three times then there! There it was, the reason he turned back to look at the oars. The whole project, everything that had happened and all, summed up and represented by one simple action. He watched the cycle for the fourth time and yep, there it was. The water seemed to be all too ready to demonstrate its impatience to leave the oars, to disassociate itself with the Ardilles.

The minute the blades rose out of the sea in one violent uplifting surge, the water seemed to be in a rather large hurry to jump back into the grey expanse. If he hadn't been caught up in this whole Ardilles affair then he would've taken this to be a natural phenomenon but, seeing as he was standing on one of the two newest natural disasters in the world, that water just seemed to represent how he felt about the whole damned thing. To him, the water leaving the oars seemed to be doing more than that, it was jumping ship. Alarmed by his discovery, and feeling very alone, he returned to his place on the viewing platform.

As he scanned the bleak and depressing horizon for the idiotic boat that the Italians had so desperately rushed into service, he could not help but think of the film 'The Cruel Sea.' That classic film, so rich in British 'hullabaloo,' seemed to have become the departmental bible. Members of the team seemed to be walking round acting out the thing, saying things like "Snorkers! Good-o!" and "There are men in the water!" He had watched it once or twice, in civilian life, but now knew it off by heart, as it had become an essential reference guide.

A classic example of this was how things were now seemingly playing itself out on the bridge, to his left. Whilst he stood, eyes glued to eyepieces, dutifully searching for 'the enemy,' over to his left stood a rather excited Sir Douglas, energetically playing with a fake communication pipe, 'linked' to the lower decks.

At first, Thomas had heard a rattling of, what sounded like a kettle lid and a chain, then "Bridge, depth charge!" After this came the rattle of kettle lid and chain again. The second time this audible sequence occurred, he just had to stop looking through those damned binoculars and look at Sir Douglas. Sure enough, there stood Sir Douglas, at the very front of the bridge.

Was he also scanning the horizon through the big and very awkward bridge windows of the Ardilles? Was he heck! He was actually too busy to look for the foe, as his mind was engaged playing with one of those many black plastic pipes that rose out of the floor. These pipes, that were just a couple of inches in diameter and were attached to the front wall of the bridge beneath its windows, were nothing more than lengths of domestic waste pipe, fixed there to mimic the communication pipes on the bridge of the 'Compass Rose,' the star of The Cruel Sea.

Thomas now remembered that Sir Douglas had mentioned several times previously that his favourite bit of the film was the bit where the officer opened a 'pipe' and sent the address "Bridge, depth charge!" down it. Now, it all became clear. The minute anything out of the norm happened, Sir Douglas took the opportunity to act out his favourite scene. Except, he didn't have a communication pipe, he had a length of black plastic waste pipe, and he didn't have a lid of a communication pipe to open, instead he had an old kettle lid affixed to the top of the pipe with a small length of chain.

Thomas thought the whole scene smacked of an amateur production and that, any minute, the scenery behind Sir Douglas would fall down. Maybe, just maybe, the guy standing at the wheel of the Ardilles would trip and fall through some curtains. It didn't really matter anyway, as the wheel of the Ardilles wasn't actually connected to anything other than a 'Left' and 'Right' sign down below, via a hastily attached cable.

He then looked around at the disjointed, unorganised

and profoundly un-sound surroundings that he found himself in and decided that, actually, what Sir Douglas was repeatedly doing, fitted in quite nicely. How could any actions seem bizarre when they were happening on board a half Trireme, half fridge door vessel, rowed by six hundred accountants? Thomas' eyes returned to the grey seas and the search for the Del Piero. All the while his eyes searched and searched his ears were subject to "Bridge, Depth Charge" over and over again. The repetition was relentless and was only broken by a positive sighting of the Italian vessel. "Del Piero off the port bow!"

Not only did this signal a frenzy of activity on the bridge, but it also stopped Sir Douglas dead in his tracks. Looking through the bridge from where he stood, Thomas could see several men running to join their colleague on the platform from where the vital sighting had been made. In no time at all came the confirmation that everyone hoped for.
"Sighting confirmed...Range...three point four miles"
Sir Douglas listened intensely.
"Heading....about ten o'clock..."
Even compass bearings had seemingly succumbed to the McJeffers Act.

Thomas had now joined Sir Douglas at the front of the bridge, looking out of the windows on the Port side.

Having heard so much about this boat, both were eager to see it for themselves. Both men looked through their respective binoculars, Government Issue, and closed in on the floating enigma in the distance at the same time. It was Thomas who spoke first.

"Christ almighty! It can't be!"

Sir Douglas, keen to present the demeanour of a military man of many years service, who knew a lot about this particular subject, tried to keep his answer composed. "That, Thomas, my friend, is the Signore Del Piero. For all intents and purposes, she is a bloody large gondola. I would hazard a guess and say that they didn't bother to install any oarsman along the hull of the vessel and that there would appear to be an overcrowding issue at the rear."

"Now, you don't say!"

The sarcasm was the result of seeing the Del Piero, and, in particular, the most obvious design floor facing the Italian craft.

The Signore Del Piero. A very large and extremely oversized gondola of some three hundred feet long with, apparently, two hundred odd feet of this protruding at a sixty-ish degree angle out of the water. The pure and simple design of the basic gondola meant that the gondolier would stand at the back of the craft and propel it forwards. With one man standing on the aft of the vessel and one or two maybe sitting in the middle, the craft was flat in the water and able to move around in it with no problem at all. In this condition, the gondola was and is a proven and reliable watercraft.

However, on seeing the H.M.S Osvaldo Ardilles on T.V, the Italian Government had decided that that kind of thing was the deal for them, and was nothing other than the way forward. In a rash act of National pride and complete ignorance, strikingly similar to that of it's British counterpart, it had been decided that Italy needed a presence of this magnitude in the water, and it needed it now. It had taken three days to decide what to do, to design, to steal parts and to build the vessel. It had then taken a morning to decide how to man the thing and, after lunch, the lucky participants were rounded up.

At this point in the Signore Del Piero timeline, a trip to Venice would've been a very bad move indeed. Anyone waiting for a water taxi would've been ok but, anyone fancying a majestic trip around Venice in a Gondola, the very essence of culture, would've found that there was an abundance of gondolas available for hire, but no Gondoliers at all. Every single one of them had been rounded up and charged with "bringing the water into disrepute."

Quite what this meant was never explained to them.

What was explained was that, either they went to prison for thirty-five years, with no questions allowed and no chance of early release, or they joined the crew of "an exciting and vital ship," which was already "the envy of the world!"

The exact figures were unknown, as the Italian Government did not wish the world to know how many Gondoliers chose prison but, what is known, is that many did. The rest were promptly shoved aboard the Del Piero with a few rations and a monogrammed handkerchief and told to "get to sea and find the Ardilles!" Quite what they were supposed to do once, or even if, they found her, no one knew, but get to sea they did.

However, before they could "get to sea," they and the Del Piero had to be given a fighting chance of staying afloat long enough to clear the harbour. Clearly, launching from anywhere in Italy wasn't going to see the Italian flagship find anything other than water rushing into the hull within minutes of casting off. With this in mind, The Italian Government flew the Del Piero to France and assembled the sections at Calais. The hastily assembled crew followed shortly afterwards. To the French locals, the scene was merely an interruption to their smoking and games of boulles.

With Italian men being extremely proud by nature, every single one of the gondoliers aboard the Signore Del

Piero wanted the honour of propelling her in the name of their country. At first, one had made a move for the platform at the rear, whilst the majority of the others stood and took in their new surroundings. He was nearly there when he was spotted by a few, who shouted some questions at him. This alerted a few more and, when he didn't answer, pandemonium broke out as hundreds rushed for the same spot.

Soon enough, the Del Piero had raised her bow about sixty degrees out of the water as the dance of the gondoliers broke out on board. Not content with pushing and shoving each other, the gondoliers had all crammed themselves on top of the platform before commencing their arguments. With all ropes cast off from the jetty, the Signore Del Piero had set sail at a rather frantic pace in front of the world. All of this, and not a hint of stability to be seen.

About two miles out and her bow was still about sixty degrees out of the water. There were still hundreds of gondoliers standing on a platform made for maybe fifty. There was still no hint of stability, but there was an air of teamwork in the offing. Steadily, tempers subsided and several hundred Italians began to work together. Inside the Del Piero, this created a picture of pride, Italian spirit and determination. Outside, in stark contrast, the picture was one of a dangerously unseaworthy craft waddling around in the water. It was this image that now filled the binoculars of both Thomas and Sir Douglas.

"Christ Almighty!"

"No, Thomas, Del Piero"

"Yes, I'm aware that that is the Del Piero, but, Christ almighty! That ship is more unstable than ours!"

"Absolutely, Thomas, my friend. If ever there was a result of testing and superior design, then it is surely the Ardilles." Sir Douglas felt proud.

"Yes, I agree, but only when the comparison is with that thing!"

Thomas felt alarmed.

Sir Douglas was on his toes, out of the blocks and at the top of his game. It was a most unusual site that Thomas now witnessed. He'd never really seen Sir Douglas so motivated or his wits so sharpened and yet, there he stood, focused.

"Ok, Thomas, I suggest we haul that translator chap you found, up here so we can brief him. He is a major player in Plan A. Plan A is to send over a Trafalgar pigeon with a greeting. A greeting in our finest Italian."

Thomas felt a slight amendment to this plan might have a more favourable outcome.

"May I suggest, Sir Douglas, that we don't send over a pigeon as they may regard it as a delicacy and eat it."

"Good God man! Have you ever seen or heard of a Pigeon Pizza?"

Thomas shook his head.

"No, well neither have I! They are Italians my friend. Men of style, a Nation of quality, well, sort of, or maybe not. Anyway, their Army is one of the finest in the world, nope, was thinking of the Isle of Wight rear-guard there. Actually, I think their Army wear trainers on their feet and are the fastest runners in the world!"

Thomas felt it about the right time to stop the mad mumblings of Sir Douglas and stamp his mark on the situation.

"Ok, Sir Douglas, here's what I suggest. Write down what we want to say, "Hello, Del Piero, how are you?" that sort of thing, throw it under the nose of Brian and send it over on the leg of a Trafalgar pigeon. What do you say?"

Sir Douglas, who was still going through his views of Italy and its people, just mumbled a brief "OK" and carried on with his opinions. Not needing a second invitation, Thomas was off down the heavily polished stairway to the corridors and rooms below. The air at the bottom of the stairs was thick with the smell of varnish, as everything on board had been saturated in the stuff.

Quite frankly, it stank. A few sharp left and right turns led him into the main corridor on the Ardilles, which ran directly above the accountants in the engine room. He tried to keep up his brisk pace, but the motion of the ship on the waves meant that he got buffeted a fair bit. But, eventually, he made it to his destination, the canteen stroke rest room. There, sitting in the far corner, sat one Brian Allcroft.

A rather tall and skinny specimen, Brian Allcroft, twenty-three and single was, and always had been, a shell of a man. He had lacked confidence in himself and his abilities from a very early age. This characteristic had, unfortunately, made him a prime target for the bullies and the beatings that school life always nurtured.

His presence appeared very much the same throughout his teens and early twenties, which meant that girls and later women, kept away. He was known to Thomas through the school life they had shared and so, when the subject of finding an Italian translator at short notice, became top of the 'to do' list, Thomas had easily remembered the geeky kid from school, who had seemingly been good at Italian.

An offer had been made by Thomas and, with no

quality of life to speak of for Brain, been accepted readily. A quick briefing on what sort of lines to prepare and a date on which to report for duties had seen that bit of business closed nicely.

"Brian, hello mate."

" Oh hi, Thomas, how's things?"

"Pretty good, but about to get weird! We've just spotted the Del Piero and we need some of your linguistic mastery please."

"Great, what do you need?"

"Well, I was thinking something along the lines of "Hello, Del Piero, The H.M.S Ardilles offers peaceful greetings on this day." Or something like that. Perhaps getting it flowing a bit more. Mention Mother Nature and stuff. You know what I mean."

" Great, I'll get that written out right now and bring it up to the bridge shortly."

"Thanks, my friend. The boys are preparing a Trafalgar Pigeon as we speak."

Conversation completed, Thomas turned and left the rest room, heading back to the bridge. Brian, on the other hand, exited the rest room as well, but headed to his quarters in order to retrieve his writing set. Once retrieved, he returned to the rest room in order to sit and compose this most vital of messages.

Up on the bridge the excitement continued. Thomas had re-joined Sir Douglas, who was relentlessly peering through his binoculars. On picking up his own set, he had not taken long to re-focus on the target, still bobbing about a few miles away.

"What are your thoughts, Sir Douglas?"

"Well...I wouldn't want to be the pigeon about to fly over there. How the hell is he supposed to land on that thing?"

Not quite the line of conversation he was expecting, he nodded in agreement nonetheless. Thomas could see that some of the crew, assigned to look after the pigeons, had completed their task and now stood there at attention. One of the crew stood, holding in his hands, a rather dirty looking bird. Attached to its leg was a small leather cylinder that Thomas could see was empty.

Just at that moment, Brian appeared on deck with a piece of paper in his hands. The sea breeze was catching the paper, which thrashed around violently in his hand as a result. Thomas noted that Brian was holding on for dear life. A quick fold and roll, made with military-esque precision, and the piece of paper was small enough to be fed into the cylinder. With his task complete, Brian stepped away from the pigeon detail and took up a favourable position a few meters back along the ship where he then leant on the side.

Thomas, still watching his every move, had decided that leaning on the side of the ship appeared to be a good idea. For him, mirroring this posture seemed to make the stresses and the strains of the impending situation simply melt away. By leaning on and over the edge of the Ardilles, Thomas somehow felt calmer and, he realised, a lot less nervous about how the approaching confrontation with the Del Piero would play out. He was rather enjoying this sense of calmness that gripped him.

Suddenly, a quick glance downwards changed all that. He had realised that a lot of the squeaks and groans, now taken for granted on the Ardilles, had ceased and this glance downwards at the sea had confirmed the reason for this. There below him, and between him and the sea itself, sat a section of the oars that powered the Ardilles. For, what felt like the first time in his memory, all the oars were stationary. All the oars appeared to be accountant-less and abandoned, which was exactly what they were, as down below decks pretty much all of the crew had left their stations and rushed over to any vantage point on the port side, which they could find. At this point everyone wanted a chance to see the Del Piero before she sank.

Nearby, Sir Douglas was still peering through his

binoculars relentlessly. He had issued the "stop engines" command, without ever removing his face from them, so strong was his desire to win the impending confrontation. He had the Del Piero in his sights and that's exactly where it was going to stay. With a hawk like stare he followed her every move. Meanwhile, approximately three miles away, the Signori Del Piero tossed and turned its way from here to there. No set course and no real stable method of control, she still had between two and three hundred proud, but panic-stricken gondoliers on board, with each and every one of them fighting for the honour of steering the ship.

As the H.M.S Ardilles prepared to launch a "confront and greet" mission, the Signori Del Piero continued to bob about in the relatively calm seas. Sir Douglas wondered to himself if the situation would've got this far had the seas been choppy? Surely, he reasoned, they would be conducting a search and rescue mission now, rather than what they were actually about to start? In all his years of loyal service, he had never seen such an unstable craft as what currently filled his binoculars field of vision. It was, quite simply, absurd.

Chapter Twenty – The meeting

The Del Piero rocked from stern to bow and side to side as every man on board struggled for his own personal space and piece of fame and glory. All eyes were focused on each other, with each man desperately trying to keep every other man in his sights. It was a scene reminiscent of a Wild West bar, as men to the left stared down men to the right and men by the bow tried to stare down men at the stern.

Hundreds still struggled for control of the excessively large gondola oar that powered her. There was an air of mistrust hanging over them. For a few brief minutes, as they had left port, there had been a spell of teamwork on board, but this had long since vanished and a kind of stand off had begun. With so much staring going on, the Trafalgar pigeon flew towards its target completely unnoticed.

Unfit, unshaven and with a peg leg, the pigeon was finding the going very tough. Just about three miles to cover and with the added weight of the leather carry case and its contents, it seemed to take an age for the inaugural pigeon to be launched from the H.M.S Ardilles, to reach it's target. Having battled all of this and a slight head wind, Sir Douglas and all of those on board the Ardilles, watched through their respective binoculars as the peg-legged pigeon reached the

Del Piero.

Having touched down with a thud of peg leg on wood and a huge cough-come-clearing-of-the-lungs, the pigeon sat perched on a handrail watching in amazement. It was just thinking to itself, if only it'd packed some cigarettes for the journey, when it was finally spotted. The spotting of the pigeon took the chaos on board to the next level. "ey,ey,ey…eets a pigeon!"

The first man to make the spot triumphantly declared to anyone that could hear him. Repeated "ey…ey" cries eventually found it's intended audience as, at first one, then ten, then twenty Italian gondoliers joined in the declaration. Soon there was a huge chorus of "ey,ey,ey!" Within minutes a natural leader had emerged from within the ranks of the gondoliers. "ey,ey,ey…shuddup everybody…shuddup!"

The rest of the crowd responded by trying to calm everyone else down. In doing so the pigeon sat startled with bulging eyes as a massive wave of "ssssssssshhhhhhhhhhhhhhhhh" rose and fell on board. The natural leader, one Alberto Nesta, seized his moment for good and started to issue instructions to those others on board.

"Guiseppe, da pigeon….picka da bird up and checka

whats in the poucha.."

Guiseppe, the man nearest to the pigeon, accepted the order and approached the bird. As he got nearer he could see, for the first time, the actual physical condition and appearance of the bird. An alarming cry left his lips...

"Holy Mary, Mother Theresa..."

Alberto heard and saw the anguish of Guiseppe and called out to comfort him.

"wadda eez eet, Guiseppe. Are you okaya?"

"eeza godda stump...da bird, eeza godda stumpa...and a beard....da bird, eeza godda stumpa and a beard....wadda da hell?"

With this proclamation came a collective gasp from all those on board. Alberto, keen to get to the bottom of things, thought some searching questions might help. He decided Guiseppe would be the recipient.

"Guiseppe, where de ell deed da birda come from?"

"Alberto, ee come from da sky!...where deed you thinka ee come from, eh? Are you stupido?"

Trying to keep calm, and not allow the presence, of a rather unkempt looking pigeon, bring the whole sense of order crashing down, Alberto tried again, but from a slightly different angle.

"Guiseppe, looka at da state of da ting...ee is a shagged, ee asn'ta flown far. Nowa, I aska again, where as da bird come from?"

Almost as one, the impending situation hit home to every man on board, as each and every one of them rushed to an available vantage point and began to scan the horizon for any clue as to just where this bird had come from. Not quite as organized as those on board the Ardilles, the men rapidly realised that a complete lack of any binoculars or optical aids was proving to be a massive hindrance.

Approximately two hundred proud Italians manned the perimeter of the Del Piero, looking at the cold, grey sea, that lay all around them. In a strange way, the presence of the pigeon had had a positive effect on the occupants of the oversized gondola. For up until the moment peg leg had touched wood, they had been just that, occupants. Now, with Alberto assuming the Captains role and Guiseppe happily slotting in as his number one, these occupants were suddenly becoming a crew. Alberto called out again to Guiseppe.

"Ey, Guiseppe. Maybe you wanna put some gloves on first before you toucha dat thing, eh!?!"
The reply was swift, proud and ignorant.
"No, no, no…Iya am Italian…proud Italian man. My country, eet build many fine and beautiful things with eez and err ands. My ands are immune to dirty pigeon, so I no

need gloves. Besides, there are no gloves on boarda…"

Declaration made, Guiseppe Alcante of Venice, Italy, stepped forward, spat on his hands, then scooped up the pigeon from the handrail and carried it half the length of the gondolier to where Alberto stood. Seeing the feathered visitor up close and personal sent a shiver of disgust down Alberto's body.

"Jeeeeeez, eet isa disgusting. Mama mia, looka at da stayte of eet. Get da message, Guiseppe, and then send eem on is way. Dirty birda…shoo, shoo!"
Guiseppe reached down and undone the small leather case, strapped to the leg of the pigeon. On opening the lid he saw a small, rolled up piece of paper and removed it. After handing the note to Alberto he thrust the pigeon upwards shouting, "shoo pigeon, you stink!" The pigeon, unimpressed with the rudeness of the Italians, was glad to leave and began his not so rapid return to the Ardilles.

Before Alberto and Guiseppe had had a chance to unroll the message, pandemonium was breaking out on board again as the proud and competitive nature of the Italian man took hold once more. Each wanted to be the first to spot whatever they were looking for and so men began declaring that they had spotted whatever they were supposedly trying to locate.

"There…Dat ting there. I see it firsta"

This declaration was met with a derisory comment.

"You idiot…that is a wave!"

Then another.

"I see it, I see it…I am proud Italian man!"

Was met by an equally derisory one.

"mama mia!...are you stupid? That is the sky!"

And so it went on, seemingly louder each time. For a moment, the spectacle of it over took the more pressing task at hand as both Alberto and Guiseppe stood watching as these ridiculous declarations and corrections began coming from all over the place. The conversations began to get really loud but, before they could reach a crescendo, Alberto, without looking up from twiddling the still unopened message between his fingers shouted, "DA BIRD!"

An almost unanimous "Eh?" came back at him.

Tutting loudly, he looked up and shouted once more.

"As anyone of you been a watching where da fatty pigeon go to?"

Surveying the faces looking back at him, he was distressed to see so many blank expressions.

"Jeesus! Da bird, ee eez fat eh? Ee eez unfit eh? Ee not a fly very a far before ee av art attack anda fall into de sea, yes?"

Nope, still blank expressions.

"Wat fatty bird fly to is a nearby as fatty can't fly very far. Sooooooooooo…."

Gestures with his hands began to encourage those before him to join in. From the starboard side mid ships came a voice willing to take up the challenge.

" We follow da fatty pigeon in da air and we see wat we look for. Fatty pigeon take straightest route as ee is a too fat, yes?"

Without showing the relief of it all, a smile and a cool, calm, "Yes!" was all it took for a mass outburst of cheers and instant celebration. The man who owned the voice at mid ships was now being kissed repeatedly by his fellow crewmembers, as though he had just saved their lives or scored the winner in the world cup final. Alberto cut this entire celebratory gesticulating short.

"FINDA DA FATTY BIRDA….NOWA!!!"

Each man turned and scurried back to their previous positions to look for a rotund bird with a beard and a peg leg, currently somewhere in the air not very far away. Whilst the search began, Alberto and Guiseppe returned to the message, still being rolled around in Alberto's fingers. Both looked at the piece of paper. A pensive look took hold of both men. Guiseppe spoke first.

"Alberto, open da message. Watta eet saya?"

Alberto gazed downwards at the piece of paper, which had

been the subject of much finger rolling recently and paused. A quick look at Guiseppe and then he launched into opening it. A couple of folds to over come and then there it was.

A message of some kind. A message that, as far as the command of the H.M.S Osvaldo Ardilles were concerned, read *"Hello Signore Del Piero, Mother Nature has brought us together and we welcome you as friends and colleagues of the sea. Yours in good faith H.M.S Osvaldo Ardilles."* But what actually read *" I would very much like to wet myself on board. If my Father had been a girl, then he would've sailed on the Signore Del Piero! Lots of loves H.M.S Osvaldo Ardilles."*

Alberto began to boil up inside. Guiseppe now grew concerned, as he watched Alberto become redder and redder in the face. Alberto, who was now beginning to growl like a dog, screwed up the message and dropped it on the deck before letting out a massive roar-like "Inglish pigs…they is insulting Italia and day is insulting all of us!!!"

He stepped forward to address the crew who, on hearing the growling, had turned to look for the source of it. On seeing that the source was a rapidly reddening Alberto, they knew something was wrong. Without stopping to calm down or even consult with Guiseppe, he began to address the men before him.

"Men of Italy, men of Del Piero. We av been spat onna by da inglish in their Armadillo thing over there. Day av insulted us and take da funny business out of us. Iya demand a war wiv them to show them ooze proud. Are you wiv me???"

A resounding cheer went up and much kissing began. Guiseppe, who, he felt, was seemingly the only cool head on board, picked up the message from the deck and opened it. On reading the message he was alarmed at the over reaction by Alberto and moved to bring a hefty dose of sanity to the party, in the form of some questions.

"Ey, ey…Alberto!"

"What is eet, Guiseppe..eh?"

"Alberto, dis a can't be right eh?...I mean, look…wat sort of man write dis eh?"

"I tell you who didn't write it, Guiseppe….proud Italian man, that's who!"

Feeling as though he was getting absolutely nowhere, Guiseppe upped the ante.

"Alberto, dis a make no sense. Dis, is written equivalent of fatty pigeon…a joke."

"It's no a joke a, Guiseppe. Eet is a war!"

"But Alberto, what are we going to war with, eh? We don't a have a any guns. In fact, look around, we don't av anything. We sail so quick we don't a pack anything. Little food, no water and no guns. So what are we going to fight with? How a we going to sink this armadildo thing, eh?"

Alberto stood silent. In fact, every man on board stood silent. Alberto, stood constructing an answer, the crew stood not sure what to do. With answer constructed and, apparently, not a man to be beaten, Alberto shouted another passionate declaration into the air.

"We a use our a shoes! We av proud Italian shoes wiv ard eels. We sink a da Armadildo wiv our ard eels. Da inglish will regret da day da stinky pigeon bring da message, eh!"

Again, a resounding cheer went up and joy spread all around. Celebrations and more kissing broke out on board and Alberto was now calm, composed and loving what he saw in front of him. Guiseppe, concerned by pretty much everything now, moved to bring some sense to proceedings again.

"Alberto, my friend, we av not even found da Armadillo yet! We a don't a even know what eet look like. It could be one undred feet high with a steel and a planes and guns and things…we ain't ever going to sink dat wiv proud Italian eels!"

Alberto shrugged his shoulders and agreed. Turning back to the celebrations behind him he shouted.

"Da fatty pigeon, da Armadillo. Find a them a nowa!!!"

Celebrations ceased instantly and all men returned to their look out positions. All men now resumed declaring and putting one another down.

"ista there, Iya see eet firsta"

"Idiot, dat isa duck, orra bird, orra something wiv feathers, sitting on da water."

Time went by. Beads of sweat ran down intense, but weary brows. Nearly three hundred proud Italian men stood at their posts scanning the grey sea, and only a slightly bluer sky, for a fat pigeon and its destination. Alberto, inwardly frustrated by the fact that a fat pigeon had only just left his ship, but was seemingly nowhere to be seen, felt it best that he not outwardly show his emotions. He stood biting his lip, eagerly waiting for a sighting. But this sighting wasn't forth coming.

Meanwhile, on the H.M.S Osvaldo Ardilles, Sir Douglas, Thomas and the many crew members watching all of this through their binoculars, were amazed to see that the pigeon, having only just spread its wings for the return journey, had, in fact, headed straight downwards to a small perch, just above the water line. This perch was seemingly the end of, what looked like, a rather hastily assembled cross member of some sort.

From what they could see and at the distance they

were, it seemed to sit awkwardly in the position it was. It didn't seem particularly well installed and appeared to have some rather alarming gaps around it and between it, and the nearest part of the vessel. This aside, it did appear to be sturdy enough for a rather unhealthy and out of breath pigeon to take up residence on.

Sitting on its newfound perch, just above the water line and completely hidden from all those on board, the pigeon nestled down for a well-earned sleep. Tucking its head in to its chest, it took seconds for it to be off in a deep sleep, farting and snoring as it did so. Whilst, up above, proud Italian eyes continued to scan the cold, grey surroundings, desperate for a sighting of either a fat pigeon with a beard and a stump or the now mystical ship that it was allegedly returning to.

Silence reigned supreme as the competitive nature of the proud Italian man gripped those on board once more. Alberto noted that, for once, the Del Piero sat quite peacefully in the water. The balance and stability seemed good. Perhaps the way to get around or, more importantly home, was to keep his men stationed on the perimeter of this most unseaworthy of vessels that they had set to sea in.

For the first couple of hours he had only seen sky straight ahead, as the bow had been out of the water, due to the high volume of proud Italian men stood on the aft platform. But now, with the aforementioned proud Italian men spread out around the edge of the vessel, things were calmer, the bow was back roughly where it was designed to be and the all round vibe was better.

With this calmness and stability came improved vision. The sun was now warming nicely and doing its best to burn off the cloud and haze. The greyness of the sea seemed to be changing to a healthy blue and the whole area seemed to be brightening. Alberto looked at his watch and noted that it was nearing midday. Almost in sync with the improving conditions came the sighting that everyone on board craved. Another passionate cry, but with the difference of no put down from his fellow crewmembers.

"Eye a see eet....eets over dare. Look everybody, look, I am a proud Italian man and eye a have a seen eet first."

Over Alberto's left shoulder, leaning enthusiastically on the hastily assembled and varnished handrail, stood the man responsible for the declaration. Alberto turned to face the man and was met by the sight of a proud Italian man with a very large grin, leaping around and pointing repeatedly out to sea. Alberto, desperately trying to remain calm, finally gave in and rushed forwards to kiss this proud Italian and most observant man.

"Tito…you are a genius!"

Before Tito, "the observant," as he'd already decided that he would be called, could react, he noticed a near stampede breaking out behind Alberto. Every crewmember became increasingly desperate to be the next proud Italian man to lay eyes on the English foe and had begun to move, at speed, towards the stern of the Del Piero. The stability on the water, that had been enjoyed by one and all on board, was now gone. A rush of bodies had meant that the vessel now began to bob and weave alarmingly. The more men that rushed towards the stern, the higher the bow began to rise out of the water. This movement remained unnoticed by all on board, as much kissing and celebrating broke out once again.

On his perch, not far below all of this celebrating, sat the Trafalgar pigeon. Woken by water on its feet and alarmed that he might be receiving a bath, it had decided that it was time to leave. The sea was rising towards him fast and so, with a quick flap of unkempt wings, the pigeon was up in the air and flying towards the Ardilles. Flying upwards, from right under their noses, the Italian gondoliers were incensed to see the pigeon, that they had put so much effort into finding, rise into the air in front of them.

"Jeesus!…eets da fatty pigeon!…shoo shoo fatty pigeon…"

Alberto came to his senses straight away and, in

response to this alarm from an unknown source, he snapped back into his captain's role.

"Shoe is the answer! I need a shoe…some proud Italian man with ard eels and pointy shoes needs to sacrifice ees footwear!"

A strange request, but met instantly by a proud Italian crewmember with hard heels and pointy shoes. In a flash, this man had removed his footwear and had made his way through the crowd, with arms and shoes aloft, to the handrail on the stern of the Signore Del Piero. Alberto felt he needed to add a touch of encouragement to this man, who was now taking aim with a stunning boot, that he'd recently purchased in Rome.

"You a miss…we a will laugh at you…you eet im and we kiss you…."

With these words, spoken into his ear, the man took aim. His target, twenty feet away and still trying to gain altitude, was the Trafalgar Pigeon.

Chapter Twenty-One – The pigeon, the boot and the mess that followed

Oblivious to the boot, currently been aimed at him, the inaugural pigeon to be launched from the H.M.S Osvaldo Ardilles, began to get a bit enthusiastic as a real burst of energy had seen him gain another ten feet in altitude in no time at all. He could hear all the noise and excitement behind him, but thought it best he get away from these over excitable humans. Flapping his wings wildly as he went, he was hoping that he'd make the three miles back to his quarters before he run out of puff and needed to look for another perch to set down on for another sleep. Concentrating harder than he'd ever had to before, his sole aim right now was to gain altitude.

On board the Del Piero, now situated twenty odd feet below him, the owner of the fine boot, recently purchased in Rome, had finished his aim and hurled it skywards. This was met with a huge cheer from his crewmates. A brief moment of silence and anticipation followed, as each and every proud Italian man studied the trajectory of the impressive boot as it tumbled, toe over heel, through the air. It seemed to be heading for a direct hit, but suddenly fell away at the last moment.

A blind man could've followed this scene, purely by the increasing and decreasing "wooooooooooooooooooooooooooooooo." Disappointment showed all around, as the superbly made boot arced downwards and into the sea. Furious that he'd missed his target, he prepared his remaining boot and, on securing the target in his sights, launched it into the air with all the gusto he could muster.

Again, an impressive chorus of, "wooooooooooooooooooooo" rose, as the spinning boot neared its target. This time it changed into an almighty cheer as stylish Italian leather met dirty Trafalgar pigeon. For a brief moment, the bird seemed to drop like a stone. As it fell, there seemed to be bits of it breaking away. In reality, whilst striving for that all-important altitude, the toe of the boot had clipped the pigeon. Being a Trafalgar pigeon and thus horrendously unfit, the shock of being struck by a missile had been too much and it had simply not had the will power to recover straight away.

The free fall had caused cold air to ruffle its feathers and that proved to be more uncomfortable than a bath and thus the recovery had begun. Flapping its wings once again, the pigeon realised that the missile had removed his stump. With the stump gone the pigeon was confused as its flight characteristics were suddenly very different. Quickly realising that a little bit of weight had been taken away he flapped for his life, continuing to try and get to safety.

This now became a tale of two ships and, indeed, a tale of two crews, as emotions, although running high on both vessels, were at vastly different ends of the spectrum. On the Italian side of things, much celebrating had broken out and kissing was present in abundance. Huge cheers had met the contact of toecap on stump and the sight of the free falling pigeon had brought a roar of approval. This had dimmed significantly as the pigeon had recovered and begun to pull out of the dive before their eyes and, as the bird cleared the maximum range for boot throwing, an air of disappointment descended on the crew of the Del Piero. They could only stand and watch as the fat, unkempt and now stump-less pigeon put distance between it and them.

On board the Ardilles, all of this unfolding escape had been watched by one and all. Sir Douglas and Thomas had stood mortified as they observed, through binoculars, the violence being unleashed against their bird. First one, then two objects had been thrown at the pigeon, from someone on board the Del Piero. The first projectile had been un-identifiable, as it had appeared suddenly, catching them by surprise, and then fallen into the sea before anyone could positively identify it.

They were, however, ready for any more objects and, when another appeared to be thrown from the Del Piero, they were ready, eyes sharpened.

"Is that what I think it is?"

Sir Douglas moved to confirm what he believed and, by the sounds of things, Thomas believed it to be.

"If you are thinking that the object currently tumbling through the sky towards our pigeon is a boot then, yes, it is what you think it is!"

Both men stood, dumbstruck, as the boot appeared to strike the pigeon and both fell seawards.

"Good God, that's barbaric!"

Thomas felt disgusted. Sir Douglas, on the other hand, was surprisingly cool and, although his many years of active service hadn't actually placed him in a war zone, he felt his superior knowledge gave him some artistic licence on the subject. An almost Clint Eastwood-esque reply of "That's not barbaric, Thomas, that's war!" left his lips.

Inwardly he smiled a massive smile. He sounded battle hardened and this suited him fine. Before Thomas could answer, Sir Douglas had realised that he'd best follow that line up with another. He quickly added, "That's all it is, Thomas, war!" Satisfied that he'd completed his summary of the situation, from the position of a war weary general, he left it there.

By now, the pigeon had recovered and had gained some altitude, all be it without his stump. The sight of their bird flying safely back towards them brought relief to all on board. But, relief was not enough for Sir Douglas. Revenge, retaliation, call it what you will, but he wanted some sort of responsive action.

"Thomas, how many pigeons do we have on board?"

"I would say we have about one hundred of each type on this trip, Sir Douglas. May I ask why you ask?"

"Yes, you may. I was thinking of sending over maybe thirty or so to, erm, mess all over the Del Piero."

"Sir Douglas, Is that wise?"

"Thomas, no-one and, I mean, no-one, throws a boot at a pigeon in the service of The Floaty Boat Brigade and gets away with it!"

"But, is it not wiser just to leave it and let bygones be bygones?"

"Nope! Have the Trafalgar's had a toilet flight today?"

Although the Ardilles had only been fully crewed, loaded and at sea for a few days in total, certain routines and practices had already come into play and had bedded down into everyday life for those on board. One of these routines was to let all the pigeons out for a 'toilet flight' two or three times a day. The birds obviously needed this time in the air and it gave the pigeon handlers, down below, a chance to clean out their quarters and fluff up their tea bag pillows.

The handlers found that the pigeons would start to return within a few minutes, a few at a time. On touching down, they would be scooped up by the handlers and carried back down below to their quarters. If no handlers were available they would just congregate on the handrail of the Ardilles and wait.

With no 'toilet flight' undertaken yet this morning, Sir Douglas' planning was perfect. Without removing his face from the binoculars he coolly issued an order. "Thomas, can you organise thirty Trafalgar Pigeons, in fact, hold that. Can you prepare every pigeon on board for a "toilet flight" please? Also, get the engine room cranked up and heading for the Del Piero."
Thomas, alarmed by the wisdom of these orders, replied with an acknowledgement.
"Yes, Sir Douglas, I'll get the pigeons ready now and I'll crank up the book-keepers."

With that, Thomas was off down some stairs and away from the bridge. His first destination was the engine room. A few well varnished corridors and stairwells and he was there, issuing instructions to the bookkeepers and the accountants. The result of this briefing was a scene reminiscent of a train arriving at London Bridge in rush hour. Men in grey suits organised, but not hanging around, cut a swathe through the mass of bodies around them and made for their own seat.

Bookkeepers, similar in appearance, also made their way to their respective seats without a fuss and without a word. Thomas, watching from where he stood, could not help but be impressed by this display of absolute precision movement. Although none of these fine men would admit it, conditions in this part of the boat were cramped, as wooden beam criss-crossed with another wooden beam.

And yet, there he stood, watching in awe as these grey suited professionals just moved amongst each other, without a single word of anger. Within minutes every man was seated and prepared for work. The engine room was ready. Thomas moved for the door that, in turn, led to the corridor that would take him to his next port of call. As he left, he noted that the bookkeepers were having a quick discussion, probably regarding direction, speed and conditions.

With one task organised and completed, Thomas was off, out of the engine room and heading along the corridor towards the pigeon's quarters. As he approached, he noticed that this seemed to be the only area of the ship where the air was not thick and heavy with the lingering smell of varnish. A few steps nearer and he realised just why that was.

The heavy and rather unpleasant smell of pigeons, up close and personal, filled the corridor. It was the first time that he had been in these quarters since setting sail with a full quota of pigeons on board. He'd had the odd walk around whilst the ship was being built, but he'd not been anywhere near the pigeons since they'd been on board.

The first thing that struck him, on entering the area, was the presence of miniature gym equipment. This, in itself, seemed absurd. Sure there were thorough bred racing pigeons on board, but it appeared to him that someone, somewhere within the Brigade, had confused macaws and parrots with pigeons. He instantly recalled several instances from his past, where he had been at a zoo or a bird sanctuary and witnessed playful parrots pedalling miniature bikes and talkative macaws lifting miniature weights with their beaks. Clearly, that someone, somewhere within the brigade had recalled the same memories and decided that, if macaws and parrots could use bikes and weights then racing pigeons could too.

To Thomas, there was no surprise that this miniature gym was empty. Opposite the gym were the quarters of the racing pigeons themselves. Not too much in the way of furnishings, but it just seemed to have a quality feel to it. The small troughs, that contained seed and the small bowls of water, all appeared to be items of quality that, on reflection, matched the quality of the birds, sectioned here. The birds themselves all sat calmly on shelving, one tier above the other. If you were a racing pigeon, this seemed like a pretty good place to be.

Thomas continued on down the corridor, which led to the heart of the quarters. Leaving behind him an air of calmness and respectability, that reflected the fine specimens that resided there, he felt the quality of the place suddenly reduce a few steps further on. There, before him, on both sides of the walkway and seemingly on one continuous perch around the stern of the boat, were around one hundred of the filthiest, unkempt and downright smelliest birds known to mankind.

A range of appearances met him from just plain untidy to untidy with beards, untidy with stumps and untidy with beards and stumps. There was a complete lack of gym equipment around but there was, however, a large shelf like platform that had several open top pots of seed and water. Thomas noted that neither the seed nor the water appeared to be particularly clean in appearance and merely served to emphasise the class difference between these birds and the thoroughbreds, situated behind him down the corridor.

Currently mulling around this area were several Trafalgar pigeons that were all cooing, gulping seed and taking the odd beak full of water. A sudden realisation hit Thomas. "No gym, but lots of food, drink and socialising. This must be the pigeon pub!"

"That's pretty much what it is, Thomas."

Having meant to think it to himself, Thomas had, in fact, declared his findings out loud. The nearest pigeon handler present had instantly replied.

"Oh, erm, is it?"

Thomas tried to brush over the fact that he'd just blurted stuff out loud. He felt the best way to deal with this and remove himself from the pigeons, their smell and the hundreds of rather dirty looking tea bags, currently being used as pillows, was to issue an order then get out of there.

"Guys, please prepare every air worthy pigeon for flight and bring them top side for launching as soon as possible"

A vague and almost distant, "Ok, Thomas," was the reply and that was the only confirmation he needed, as proof that his instructions had been received, for him to be retreating back down the corridor and swiftly heading for some fresh air up top.

On his brief journey back to the bridge, Thomas had noticed that the Ardilles was back under way. The familiar noises, the creaks and groans, the roar of the water as it escaped the blades of the oars, all indicated that the accountants were rowing. Apart from all this, the almighty lurch forwards through the water, as the oars, acting as one, ploughed into the water each time and pulled the Ardilles through it, made Thomas stagger slightly on every certain part of the engine room's stroke forwards.

With fresh air roaring up his nostrils, Thomas knew he was close to the open air. The last few steps up the final ladder took him onto the upper deck. Looking upwards he could see Sir Douglas still peering out to sea through binoculars. Climbing up the stairs to the bridge, two at a time, he approached Sir Douglas and confirmed that his initial order had been carried out.

"All pigeons being prepared for flight and should be top side within a few minutes, Sir Douglas."

"Excellent, Thomas. Thank you for sorting that out."

"My pleasure, Sir Douglas. How are we doing, anyway?"

"Well, Thomas, these Italian fellows seem to be a bit barmy, if you ask me. Take a look for yourself and you tell me if their behaviour is that of sane and rational men."

Thomas picked up his binoculars from the coat hook, hastily screwed into the wall of the bridge before they set sail, and took a look for himself.

"Oh, I see what you mean, Sir Douglas. Would I be correct in saying that they all appear to be waving footwear at us?"

"Yes, I would say they are indeed waving footwear at us. I ask you, Thomas, are we doing the right thing? I mean, sailing towards a clearly unstable structure, full of men willing to remove their footwear and wave them in the air? Is this what we should be doing?"

Thomas moved to re-assure Sir Douglas with a nice, warm, comforting answer, but that went a bit wrong during delivery.

" I would suggest, Sir Douglas, that we don't get any nearer to them than we have to. Keep our distance and all that sort of thing. If they couldn't hit the pigeon at twenty odd feet then they won't be able to hit us at a couple of miles. Meanwhile, having thought about it, I'd agree with you and concur that we should launch all available pigeons in their direction and, how can I put it, poo all over them."

With the Ardilles back under way and making short work of the three odd miles between the two vessels, the view through the binoculars was now vastly improved. The exhausted and severely stressed out Trafalgar pigeon had not long touched down from his eventful mission to the Del Piero and, because of the events that had unfolded, the pigeon had long since forgotten about his missing stump. Thus, on landing on the handrail of the Ardilles, had promptly fallen off onto the deck.

Slightly bruised, both physically and emotionally, the pigeon had been quickly collected by a handler and taken down below for some well-earned seed, water and rest. But, before the pigeon could taste any of this, it was critical that he under go a new stump fitting and a quick debrief, as this is what the flyboys did. The handler, who was taking care of the pigeon, had quickly realised that a debrief wouldn't work and so had scratched this from the list. This now left the stump fitting, a quick health check, and then food, drink and R&R.

Sir Douglas, thinking about what Thomas had said and, another chance to quote the Cruel Sea, didn't hesitate in issuing the one order he'd been wanting, secretly deep down, to issue.

"Stop all engines! Erm, accountants. Stop all accountants! Erm, STOP!"

The message was instantly relayed, one crewmember to the next, down from the bridge, where Sir Douglas stood, along the walkways and down the stairs, through the corridors to the bookkeepers and accountants below. Thomas peered over the side and noticed that, once again, the oars were still. The creaks and groans were gone once more and the only discernible noise was now coming from the stern of the boat as one by one the pigeon handlers began to appear from down below with a varying number of pigeons sitting on them.

The lesser-experienced pigeon handlers had one bird on each hand, whereas the more experienced ones appeared from below looking like a pigeon tree. There were pigeons on hands, pigeons on arms, shoulders and heads. A vastly different image, to what he had just seen down below, now appeared on the rear decks, as very organised and apparently focused Trafalgar pigeons had replaced the scene of disorganised Trafalgar pigeons.

Seemingly, one handler after another appeared from below decks and transferred pigeons from his/her body to the rail of the Ardilles. Thomas thought to himself that he hadn't realised just how many of these people there were on board, but apparently there were quite a few, as more just kept coming up from below. Within a few minutes Thomas received a double thumbs up from the senior handler, which signified that the pigeons were ready to go. Before giving the order to launch, both Sir Douglas and Thomas watched admiringly as the senior handler picked up four racing pigeons and appeared to show them the target. His actions seemed so simple and yet so thoroughly professional.

Something akin to a martial arts expert quietly motioning his/her moves. These few minutes were so engrossing that, on looking around, Thomas noted that everyone on deck stood silently watching this as well. There didn't appear to be any audible words coming from the handler, but whatever was being communicated to the pigeons was done very calmly and quietly. The pigeons themselves seemed to be in some kind of hypnotic state. Sitting motionless and quiet, but with eyes enlarged and fixed on where their handler pointed.

Several minutes elapsed before the handler suddenly became active again and looked up at Sir Douglas and Thomas on the bridge. Seemingly, when the handler became active again, so did everyone else on deck. To each and every man and woman on board, a sense of awakening and a kind of cleansing came over them. They had just watched something so deep and yet so beautiful, that they all found themselves suddenly feeling remarkably good and refreshed. Now the mood on the Ardilles was excellent.

Sir Douglas looked at Thomas and raised his eyebrows in a kind of "wasn't expecting that!" way. Thomas knew what was meant and nodded in agreement. Thomas looked at Sir Douglas and then down at the senior handler. "It's over to you, Sir Douglas. It would appear that our feathered friends are ready to go."

Sir Douglas acknowledged Thomas and then, waving his arm and not being able to recall a line from the 'Cruel Sea' that he could use, he simply shouted, "LAUNCH!"

With that command, the handler edged the four racing pigeons into the air. Within seconds they were off, heading for the Del Piero. Swiftly followed by the remaining birds. In no time at all the class and fitness difference had shown itself, as a gleamingly clean squadron of racing pigeons flew as one and at speed towards their target, whilst, already many meters behind, came the un-gamely and awkward looking group of Trafalgar pigeons. After launching amongst a flurry of loose and very dirty feathers, most Trafalgar birds realised that their toilet for this morning was actually some way off and began to look for something closer to mess on. With nothing around, they all begrudgingly headed after the racing pigeons.

Seeing this from the bridge, Thomas realised that this delay, and reluctance to fly any great distance, had actually made both him and Sir Douglas look great. Now, and totally unexpectedly, they had effectively two flights of birds heading across the open sea to their target. This hesitation by the Trafalgar's had, unintentionally, created a first and second-strike wave. Thomas moved quickly to discuss this with Sir Douglas.

"Seems our fat and dirty friends didn't fancy the journey, Sir Douglas!"

"It would appear not, Thomas. It has, however left us in a stronger, yet fortunate, position."

"Would you be alluding to the fact that we now have two flights heading their way? Thus a first and second-strike wave, by any chance?"

"Aaagh yes, Thomas, that'll be the one!"

A warm smile from Sir Douglas met a warm smile from Thomas. Both men realised that, through the pure laziness of the Trafalgar pigeons, they now looked a lot more militarily enlightened than they ever had done before. A point acknowledged readily by Sir Douglas.

"Those fat little buggers have made us look rather good, Thomas! Anyway, we haven't given our mission a name yet, any suggestions?"

Remarkably quickly, Thomas came back with "Operation Del Poo-aero?" Sir Douglas couldn't help, but laugh in admiration and declared "Outstanding, my friend! Operation Del Poo-aero it is!" Thomas, still smiling, agreed.

By now, the newly designated, "first strike wave," was closing in on the target. With under a mile to go, the group of racing pigeons, flying in tight and impressive formation, looked stunning. The same thing couldn't be said of the second wave, languishing over a mile behind. Appearing to be scattered all over the place, the un-healthy birds flapped and flustered their way forwards.

Every so often one would drop slightly from its level flight as a sudden gasp for breath caused an involuntary lapse of flapping. Whereas, the first wave of pigeons would tick every conceivable box for precise and stunningly executed flying, the second would not. They flew in the same way as they stood, just about. There were no tight formations. In fact, there were no formations at all. The best way to describe the second wave was "scattered."

"Scattered." A term favoured by the military for many years. When used to describe patterns, be it bomb or otherwise, there would always be a hint of disappointment in the air. Almost as though they had failed. "The bombing patterns were scattered," would hint at real internal misery, maybe even a vision of hope and determination left floundering on the rocks. Indeed, the term "scattered," was rarely used in a positive way. No surprise then, for Thomas to hear Sir Douglas point out in a very sullen manner, "The second wave are very scattered, Thomas. That's not cricket!"

Thomas, by now a nigh on expert on the Cruel Sea, was struggling to think of the scene where "That's not cricket!" may have been said. Sir Douglas, on the other hand, had surprised himself with this latest remark and inwardly cursed himself for saying something not apparently from his beloved film. Although he cursed about the situation, he was right. The second wave were scattered and they were struggling to reach their target.

As those on board the Ardilles watched the two groups venture ever onwards towards the Del Piero, Thomas felt the time was right for a little clarification.

"Sir Douglas."

"Yes, Thomas?"

"May I ask what we are expecting from our air strikes today?"

"What exactly do you mean, Thomas?"

"Well, what I mean is, just that really. What are we expecting?"

"Not really with you, my friend, do explain."

An edgy cocktail began to show in Thomas' voice. Ingredients included panic, doubt, nervousness and a healthy shot of the unknown. He tried to explain.

"Well, Sir Douglas. What I mean is, we're standing here

awaiting the impact of two air strikes on "old wobbly" over there. In any other zone of combat, that would probably entail fast jets, laden with missiles, zooming over the targets or firing missiles from distance. Either way, speed, missiles, explosions, barrel rolls, home to Blighty, smoked kippers and bags of hurrahs!"

"Okay, continue!"

"As I said, in any other zone of combat! What we are awaiting the impact of is two flights of pigeons containing a little speed, granted, but no missiles and certainly no explosions. With that in mind, what exactly are we expecting our air strikes to actually do?"

"Oh, I see now. Being pigeons, we can't actually brief them. The nearest we've got to that is old Obi-feathers-Knobi down there with his pre-flight pigeon Pilates class. Right, erm, with you. Don't actually know is the answer!"

Thomas was about to expand on this newly recognised unknown area of the mission when a voice shouted out "Helicopter over on the starboard side…about ten-ish in the air." Sir Douglas made a mental note to get the men trained in navigation, if they made it home. Once duly noted, he ran to the other side of the bridge to have a look and was joined shortly afterwards by Thomas. It was Thomas who identified the visitor.

"Oh look, just marvellous. We have two waves of pigeons heading for "old wobbly" and we haven't got a clue what they're going to do when they get there. And, with almost impeccable timing, the Sky Copter shows up! Just great!"

Sir Douglas, for the first time on the voyage, became almost realistic. Almost as though he had climbed out of the bubble that was the H.M.S Ardilles and The McJeffers Act. For the first time, he acted and spoke differently. Thomas couldn't quite put his finger on it, but it was there. With no time to lose, Sir Douglas barked some orders. "Thomas, you get back to the mission. The pigeons will either fly past the Del Piero, mess on it without landing or, my preferred option, settle into the mast type structure and poo for Queen and country. You watch and deal with any returns. I'll get some men for the starboard decks, a walkie-talkie and then deal with Sky. This is our moment!"

With no time to think about what "This is our moment" meant, Thomas ran back across the bridge to his original position and resumed staring at pigeons through his binoculars. His timing was impeccable as he was just focusing on the first wave when the Del Piero came into the same piece of viewfinder. With relief in their eyes, the racing pigeons cooed in delight as they realised they had reached their toilet. Almost as one, they flew on past the "mast type structure" and then arched backwards onto it, using it like some gigantic perch. On touching down, the movements began.

For one crewmember, on board the Del Piero down below, the sight of the on-flying pigeons was enough for the red mist to descend. Tito, "the observant," as he now proudly slipped into conversation at every given opportunity was, again, the man to spot the on rushing birds. Whilst commotion still reigned supreme on board and much shoe waving was till being undertaken, Tito had taken a step back from his comrades and began surveying just what was happening.

Sure, they had missed the fatty pigeon, but none of his fellow crew members had actually taken time out from shoe waving to see another lame duck, but one seemingly happier in the water than theirs, close in on them. But, just as he had made up his mind that he had seen enough and was about to raise the alarm, this ship had stopped and began to keep a distance between them and it.

And if that was not enough, a few minutes later he had witnessed some sort of cloud emerge from this ship and head for them. Whilst, all around him, men shouted at the ever-distant bird that had evaded all fine Italian boots, he had studied this airborne cloud type "thing" heading his way. With no optical aids to assist the identification process, Tito had simply stood; mouth open, studying through naked eye whatever it was that drew or flew closer.

Now that they had arrived, landed and began their morning bowel movements, it was clear to Tito what this airborne cloud had been. Pigeons, and whole a lot of them. As the noise of pigeons going about their toiletry habits intensified, so did the end result falling on all and sundry down below. On seeing what was happening, Tito erupted. "Ey, ey ,ey…whatta da ell!….da stinky bird…ee hava maytes and they be poo poo all over us!"

The taunting of the now non-existent Trafalgar pigeon suddenly stopped. To a man, the crew of the Del Piero turned to Tito, who was now shielding himself from falling pigeon droppings. All fine Italian boots were slipped back on to Italian feet and much shouting and taunting broke out in an upwards direction towards the birds high above them, nestling in and on the tall mast type structure towering over them. As each man now fought his own private battle to evade droppings, the vitriol began to spiral out of control.

Peering through his binoculars, Thomas could see this developing. It became ever clearer to him that those on board the Del Piero had lost, or were in the speedy process of losing, all control of emotions. First, boots were waved, then they were seemingly replaced on feet, then all angst appeared to be aimed at the newly landed first wave of pigeons. And with the angst came more boot waving and throwing. First one boot climbed upwards but fell short, then another, then another. Things appeared to be out of control.

On board the Del Piero things were now the worst they had been since they bobbed out to sea earlier that day. With all the anger being directed upwards at the newly lightened pigeons, there now came a down side. Not only were droppings falling on them, but also the boots that had arced upwards and fallen back earthwards without success each and every time. Tito and Alberto looked around at the carnage developing around them. As fast as a man could shout an obscenity at a bird and hurl a boot upwards, he then had to quickly shield himself, from fine crafted Italian leather, falling in his general direction. This was the same everywhere around them.

Suddenly, from one and all on board came a massive cheer. It was as though Italy had won the world cup. It appeared to each and every man as though the pigeons had had enough of the taunts and obscenities coming at them thick and fast and had decided to spread wings and leave. Much celebrating and kissing instantly broke out.

Tito was unmoved and Alberto saw this. "This man, this Tito," he thought, "what a wise man!" Within minutes of surveying the situation, Tito knew why the pigeons had left. It wasn't true that insults had won the day. The pigeons didn't understand anything anyway. There was only one reason why they had taken flight. More pigeons. Tito scanned the skies and was mortified to see a second wave heading their way.

Having issued his sternest of orders, Sir Douglas had grabbed a walkie-talkie and waved both arms above his head in the direction of the helicopter, hovering alongside. When he appeared to get an acknowledgement from someone on board, he waved the walkie-talkie in the air and signalled, with one hand five, five. A quick thumbs up from the chopper and Sir Douglas was turning on and tuning in. On selecting channel fifty-five, he spoke into the mouthpiece. "This is Sir Douglas Squires of the H.M.S Osvaldo Ardilles calling the Sky Copter, over!"

Before he could repeat his address, a voice came back through the hand held device.
"Hello, Sir Douglas, this is sky reporter Peter Preston on board the Sky Helicopter. Pleased to make your acquaintance, over!"
Sir Douglas smiled and replied; almost amazed at the success

he had had so far.

"Aaagh, Peter, I know you well. Always have produced good work, if I may say so. What brings you out here? Over."

"Why, thank you, Sir Douglas. It is very kind of you to say so. We are here to update the populace back home on your momentous voyage. It would appear that such an unorthodox craft, if I may say, is grabbing the imagination of the world. And now, it would seem, you have a challenge laying in your way in the shape of that Italian craft over there! What can you tell us? Over."

A peaceful conversation now guaranteed, Sir Douglas calmly answered, "Well, what can I say? We all felt very strange about this project from the off, but we have grown to love and believe in it more and more each day. Agh, yes, the Italians. That, my friend, is the Signori Del Piero. It would appear to be a most un-seaworthy vessel, seemingly manned by lunatics!"

"Oh, I see, Sir Douglas. May I ask what your plan is? Over."

"Well, Peter. We never set out to be confrontational. We actually sent over a message of good will. It was the Italians that tried to shoot down our carrier pigeon and that is why we have had to act. We have sent over a few pigeons in an attempt to de-stabilise their vessel. Once that is done, we shall head for home. I would appreciate it if you could stay around and report on their plight rather than ours. I think they'll need some sort of assistance soon. Over."

"I understand, Sir Douglas. But, what about you and the H.M.S Ardilles? Over."

"Peter, we'll be fine. Things look and feel strong on board. We'll make it home and continue our evaluations until we get there. If you can focus on the Del Piero then its' men will be saved. I don't see that staying afloat too much longer. In a few days we can meet, once the dust has settled, and I can give you a full interview. How does that sound? Over."

Sir Douglas split his time, whilst waiting for a reply, between looking at the chopper and looking at the handset. After, what felt like an eternity, a reply came through. "That sounds fine to me, Sir Douglas. We'll go and locate near the Italians and report from there. Good luck and God speed on your return voyage. I look forward to a victory drink soon. Over and out."

Conversation over and a wave from Sir Douglas, which was promptly met by a cheery wave from the crew of the helicopter, brought the episode to a close. The Sky copter flew off in the general direction of the Del Piero. Aware of the pigeons nearby, it kept close enough to report, but distant enough so as not to cause harm. It's close proximity to the

Italians merely added fuel to the ever-growing fire, now raging on board.

The approximate point, where the returning first strike-wave met the still-struggling-to-get-to-the-toilet second wave, was about two thirds distance from the Ardilles to the Del Piero. With each breath hard to come by, the struggling Trafalgar pigeons really didn't appreciate the gesture as the sharp and sleek racing birds cut a swathe through them.

Swift, clean and precise, the first wave powered on through, without so much as a blink of an eye or twitch of a feather. Heading straight towards the second wave, it was they who would have to take evasive action and that is exactly what they did. Feathers, dirt and general debris left the panic stricken Trafalgar birds and filled the air seconds before the thoroughbred racers roared past, heading back to the Ardilles.

Regaining some sort of formation, the Trafalgars headed onwards. As they got nearer the Del Piero they could finally identify their toilet for the morning. Out of breath and very scared, they couldn't help but be impressed with the close proximity pooing of the first wave. As they prepared to land on the mast type structure of the Del Piero, they couldn't help but notice the seemingly very irate people down below.

On landing and getting down to business, they found objects rising up towards them but not quite reaching. Undeterred, they continued with their morning movements.

Down below, and more irate than ever before, the crew of the Signori Del Piero simply couldn't take it anymore. Agitated beyond sanity, their actions reached fever pitch. With the entire boot throwing onslaught seemingly failing miserably and the vitriolic abuse falling on deaf ears, they were now unaccountable for their actions. All filmed from above by the nearby Sky copter, the world was tuning in to see a severely unstable vessel begin to take on water as the irate crew jumped around gesturing more and more.

It was certainly gripping TV. With movements pretty much complete and their toilet beginning to sway dangerously, the pigeons took to the air for the return journey back to their quarters. This simple act of getting airborne merely served as another insult to the Italian crew, who took their gesturing and jumping around to yet another whole new level. Water was now pouring in from various holes in the super structure and it was decided, by the crew of the Sky copter, that now would be a good time to put out the inevitable May Day call. With the world still watching the unfolding drama, Sky knew they were on to a good thing.

Back on board the Ardilles, Sir Douglas watched with

pride, as the second wave cleared the range of finely crafted Italian boot and ploughed onwards towards him. With a smile on his face he turned to Thomas.

"Thomas, my friend, as soon as they're back on board, let's set a course for home and slip out of the big picture."

Thomas, returning the smile, declared, "Yes, Sir Douglas, I'll go and brief the crew."

Before he could get two steps towards the ladder, that would take him off of the bridge, the voice of Sir Douglas grabbed his attention again.

"Oh, and Thomas…"

Thomas stopped and turned to answer.

"Yes, Sir Douglas?"

"One more thing. That idea of yours, you know, for the bird or aircraft carrier. Stroke of genius, Thomas!"

"Oh, why thank you, Sir Douglas"

"In fact, I'm going to recommend, to the men in suits and wigs, that we proceed and build the H.M.S Brian Cant immediately!"

With a gleam in his eye, Thomas removed himself from the bridge and made plans for home and the next chapter in these most eventful of times.

The End

www.spoonbooks.co.uk